The river is the river

JONATHAN BUCKLEY

Sort Of
BOOKS

for Susanne Hillen and Bruno Buckley

Published in 2015 by
Sort Of Books
PO Box 18678, London NW3 2FL
www.sortof.co.uk

Typeset in Melior to a design by Henry Iles

Printed and bound by CPI Group (UK) Ltd, Croydon, CR0 4YY

10 9 8 7 6 5 4 3 2 1

288pp.

A CIP catalogue record for this book is available from the British Library

Print ISBN 978-1908745-54-5

The river is the river

JONATHAN BUCKLEY

I can no longer write, for God has given me such glorious knowledge that everything contained in my works is as straw.

Thomas Aquinas

I

1.

In the middle of a Tuesday afternoon in September a woman named Kate Staunton, at home, at her desk, takes a call from her sister. We will call the sister Naomi; the author's name is Kate and she had a sister who resembled Naomi as the author resembles Kate Staunton, which is not the author's name. Words recorded here were actually spoken.

2.

The sisters last spoke to each other months ago. Their previous conversation had been in essence an announcement: Naomi was going away for an indeterminate period, to a place somewhere in Scotland, with people of whom Kate had never heard: Bernát, Connor and Amy. The introduction of these hitherto unknown companions was not in itself remarkable; there had been precedents. It was something of a surprise, however, that the company was not to include Gabriel, as we shall call the man who had been Naomi's partner for some time; 'partner' is perhaps not a wholly appropriate word – 'companion' might be preferable. The quartet did not constitute two couples, Kate was to understand. Gabriel was staying in London because he could not get the time off work, said Naomi; this did not convince, but the subject was not pursued. It was strange that walking the hills seemed to be the main purpose of this holiday; not since she was a girl had Naomi shown any enthusiasm for strenuous physical activity. 'It'll do me good,' she had said, and her sister could not disagree. They would be staying in an old farm building, near a loch; she could expect to see otters and buzzards and falcons, Naomi enthused, though wildlife had not been an interest, never mind an enthusiasm, as far as her sister knew. 'There's no phone signal,' Naomi told Kate, in the tone of a woman who was tired of being pestered. She would ring as soon as she returned, she promised.

Now her first words are: 'I'm back.' She almost sings it, as if she has only that moment returned, and the expedition has been a delight. It turns out that she has been in London for two weeks already. 'Can I come and see you?' she asks immediately.

'Of course,' says Kate, despite the recollection of her sister's last visit.

'I have things to tell you,' says Naomi. 'Big changes. Big big changes.'

The urgency and brightness of Naomi's tone is familiar; in the past this voice has been indicative of a crisis. 'You sound excited,' says Kate.

'I'm leaving London. I've decided.'

This is not the first time that Naomi has decided to leave London; she has never done it. 'When a woman is tired of London she has finally seen sense,' says Kate.

'I am changing my life,' Naomi states, unamused. It sounds like a declaration made to a meeting of addicts.

'You have something specific in mind?'

'I know what I'm going to do, yes.'

'So—'

'Back to the hills.'

'What?'

'I'm going back to Scotland. I'll tell you about it when I see you.'

'And what about work?' asks Kate.

Naomi has had enough of teaching. The thought of another year of listening to little Imogen and Grace puffing through their grade two pieces is more than she can bear. 'And no more pushy parents,' she says.

'How are you going to live?' asks Kate.

'The income, you mean?' says Naomi, as if income were an inessential detail.

'Yes. How are you going to support yourself?'

'I have some ideas, don't worry.'

'Such as?'

'Don't worry,' Naomi repeats.

'I won't worry if you tell me what you're going to do. Perhaps.'

'I might keep bees.'

'What?'

'Become a bee-woman. Make honey. Sell it.'

'Bees? In Scotland?'

'It's not the arctic, you know. The little chaps do fine with heather. Look it up. They're tough little buggers.'

'Naomi, when did you become an expert on bees?'

'Not saying I'm an expert. But I'll pick it up. I've done some homework. It'll be a challenge.'

'Well, that's one word for it. And you'll be selling how many gallons of highland honey a day?'

'Don't be unpleasant, Katie.'

'I'm not being unpleasant. I'm only—'

'Being practical.'

'Quite.'

'I'm not going to need to earn a lot. It'll be fine, believe me. We've got it worked out.'

'"We"?'

'I'll explain when I see you,' says Naomi, as though soothing someone who's making an extraordinary fuss of things. 'I was thinking of coming down tomorrow. Just for a day or two,' she adds, having heard, of course, the silent reaction at the other end of the line. 'Is that inconvenient?'

'I don't think so.'

'You sound unsure.'

'I'll need to check with Martin. I don't think we have anything planned.'

'Katie, you know if you've got anything planned,' says Naomi, in the tone of a loving mother admonishing her teenaged daughter for a ridiculous alibi. 'You know what's on the schedule for the next six months. What you mean is: you have to ask Martin how he feels about having me in the house.'

'That's not—'

'You can assure him I'll be on my best behaviour. I give you my word. Promise.'

'I'll call you this evening. But I'm sure tomorrow will be fine.'

'Tell him I won't cause any trouble. I'm on an even keel.'

'You sound happy.'

'I am. The sun is out.'

'That's good,' says Kate, thinking: the sun may be out today, but tomorrow might still be a downpour.

'I know what you're going to ask me,' says her sister.

'And the answer is: nothing.'

'You've lost me.'

'Come on, Katie. I know what you're thinking. But I'm not taking anything.'

'Nothing?'

'Not a thing.'

'Since when?'

'Months ago.'

'And you're OK?'

'What does it sound like?'

It is arranged that Naomi will take a train around five o'clock the following day.

At half past five she calls, from home. Her last lesson overran, she explains; from the explanation it becomes clear that even if the lesson had not overrun, Naomi could not possibly have caught a train around five. She'll be on the seven fifteen, she promises; she'll be at Kate's house by eight thirty. At eight o'clock she rings again; it's after ten when she arrives.

Standing on the doorstep, in the half-light, Naomi looks regal, and rather tired. She's wearing her black turban-like thing, adorned at the front with a huge acrylic brooch; the black woollen coat is half unbuttoned, exposing a sky-blue sari; on one wrist hangs a massive cuff of glossy blue plastic; several fingers are adorned with rings, studded with faux stones of various colours. She steps into the light of the hall, and passes the coat to her sister. Now she looks worse. The skin below her eyes has the texture of a perished balloon, and her mouth is bracketed by deep lines; her arms are slack; her ankles are swollen. She removes the turban, revealing hair that has been clumsily cut, and is as lifeless as towelling; it's been dyed badly too – a cayenne sort of colour. She is thinner; very much thinner.

Martin is out, but Lulu – as we shall call the daughter – is at home, in her room. Called, she emerges a minute later; at the turn of the stairs she hesitates for a second, taken aback by her aunt's appearance.

Pretending to have noticed nothing, Naomi spreads her arms to invite a hug. 'Hello lovely,' she murmurs, holding onto her niece as if to absolve her of blame for her alarm. 'How are you?' she asks. Lulu answers as almost any teenager would, in a phrase or two. Another question is asked and similarly anwered, then another, before Naomi says, fondly: 'I'm keeping you from something.' A blush begins below her niece's eyes. 'I've interrupted a conversation, haven't I?' says Naomi.

'It can wait,' states Lulu.

'No it can't. Off you go,' says her aunt, inviting another hug.

The sisters go into the kitchen. Naomi has not eaten since lunchtime. There follows a discussion of what Naomi can and cannot eat; she has been on a sort of diet, she says; she will explain later. Blandness is required, because her taste buds have become very sensitive. Likewise her sense of smell. Garlic is intolerable, and spices are out of the question. When Kate opens the fridge door, Naomi recoils; she can smell the steak from the other side of the room, she says, wincing at the supposed stink. A stir-fry of vegetables with unsalted noodles is acceptable; the portion is small, yet she eats little more than half of what's on the plate. Water is all she will drink. She takes an apple; the first bite leaves streaks of blood on the white.

'You've lost a lot of weight,' Kate remarks.

'I have,' says Naomi, cheerfully commending her belly with a pat. 'Want to guess?'

'Forty pounds?'

'Fifty.'

'Fifty pounds in one summer – that's too much,' says Kate.

'Never felt better,' Naomi insists. Her fingernails, Kate observes, are the colour of curdling milk.

'You look exhausted.'

'It's been a long day.'

Kate carries her sister's bag up to the guest room, at the top of the house; Naomi follows, breathing heavily once they have passed the landing, but no more heavily than would have been the case before. Since her last stay, the room has been redecorated; Naomi makes no comment. 'Quite enough exercise for one day,' she sighs, sitting on the bed. She slips off her shoes and eases herself onto her back; she closes her eyes. 'I'll be out of your hair in a couple of days,' she says, and perhaps she believes it. She smiles and reaches for a hand; there is no strength in her grip. 'I'm going to live with him,' she says. 'With Bernát.' Cohabitation is a form of oppression, she and Gabriel had always agreed; this was one of the founding principles of their relationship, as Kate remembers. 'I'll tell you everything, tomorrow,' she murmurs, then a cat shrieks in the garden, and she flinches as if at a gunshot. Her eyelids tighten. She pulls her sister's hand, palm down, onto her breastbone; the bone feels like a piece of brick under a sheet of paper; the pulse is much too fast. 'Goodnight,' she whispers, moving her sister's hand to her lips; the kiss is prolonged.

'Anything you need?' asks Kate.

'Nothing at all,' answers Naomi, now opening her eyes. She looks at Kate as if at a nurse in whom she has absolute trust.

'You sure?'

'Positive,' she murmurs. 'This is perfect. Thank you.' Then she releases the hand.

3.

Kate is struggling with her new project. The story will be set in Prague, or perhaps Berlin, some time in the 1920s. The central character is to be a woman, called Dorota (or Dorothea, or Dora). Her husband, Jakub (or Jakob), has been killed in the war. Dorota is an attractive woman, and has remarried; her second husband is a decent man; she believes herself to be happy. One day, perhaps ten years after the death of Jakub, she is returning from the shops when she sees a man who might be Jakub – he looks as Jakub would now look, had he survived, she thinks. In the following months she glimpses this man several times, always at a distance. She has no idea what is happening to her: is the man a ghost or a phantom of her imagination? Might he be a double, or a man whose resemblance to Jakub exists only in her mind? Could he even be Jakub himself? Perhaps he had not been killed after all. If he is the real Jakub, why has he not come back to her? Has he lost his memory? There are many possibilities.

II

4.

After Martin and Lulu have left, Naomi comes downstairs. She is in her pyjamas; they are terrible old things, with deckchair stripes. Formerly owned by Gabriel, Kate assumes. Naomi's feet are bare, and she drags them on the floor like a patient shuffling across the ward. The nails have not been trimmed for some time. Her skin is grey and her eyes half shut, but she has slept well, she says. Looking out at the garden, she says: 'Shouldn't you be at your desk?'

Kate tells her that she worked late last night, and needs another coffee to wake herself up.

'Going well?' asks Naomi, ten seconds later.

'Early days,' Kate answers; this does not prompt any further enquiries. Kate busies herself at the coffee machine, and Naomi watches closely, as if this procedure were new to her and hard to understand.

Kate takes her cup to the table, as Naomi takes an apple from the bowl. A bite is taken and the bitten part is examined; the red stains are visible across the room. Not a word is spoken for a full two minutes.

'I've time to listen,' says Kate.

Naomi turns, holding the apple up to her mouth; she looks at her sister over the horizon of the fruit. It's as though Kate has just offered her some sort of deal – a deal of extraordinary complexity and doubtful benefit. She sniffs, three or four times, quickly; something unpleasant has been detected. She lowers her nose to an armpit. 'I offend. I need a shower. Let's talk at lunchtime.' In passing, she strokes her sister's hair – or rather, she wipes a hand over it, as if performing badly an act of affection.

5.

Naomi is waiting at the kitchen table. She has assembled a salad for each of them, and poured two glasses of juice, and set a place for Kate on the opposite side of the table, dead centre. Her hair has been washed and left to dry in its own time. She is wearing a red kaftan, which appears to have been ironed this morning; she wants it to be observed that an effort has been made, Kate assumes. And so the talking begins.

The 'fateful meeting' – as Naomi terms it, with irony of uncertain direction – took place at a bookshop. She had gone there, with Gabriel, for a talk and reading by someone called Daffyd Paskin, author of a recently published book on the Romani of Britain. Daffyd Paskin had also presented a TV programme on the subject. The programme, says Naomi, had rankled with Gabriel, who had known this Paskin when he had gone by the name of David. The revision of the name, thought Gabriel, told you a lot about the man.

When he was working on his never-to-be-completed doctoral thesis, Gabriel had earned a little money by teaching the occasional seminar group. He was, says Naomi, a lacklustre teacher; Gabriel has always said so himself. Nobody emerged from one of his seminars inspired to become an anthropologist. He was ponderous and tactless; instead of being a catalyst, his interventions tended to smother debate. He could not improvise, he admitted. Another consideration: Gabriel was bored, and what bored him more than anything else was his own work. Every morning, at his desk, he had to battle against huge gusts of futility, he told Naomi. But onward he plodded, day after day, dogged as a polar explorer. Six days a week, ten hours a day, he toiled across the barren wastes of his research. By the time he came to teach the group that had David Paskin in it, he was beginning to lose his way. Week by week the pages multiplied. Arguments and counter-arguments proliferated. He could not impose clarity on the material that he was gathering. And, to make matters worse, he was coming to feel that being lost was a more authentic condition than the assumption of authority would have been. He knew that he was approaching the end of a phase of his life. The thesis would never be completed, and he had no idea what he would do after he had put it aside.

This was the situation when Gabriel came into contact with David Paskin. Initial impressions were unfavourable. Waiting for the new batch of students to arrive, Gabriel looked down from the seminar room and saw a small young man walking across the courtyard. The walk of the small young man was immensely irritating: he had a quick and bouncy gait which – in combination with the somewhat self-satisfied expression – made it seem as if he were crossing a stage to receive a prize. This was Paskin. A small gold earring dangled from his left ear – a silly affectation, in Gabriel's opinion, and a passé one at that. Paskin had a predilection for plain white shirts, usually with the upper two buttons undone – three, when it was imperative to make a good impression. Though short-sighted, he rarely wore glasses, and he eschewed contact lenses; the consequent squint imparted a few extra volts to the dark-eyed gaze. David Paskin was loquacious and not unintelligent. He was smart enough to steal his *aperçus* from books and articles that were not on the reading list.

'Gabriel has always been honest with himself,' Naomi tells her sister. His academic work, Gabriel would tell you, was never lit by flares of inspiration. He was industrious and meticulous; he was able to compose a cogent essay with ease; his mind was absorbent and retentive; he could process large quantities of information quickly, and recombine the elements in structures that were original in the juxtapositions that they created, if in no other respect. He was mediocre, he would often tell Naomi – too often, she now says. But he never passed off the ideas of others as his own, which was not the case with David Paskin. When Paskin held forth, Gabriel was often tempted, as he put it, to 'take a blade to his sails'. He never did take a blade to Paskin's sails, though. Gabriel is a gentle character; timid, even. He has a pathological aversion to conflict, says Naomi. And, besides, there was something impressive about the confidence of David Paskin, and the liveliness of the seminars in which he participated was largely to his credit, Gabriel conceded. Paskin was popular, and attractive to many, it appeared.

The programme about the Romani had annoyed Gabriel. The billowing shirt, the artfully unkempt hair, the quasi-Latin gaze – the whole gypsy-scholar routine was ridiculous. 'It really was,' Naomi assures her sister. It should be remembered, she says, that the title of Gabriel's aborted thesis was: *'A people without writing': the representation and self-representation of the British Romani.* 'You'd want to read that one, right?' she says. Before abandoning the thesis, Gabriel had published an article derived from it; a couple of sentences from Paskin's script, he said, had been taken verbatim from that article. Gabriel had also despised Paskin's first book, on cannibalism; it was nothing more than a cut and paste job, of course.

Naomi accompanied Gabriel to the bookshop event, to keep his spirits up and the resentment down. 'I tried to talk him out of it, but he said it had to be done,' she tells Kate, as she scans the ceiling, smiling at what she's remembering. Then she laughs – a quick dry cackle, which provokes a sequence of small coughs. 'It was even worse than expected,' she says, almost gleefully.

David/Daffyd Paskin read two brief sections from his book, then talked for twenty minutes about the experience of making his TV programme. Questions were taken from the audience; there were many questions, and they were answered with some wit. It appeared that he had reconciled himself to contact lenses, but the armour-piercing gaze was still in use: he trained the squint frequently on three young women in the front row. There was a preponderance of women in the audience, as Gabriel remarked. Gabriel was considering an intervention: he had a question about George Borrow, because he was sure that Paskin was not as familiar with the work of George Borrow as he made out to be. But before he could speak, someone sitting behind them wanted to know if Mr Paskin was aware of the church in Birmingham that was offering its congregation classes in the Romani language. The question was put in the manner of a benign examiner, and the voice was 'gorgeous', says Naomi: a grainy bass, extremely precise in its enunciation, as if English were not the speaker's first language, though there was no accent that

Naomi could hear. Naomi turned to see the speaker. His appearance did not disappoint: dark and deep-set eyes behind expensive-looking horn-rimmed spectacles, broad cheekbones, aquiline nose, a grey-and-charcoal beard, and thick greying hair, finger-combed back from his brow. He put Naomi in mind of pictures of Brahms in later life; a slightly less paunchy version of Brahms.

When the questions were done, the author signed copies of his book. Though he had not bought a copy, and had no intention of ever buying one, Gabriel joined the queue; he wanted to introduce himself. The man with the gorgeous voice was two or three places behind them. Naomi heard the voice murmuring, and a female voice, possibly Polish, whispering in reply. The woman was magnificent: considerably taller than the man, slender, with hair that had the colour and gloss of crude oil; her skin was as pale as writing paper, with invisible pores. She was young enough to be the man's daughter, but she was not his daughter – in fact, nothing in her expression or stance suggested any intimacy. Becoming aware of Naomi's attention, she returned it; her eyes were as cold as cameras. The bearded man nodded at Naomi, like a fame-weary actor or politician.

Arriving at the author's table, Gabriel told him that he had enjoyed the talk, and the book; he had a particular interest in the subject, he explained, as he had once worked in local government as a gypsy and traveller liaison officer. A brief conversation ensued; David/Daffyd glanced two or three times at the queue; he took note of the magnificent woman. More than two decades had passed since Gabriel and David Paskin had last been in a room together, and in the interim Gabriel had deteriorated to a greater extent than had the younger man. The contours of the face had slumped; the girth had slackened. Back in the days of his thesis, he had been clean-shaven; now he was not. His hair was considerably sparser. Nevertheless, it surprised him that there was not the slightest glimmer of recognition in Paskin's face. It crossed his mind that Paskin knew who he was, but thought it necessary, for whatever reason, not to show that he did. It was possible that he had disliked Gabriel as much as Gabriel had disliked him. But this explanation was weak: Paskin could not be so accomplished an actor. He was perfectly at ease, and he was talking to a stranger. It was hard to believe, but it must be true: he had entirely forgotten Gabriel. They shook hands. 'A pleasure to meet you,' said Gabriel. 'Likewise,' said Daffyd Paskin. 'Hope it sells,' said Gabriel.

Outside, fifty yards down the road from the shop, Gabriel hesitated at the door of a pub. 'I'm such a fucking toady,' he moaned, then out of the bookshop came Paskin, with the bearded man and the amazing pale-skinned woman. The trio walked off in the opposite direction; Paskin laughed, as loud as a trumpet; the young woman walked two paces behind the men, head lowered, swiping her phone.

'That's where it began,' says Naomi, getting up from the table. 'More later. I need a lie down,' she says faintly, pressing the back of a hand to her brow, in a self-parodic mime of exhaustion.

6.

Instead of working, Kate watches Daffyd Paskin's programme online.

The presenter sits on a stone wall. A light breeze tickles the hair, which has been tended with great care to look as if no trouble has been taken with it. The shirt, striped blue and white, is soft, capacious, untucked; the jeans are mildly distressed. He is easy on the eye; the darkness of hair and eye do make an impact, Kate allows. An adjust-ment of the camera angle reveals, over his shoulder, the quivering sea, gilded by the setting sun. The camera moves to the front and pulls back; a book is open on Daffyd's knee. The set-up is contrived, but this is what the genre requires. He reads:

Coin si deya, coin se dado?
Pukker mande drey Romanes,
Ta mande pukkeravava tute.

He lifts his face and addresses us: 'These three lines, dating back to the time of the first Queen Elizabeth, and perhaps beyond, are the oldest recorded specimen of the gypsy language of Britain.' He translates:

'*Who's your mother, who's your father?*
Do thou answer me in Romany,
And I will answer thee.'

The Romani people of our island, he tells us, are our most misunderstood and maligned community. 'Or rather, communities,' he corrects himself. After imparting a little history, he conducts us to a rank of caravans; we follow him to a door; it opens, and a weather-beaten woman – her name is Judith – welcomes her guest with an awkward pretence of spontaneity. Two men and a woman are seated by the far window, talking incompre-hensibly. They are Kalè: Welsh gypsies, originally from Spain and France. The Romani dialect of the Kalè – a stew of Sanskrit, Arabic, English, French, Greek, Welsh, German, Romanian and other ingredients – survived into the 1950s, Daffyd informs us. Today they speak a species of Angloromani, which is English in grammar and syntax, but heavily spiced with Romani words. Room is found for Daffyd on the window seat. 'We breed ponies and run

them on the beaches,' says one of the men, then he says it
again, in his own language. Daffyd wants to know if they
use this language only at home.

'No,' answers Judith. 'We use it when we don't want
gadjos to understand.'

'What are gadjos?' Daffyd enquires.

'You're a gadjo,' Judith teases, to general laughter. They
seem to like him; he is likeable. After a lesson on the
subject of Romani hygiene and the exalted status of the
horse, Daffyd drives to Southend for a chat with an aged
lady called Lillian, who has colourful memories of travelling to Kent in the spring to train the hop vines, and of
returning in the autumn for the harvest. Her son is a boxer;
she shows Daffyd a small sign – gold lettering on black
plastic – that her son stole from a London pub: No Blacks,
No Dogs, No Gypsies. In a vox pop interlude, selected
members of the public duly play their pig-ignorant part.
'Don't believe in work, do they?' responds a fearsome
London matron in a supermarket car park. A rheumy-eyed
old bloke declares that gypsies should be put in camps,
'with a barbed wire and all'.

For the final segment we return north, to a dismal
housing estate somewhere by the north Yorkshire coast.
We see an end-of-terrace house, its side wall stained
with imperfectly erased graffiti. Daffyd stands in front of
the wall to tell us that in addition to the Romanichals,
who have been his subject hitherto, Britain is home to a
sizeable community of Romani who have arrived since
the last war, chiefly from central and eastern Europe.
These people are not travellers; the family who live in this
house have been here since 1970. At the door his hand
is shaken meatily by a black-haired and handsome man,
forty-ish, with eyes as dark as obsidian. This is Budek,
who leads us to the living room, where the head of the

household, also Budek, awaits, enthroned in a leather armchair. The cameras film the entrance of Daffyd; he affects the delight of a discoverer; it's a routine piece of play-acting. A cimbalom has been set up in the room and the younger Budek proceeds to play for the visitor: the music is of extraordinary delicacy and complexity, and his hands fly back and forth across the strings like feeding swallows. He grins as he watches his hands at play, as though they were no part of him. The old man's smile, almost toothless, is tinged with what we are invited to perceive as the melancholy of exile. Younger Budek's wife – a buxom nut-brown woman with arms like bowling pins – declaims a song, unaccompanied; it sounds like a lament, but we are not told what she's singing about. The last shot of Daffyd shows him agog, as well he might be.

The programme is a performance, as all such programmes are, and Daffyd Paskin's performance is very professional, thinks Kate; he patronises neither his audience nor his subjects; he is personable; perhaps rather vain, but not without reason.

7.

Mid-afternoon, in the kitchen, Kate asks: 'And how is Gabriel?'

'He's all right,' says Naomi.

'But you're no longer—?'

'No, we're not,' says Naomi.

'I'm sorry to hear that,' says Kate.

'All good things come to an end,' says Naomi, with a quick and overbright smile. 'Anyway, how goes the writing? Anything you could share?'

'Not yet,' Kate apologises.

'So shall I resume?' asks Naomi, as if assuming respon-
sibility.

A couple of months after the bookshop event, Naomi
tells her sister, she and Gabriel went to a concert, a recital
of piano music by Ravel and Debussy. The pianist, a young
and glamorous French woman, was dazzling; for Gabriel's
taste, however, Ravel and Debussy were still too sweet. He
was not in the best of moods that evening. In recent months
they had often been in less than perfect accord, Naomi
tells her sister. He was frequently morose. Gabriel, as Kate
knows, is a man who has no interest in fashioning a career
for himself, but life as a shop-floor drone was beginning to
oppress him. 'Humility has its limits,' says Naomi. On the
way to the concert Gabriel had been particularly irascible,
she recalls. He had been determined to have no pleasure,
and no pleasure was duly had. When the applause was
finished, Gabriel took his time fastening every button of
his raincoat, as if he were about to step out into a storm,
though the evening was dry and mild.

Naomi was standing in the aisle, waiting for him, when
her attention was caught by a piece of gorgeous colour –
a broad and bright red beret, an authentic Basque *boina*,
which was being settled on a thick crop of silver hair. The
silver-haired woman must have been in her seventies,
says Naomi, but she was immensely stylish: she wore a
full-skirted black coat and a dark grey high-necked top,
probably cashmere, with a necklace of garnet-coloured
beads that were the size of peach stones. So impressive
was this woman that Naomi did not immediately notice
that her companion, still seated one place from the end
of the row, was the Brahms-like man. He stood up, and
the woman took his arm; from the quality of the gaze she
directed at him, and vice versa, it appeared that she was
his mother. Naomi looked towards Gabriel, but he was

facing the wrong way, adjusting his collar and glaring at the piano as if he blamed it for his ill humour. By the time he joined her, the elegant woman and her son had left. Naomi told Gabriel that she had just seen the man who had been at Paskin's reading. Gabriel was not in the slightest bit interested.

Many apparent coincidences are in fact nothing of the sort, Naomi believes. At all times, she is inclined to see significance where others – nearly all others – would see none. Three yellow cars bumper to bumper in a queue; the discovery that a likeable stranger's name is Naomi; the sighting of two pairs of identical twins in the same day; the sudden appearance, on the radio, of a piece of music that had been in her mind only an hour before – such occurrences are not messages, necessarily, but signs that something beyond our understanding is at work. That the second sighting of Brahms's double was a meaningful event rather than an unremarkable example of the workings of chance was proven to Naomi two months later, when she saw him for the third time.

This decisive encounter also took place in a concert hall, at another piano recital. This time, the main item consisted of a single ninety-minute piece by Morton Feldman – ninety minutes of slow repetitions and gradually shifting chords, 'never louder than pianissimo, with no melodies, no expression', reports Naomi, as if such a thing were marvellous. It was, she says, 'a transcendental experience'. Gabriel would have made a run for it after ten minutes, had it been possible to remove himself inconspicuously.

The intriguing man was there. In the foyer, after the concert, he glanced over the shoulder of a man who was talking to him and recognised Gabriel and Naomi, a split second after Naomi had spotted him. It was as though he had heard her call his name, she says. He went outside, and waited.

'It was incredible,' says Naomi. 'What are the odds?'

The odds against two Londoners with an interest in twentieth-century classical music attending the same two concerts of twentieth-century classical music in London would probably not be terribly long, it seems to Kate, but she feigns a befitting astonishment.

It surprised Naomi that the man evidently remembered them. His first words to her were equally surprising. He asked simply, with no preamble: 'What did you think?' It was as though they were already well acquainted; more than that – it was as though she were a friend whose opinion was of value to him. She made an observation that was inane, she says, but he agreed with what she said, and with such genuineness that her self-conscious-ness evaporated in an instant. He introduced himself; she misheard his name as Bernard, so he repeated it.

'Naomi,' she responded.

Shaking her hand, he said: 'My delight.'

She did not know what to say to this; it was pronounced with a smile, as if it were some form of courtly greeting.

'Naomi – my delight,' he repeated. 'That's what it means.' He had known a Naomi many years ago, he explained; another coincidence.

It was established that they were walking to the same Tube station. Bernát seemed to intuit that this had been Gabriel's first exposure to the music of Morton Feldman. 'A tough introduction,' he sympathised. Gabriel, self-deprecating, remarked that he felt more at home in eighteenth-century London or Paris than in twentieth-century New York; ninety minutes of murmuring piano were an ordeal, but four hours of Handel were quite the opposite; he could listen to da capo arias until the cows came home. Bernát understood: whenever he listened to Handel, or to Bach or Vivaldi or any of a dozen others, he felt a 'terrible nostalgia', he said. In the space of two minutes it became evident that this was not verbiage, says Naomi. Bernát was a man of profound sensibility and knowledge. God, he quipped, was Bach's right-hand man; the joke amused Naomi rather more than it did Gabriel.

The conversation turned to the music to which they had just been listening, and what followed, Naomi tells her sister, was remarkable. She found that she was strangely at ease; her thoughts were not entirely articulate, but she was not ashamed to expose them. The tone was serious; it was as though she and Bernát were 'scientists engaged in the same problems'; Bernát, of course, was the senior figure; Gabriel said very little. Gabriel has many fine qualities, says Naomi; he is an intelligent man, but she cannot recall ever having had a conversation with Gabriel that was like this one with Bernát. She could never have talked to Gabriel about music in the way that Bernát made possible. Bernát, she says, had a 'philosophical mind'. Duration, in the ninety-minute piano piece, was a means of focusing attention, Bernát proposed. In a piece of such extraordinary length, one perceives not form but scale, he said. The absence of melodic incident has the effect of eliminating the action of memory; and because, in the absence of memorable patterns, we do not – cannot – remember precisely what has come before, we do not anticipate what is to come; we experience time as a perpetually self-renewing moment. A saturation of time was what this music gave us, said Bernát, Naomi tells Kate. She is aware that this might sound pretentious; Gabriel used that adjective, later in the evening. But if Kate were to hear the music she would understand what Bernát was saying. She has it on CD. 'You're welcome to borrow it,' Naomi offers.

Kate is prepared to take on trust her sister's assurance that Bernát's comments on the incident-free ninety minutes of piano music were acute and illuminating.

They were standing on the kerb, waiting for the traffic lights to change, when Bernát remarked that he had seen Naomi and Gabriel in May, at a concert. It could only have been the concert at which she had seen him with the woman she had assumed to be his mother, but she did not reveal that she had seen him too. 'Oh really?' was all she said. He had been sitting five or six rows behind them, he told her, and from his smile it was clear that he had observed that there had been some tension in the situation. At the station they halted, prior to taking separate lines. From inside his jacket Bernát produced a notebook; from the opposite pocket he took not a pen but a propelling pencil – antique, tortoiseshell. He told Gabriel about a CD of Handel cantatas that he had bought a few days earlier; he thought Gabriel would like it, he said, and he wrote down the details. Underneath, he wrote an address. Once a month, on the third Thursday, his house was open to anyone who cared to visit; around a dozen people usually dropped by, 'to listen to music, to talk'; it was 'a kind of salon, if you like,' he said, with some self-mockery, but his eyes were expressive of seriousness. The next gathering was a fortnight away; a friend of his, a violinist, would be playing sonatas by Geminiani and Giardini, he told Gabriel – plus some Bartók, he added for Naomi. 'You would be most welcome. Both of you,' he said, and he shook hands, with Gabriel first. He gave Naomi a smile of intense cordiality, as if their meeting had been a planned event, and had been even more fruitful than he had expected.

The social life of Naomi and Gabriel was meagre. Teaching children how to play the flute is no way to establish connections with interesting adults, and from the outline of Gabriel's career, if career it could be called, it might be concluded that this was a man intent on maximising the tedium and isolation of his life. After abandoning his thesis, he had worked as a Gypsy and Traveller Liaison Officer for ten unhappy years, spending too many hours, as he put it, 'arguing with people in muddy fields'. He'd had dogs set on him several times, and a Calor gas canister thrown at his car; the final straw was a punch in the face. The punch was delivered by an eight-year-old with fists like lumps of volcanic rock; the boy was applauded by his father, who earned a living by tipping asphalt over people's driveways and leaving the job half done; the father's van had the promise *All work guranteed* painted on the side. Enough was enough, Gabriel had decided. A sequence of undemanding and unremunerative jobs had followed, a downward trajectory that had brought him, by the time he met Naomi, to the payroll of a large London bookshop, where all of his colleagues were younger than him, by some margin, and none could be regarded as friends. No friendships remained from earlier years. This situation did not bother Gabriel greatly, but Naomi, though by no means gregarious, had begun to chafe, she says. The invitation from Bernát would have been welcome even if he had been less intriguing.

Having a low tolerance for the music of Bartók, and none of the skills that one needs to negotiate a room full of strangers, Gabriel decided to absent himself from Bernát's soirée. The following month, he again preferred to stay at home; he always preferred to stay at home. He could not allow himself to go, says Naomi, because it was important to make it appear that he was not jealous, which he was, even though she told him over and over again that she was not going to have sex with Bernát, ever.

Bernát's house was a nondescript semi, postwar, in a cul-de-sac of miscellaneous houses within ten minutes' walk of Wimbledon Common. It was sizeable, with an extensive garden, but Bernát lived alone; there had never been a wife, it was ascertained, somewhat later. On the evening of the first gathering that Naomi attended, eight or nine other people turned up. They gathered in a room that ran from the front of the house to the back. By the garden window stood a piano, a Broadwood baby grand of considerable age. The floor was bare boards, sanded and varnished, and the walls and ceiling were white; there were some photographs, framed, monochrome, of grass-lands and forests, some of them populated by hunting parties of moustachioed men with long feathers in their caps and large dogs at their feet, or dead deer. Three chrome and black leather armchairs, placed against the walls, were the only furnishings. Cosy was not a word that would come readily to mind when you looked at this room, says Naomi; the implication is that Kate would not have liked it, because Kate is a woman for whom cosiness is a domestic necessity.

Bernát greeted Naomi with warmth, as if her arrival were a guarantee of the evening's success. First he showed her the kitchen, where a table was laden with plates of bread, pretzels, sausages, cold meats, cheeses, pickles and bottles of Hungarian wine; it did not cross her mind until she was going home that Bernát had perhaps assumed that, being a large lady, she was someone for whom the food would be of paramount importance. After the presentation of the kitchen he introduced her to Helen and Amy, whose conversation seemed to be in need of refreshment. Helen was a demure but powerfully perfumed woman of about sixty, with damson-coloured eyeshadow, lavishly applied. Amy, perhaps thirty years younger, was thin and twitchy, with the corroded teeth of a long-term bulimic and a tendency to laugh at moments when a smile would have sufficed; her mouth barely opened when she laughed, and the sound was like a small yelp, as if she had been jabbed with a pin. She was a maths teacher, she told Naomi, in a tone of insincere apology; Bernát was also a mathematician, she said; she had met him at a concert, whereas Helen had met him at the cinema, at a screening of a film by Miklós Jancsó, the title of which was now eluding her, but it was set during the Second World War and Bernát had made some very interesting comments about it.

Amy told a joke. Enrico Fermi was once asked by colleagues at Los Alamos why, if there were intelligent beings elsewhere in our galaxy, we hadn't yet heard a peep from them. And one of those colleagues, a Hungarian, replied that extraterrestrials hadn't merely made contact – they were living among us, and were quite easy to spot, because they roamed all over the planet, spoke a language that was unlike any other, and were much more intelligent than humans. They called themselves Hungarians. The violinist, who was now tuning up, was Hungarian too, Helen believed. Her name was Marta, thought Helen, and she was an unusually handsome woman, tall, forty-ish but slim as a highjumper, with oaken hair and glacier-blue eyes. Hungarians were also known for their beauty, Helen remarked; she had a list of good-looking Hungarians – Zsa Zsa Gabor, Paul Newman, Tony Curtis. Until this point, there had been no male guests, but now a man arrived – the one who had been talking to Bernát after the Feldman concert, Naomi thought. He took possession of an armchair after a businesslike greeting for Bernát, and listened to the recital with the impassivity of an almost unimpressable connoisseur; he left within minutes of its finishing, having fiercely congratulated the violinist and the pianist who had accompanied her for the Bartók piece. The performance was of professional standard, says Naomi.

The following month, some Bach preludes and fugues were played by the pale woman who had been with Bernát at the bookshop; her name was Jolenta; she was often at Bernát's house and she was never seen to smile. Jolenta's face registered no emotion whatever as she played; her eyes tracked the movements of her hands as if observing the workings of a pianola. Her style was too austere and analytical for Naomi, who warmed rather more to the young flautist who performed a fantasia by Telemann one evening. Her breath control was astounding, says Naomi, and she was a remarkable sight too, with a wild thatch of stiff auburn hair, which veiled her eyes completely. Upon discovering Naomi's profession, Bernát asked her if she might play for them one evening; having heard the auburn-haired flautist, she demurred, and Bernát did not press her to reconsider.

Sometimes, when most of the guests had gone home, Bernát himself would sit at the piano and play. His technique was unremarkable; at the age of twelve Naomi could play things that would have been too difficult for Bernát. Yet he was, she says, 'deeply musical'. The compositions that he played were simple and brief, but they were far from trivial, and his playing was of great sensitivity and eloquence. He understood what lay 'beyond the notes', Naomi tells her sister, who declines to ask what this phrase might mean. There was a 'powerful sincerity' to Bernát's playing, says Naomi; he knew how to phrase the music, how to give it shape. His preference was for music that was quiet and contemplative. Three or four times he played a short piece called *Angelico*, from Mompou's *Musica Callada*; it's a delicate and melancholy miniature, in which the left hand conjures the chime of church bells, Naomi explains, and Bernát's performance of it moved her deeply. It was like 'an act of devotion', she says.

Another room was set aside for Bernát's hi-fi system; the equipment was self-evidently engineered to the highest specifications, and the collection of CDs was vast, filling two entire walls. For his guests he would play recordings that he had recently bought, and there was rarely an occasion on which he did not bring to Naomi's attention a composer who was unknown to her. His knowledge of the repertoire was 'astounding', she says. Sacred music was a particular interest: Morales, Victoria, Palestrina, Tallis, Guerrero, Josquin, Schütz, Lassus – these were of the greatest significance to him, and Bach, as goes without saying. He did not much care for Beethoven and his successors. The high artifice of the Baroque was healthier than the self-advertisement of Romanticism, he declared, says Naomi, as if this pronouncement were something one might wish to write down.

Music was not the only attraction of Bernát's salon. For some of the guests, it seemed, the place was akin to a private club, and they came in the expectation of good conversation. In the months that Naomi attended these gatherings she met as many as fifty different people, she estimates. The company was remarkably disparate. In the course of a single evening Naomi met a physicist who was working at CERN, a film-maker who had spent six months alone in a forest in Siberia, a tree surgeon who had been struck by lightning twice, and a designer of artificial limbs. On another occasion she passed an hour with a mountaineer who had fallen five hundred feet in the Andes and broken only a wrist. She came to know a woman who had worked on the Tube Alloys programme, and an ex-jockey who had become a stuntman. The stuntman had many tales to tell and alarming scars to display.

Even tougher than the stuntman, though, was the young man named Connor; this was the Connor who had been in Scotland. Naomi met him on her third or fourth evening; she went out into the garden and came upon him, sitting on one of the benches by the magnolias; he was smoking, and staring at the wall in front on him. He did not look like any of Bernát's other guests: to be frank, admits Naomi, he looked rough. He was wearing a T-shirt and jeans, and both items were less than pristine. It was immediately noticeable, too, that he was powerful: the biceps were substantial, and the whole neck and head arrangement, says Naomi, had the shape of a lump of cement that had been cast in a bucket. Above one ear, visible through the crewcut, he had a tattoo of a sniper's cross-hairs; the forearms were heavily inked. What's more, his expression as he stared at the brickwork suggested that some grievance was uppermost in his mind. But when he caught sight of Naomi his expression changed entirely, in an instant; he raised a hand and smiled, and the smile was disarmingly diffident. 'Nearly done,' he said, indicating the stump of the cigarette; it was as though he thought she had some prior claim to the garden.

'Don't go on my account,' said Naomi; despite herself, she sounded like the lady of the manor, she thought. She made some remark about the mildness of the evening; he responded in kind.

'I'm guessing you're a singer,' said the young man.

'Big lungs, you mean?' said Naomi. 'The proverbial fat lady who sings before it's over.'

'Not what I meant,' he lied; he had beautifully thick-lashed eyes, she noted, and eyebrows as sleek as a woman's.

'No, I'm not a singer,' said Naomi.

'Come out for a fag?' he asked.

'Don't sing, don't smoke,' said Naomi.

He stubbed out the cigarette on the underside of the bench. 'How's the show?' he asked, nodding towards the house.

'Excellent,' said Naomi; it was one of Jolenta's evenings.

The music wasn't his kind of thing, he said, but there were some fine-looking women here. 'Pity I'm not their type,' he said, lighting another cigarette.

Jolenta was quite a woman, Naomi agreed.

It was a nice house, he remarked – the nicest house he'd ever been in, unless you counted the ones he'd entered without permission.

Naomi did not react in any way, so Connor made sure that she understood: he had been in prison, he told her.

'Is that how you met Bernát?' she asked.

'Fuck me, no,' he guffawed.

She had to tell him that she had been joking.

'Well, you can never be sure,' said Connor.

'So how do you know him?' she asked.

'We drink together,' Connor answered. There was a pub in Wimbledon where Connor often went, and that's where he had come across Bernát. One evening Bernát turned up, on his own, took a pint to a corner table, and sat there with the newspaper; after an hour or so, and a couple more pints, he left. He was noticeable, said Connor; he looked like some sort of wizard, with the grey beard and the all-black outfit. A few nights later, he was back; the same routine – in the corner with the paper, on his own, two or three pints, go home. He kept coming back, and it was always the same routine. Then Connor said something to him at the bar, and they hit it off. Connor was a mechanic, and he liked motorbikes; Bernát's father had been a mechanic, and he had built motorbikes; there were things to talk about, and 'you know how he can talk', said Connor. 'Can hold his drink as well,' said Connor, and this was something that Naomi had already noticed; Bernát never appeared to be drunk, but he put paid to at least one bottle of wine in the course of an evening.

So they became acquainted, and then an incident occurred that made them more than acquaintances. They were sitting in Bernát's corner, chatting, when a man at a nearby table got it into his head to take exception to the way Bernát was looking at him. This character was someone who wanted to be noticed, said Connor: a loud bastard, a gym bunny. And Bernát duly noticed him. All he did was glance at him once or twice, when the dickhead was yelling into one of his phones (he had two, laid out on the table), but 'you know the way Bernát looks at you', said Connor; Naomi knew what he meant – when Bernát looks at you, even if it's only for a second, you know you've been looked at. The 'laser vision', Connor called it. 'What the fuck are you looking at?' the dickhead enquired, and words were exchanged, with Connor acting as Bernát's spokesman. At closing time, out in the street, more than words were exchanged.

'I have anger issues,' Connor admitted. 'When I lose it, I really lose it,' he said, eyes widening at the enormity of his rage. He had been in the army, and the things he had seen had done his head in. Before the army he had been a bit of a handful, he told Naomi, but after the army he'd really had problems keeping the lid on it. 'Not that the army wasn't great,' he said, to clear up any possible misunderstanding. Many men have confided prematurely to Naomi. In recent years, some of her dates – for want of a better word – have quickly become something more like confessionals. Her 'maternal bulk' is the explanation, she has concluded.

'Don't go looking for trouble, but if trouble finds you, strike first, and always go for the face.' This was Connor's golden rule, and he had put it to the test several times since learning it from his father at the age of ten, a few months before his father had buggered off. In accordance with the rule, a fist was brought to the dickhead's nose with all available force, and down he went, 'like his legs had become balloons', as Connor put it. 'I didn't start it, but I sure as fuck finished it,' he told Naomi, with some pride. But things had gone a bit tits-up after that. It came to court, where Bernát gave evidence, to no avail. So Connor was back in the slammer for a while and when he came out he didn't have a job; then his girlfriend decided she didn't want him living in her flat any longer, because it was just one thing after another with him – and she had a point, Connor conceded. This is where Bernát stepped up to the plate: he had a spare room that he offered to Connor, rent-free, until he got himself sorted out. And he was getting himself sorted out quickly, he told Naomi; through a friend of a friend of a friend of Bernát's he'd got a job – a crappy job, in a warehouse, working nights, but it was a start, and he was going to do a flatshare with one of the blokes from work, so he'd be out of Bernát's way in a week or two. Bernát was a great bloke, Connor asserted; he was like the uncle you always wanted, he said. 'How many people do you know who would have done what he did?' he asked. Bernát was an unusual man, Naomi agreed.

Bernát in turn was fond of Connor. Given what Connor had experienced as a boy, it was a wonder that he was able to function in society at all, said Bernát. A sister had died of meningitis; the girl might have pulled through had the parents not been too pissed to notice that something was seriously amiss. After his sister's death, Connor was taken away for a while, but then he was returned to the parents, who spent most of each day in a stupor. The father seems to have been his wife's pimp; Connor's reading of the situation was that his father absconded when she became too much a wreck to earn any sort of income. Then, when Connor was twelve, his mother took him to the shops one morning. In his mind's eye, Connor could still see her: she was wearing flip-flops, though it was November, and a red sweatshirt; in his memory, she was wearing that sweatshirt all the time. When they reached the checkout she realised she had forgotten something. 'Wait here,' she told him, pressing down on his shoulders, as if to plant him in the ground. Connor watched his mother slouch away. Five minutes passed, and she did not come back. He waited for another five, then walked down the aisle to the place where his mother had last been seen. There was no sign of her. She was gone for good.

Connor had been through some terrible things, Bernát told Naomi one evening, when every other guest had gone. Connor's time in the army, for all its danger and horror, had been the best part of his life, Bernát believed. Bernát knew that he could not have endured the things that Connor had endured. 'I am not courageous,' Bernát confessed, as though he had once been found wanting. 'But my father, he was brave, like Connor.' Now, many months after their first meeting, Naomi was told about Bernát's family.

His father's name was Zsiga, and he had worked in the Pannónia factory in Csepel, alongside his brother, Gyuri. Bernát's mother, Anikó, was a secretary in the same factory. When the Russians came in, Zsiga and Gyuri both fought on the streets. Gyuri was wounded on November 11, and before Christmas the brothers had fled, taking Anikó, Bernát and Bernát's brother, Oszkár; Bernát was three years old, Oszkár four. After some months of wandering, they had settled in the West Midlands. Gyuri found work with Guy Motors, in Wolverhampton, and Zsiga was taken on by Villiers, a few miles away, on the other side of town; Anikó, however, was a housewife for many years, and it was hard for her, said Bernát, because she was adrift for a long time. She used her first language only with her husband and his brother and her children, who were growing up quickly in the language of England, which she was struggling to acquire, through exchanges with neighbours and shopkeepers. As time passed she would have felt that she was losing the words that had formed her, because they were not the words of the world she was now inhabiting. It was important to her that her children should not speak only the language of their place of refuge – she wanted them to retain the language of their true home, because she hoped that they would one day return to Budapest. It was not until 1992 that Zsiga and Anikó went back; Zsiga died in 1995, and Anikó four years later; Gyuri had followed them to Hungary in 1993, and still lived there; but Bernát and his brother had not returned, because they 'belonged nowhere', he said, says Naomi. Belonging nowhere, Naomi seems to be telling her sister, was as much a blessing as an affliction.

'When my brother and I become extinct, the language of the motherland passes out of our family,' said Bernát, with some regret, but not much. He had no children, and would never have children, and Oszkár's sons knew no more than a few phrases of Hungarian; Uncle Gyuri had produced no offspring, because it had turned out that he did not like women in the way a man should like them, which was a big disgrace for Bernát's father, whose ideas on such matters were not sophisticated. But his father was a fine man, said Bernát, and he had worshipped his wife as if she were a gift of heaven. And Anikó had taken some solace from his devotion; it was partial recompense for the discontents of exile.

His mother, said Bernát, was too much taken with the idea of Hungarian uniqueness. Hungarians, she would tell you, are 'idealistic, quick-tempered, sometimes too soft-hearted, with a tendency to dreaminess', and Anikó accordingly did her best to be idealistic, quick-tempered, soft-hearted and dreamy. 'I am not many of those things,' said Bernát, 'but I do have her eyes.' At this point, says Naomi, Bernát directed into her eyes a gaze that made her flinch, a gaze 'stripped of all camouflage'; it was as if a trapdoor had been opened for a moment, she says; it was uncanny, like the revelation that some portraits throw at you; what she saw was a mind of terrible depth and unhappiness. Then he blinked, and smiled, and the trapdoor was shut.

Bernát continued with his story. His mother, he said, was delighted that he had become a mathematician, because to her way of thinking mathematics was a form of dreaming. Mathematicians were idealists, living in a pure and other-worldly realm of abstract symbols, where nothing was solid. Bernát went to a good university to study maths, and did well there. Tutors encouraged him to undertake postgraduate studies. His mother was therefore dismayed when Bernát instead went into finance; he was recruited by an investment bank in London. And for some time he enjoyed his work, he admitted to Naomi, she tells her sister, as if recounting a morality tale. He took pleasure in the analysis of immensities of data, and in the calculation of complex probabilities. His work was of benefit to all, he believed: at his word, money was bestowed on companies that in consequence thrived, and everyone profited, and so the great turbine of finance was kept spinning. But the wider benefit was rarely at the forefront of his mind, he confessed. He was a master of a mighty game, a game that required the application of knowledge and intelligence, and he was being paid royally for playing it.

He liked having money, Bernát admitted to Naomi, she tells her sister. For a long time he had wanted to live in London, and London was an expensive city – particularly if you had to live in a safe part of town and wouldn't settle for anything less than the best seats at the opera, Bernát joked. And his parents were proud of his success. They accepted a car from him; they allowed him to pay for holidays. But there was some ambivalence in their pride, said Bernát. It took a long time for his mother to wholly relinquish her fantasy of a professorship for her son, while his father would never abandon his belief in the supreme moral value of virile labour. To his father's way of thinking, Bernát knew, making money from money was not true work. And Bernát, increasingly, was ambivalent about himself. Factories were becoming ruins all around the town where Bernát and his brother had grown up, and their father had come to understand that the company bosses in England were as bad as the party bosses back home, or worse. Where the steel mill had stood for a hundred years there was now a shopping centre; in the centre of town, in consequence, shops were going out of business. 'A victim of the vampire,' his father commented, as they passed another defunct premises. Bernát might have attempted to talk about 'the bigger picture' and the better times that would follow this 'difficult period of restructuring', he thought, he told Naomi, who is at pains to ensure that her sister hears the inverted commas. Father and son had disagreements. Heavily armoured by theory, Bernát emerged from these arguments unscathed, or so it would have appeared. But, he told Naomi, with each argument he suffered a fresh wound, a wound that was invisible but could not be healed. With each visit to the home town he was weakening. The visits became infrequent; this was attributable, he later realised, to a burgeoning but unacknowledged shame.

Queen Victoria is said to have pulled down the blinds of her train carriage to protect herself from the sight of the Black Country, and that's what Bernát was like, he told Naomi: he pulled down the blinds rather than think about what he had seen there. But in the end the blinds came up. It was no longer possible to carry on as if this money-making had no victims. With capitalism there are always victims, by definition, Bernát acknowledged to himself at last, Naomi reports, relaying the slogan to her sister as if it were the insight of a provocative mind. But Bernát did not leave the system: he repositioned himself within it, putting his money – and no one else's – into 'sustainable enterprises'. In this way, he said, he made amends for his sins and assuaged his guilt, to an extent. Bernát was hard on himself, says Naomi. It was easy enough to recalibrate his position, he said, having already earned so much. He lacked the courage for anything more radical, and he did not believe that there was any prospect of victory anyway. The banks crash and whole countries are ruined, and we are told that nothing will be the same again, that the system has to change now that people are going hungry in the cities of the civilised world. But time goes by and things remain the same, albeit with some background noise of protest. The masters are invulnerable, says Naomi, quoting Bernát.

In lieu of more direct action, Bernát also paid a tithe, he revealed. Ten percent of his income went to charities.

'So he told you about his generosity,' Kate comments.

This is an ungenerous response, her sister tells her. Bernát was not praising himself – far from it. He was entering a plea in mitigation, she suggests. 'And I don't find him attractive,' she says, in answer to an imagined remark. 'Not in that way.'

Naomi's naivety can surprise her sister, still. 'But you're going to live with him,' says Kate.

'We're going to be living in the same place, yes.'

'Just the two of you.'

'Yes, just the two of us. One plus one. Not a couple,' she says, getting up. 'Bizarre, eh?'

'I wouldn't go that far. Unusual, though.'

Naomi bends to put a kiss on the crown of her sister's head. 'See you later,' she says. 'Get back to work.'

8.

Richard Staunton, father of Naomi and Kate, was an actuary. Marine insurance was his field of expertise, and he was highly competent; within a decade he was made a director of the company for which he worked. His daughters, to whom the details of his work were as incomprehensible as the formulas of astrophysics, admired him; there was some fear in the admiration, especially in the case of the older daughter, who had seen her father angered. His intellect was unfathomable; his job involved the consideration of potential misfortune, but he looked on those misfortunes as if they were abstract propositions; he was a master of esoteric knowledge, and this knowledge had an aura of the fateful. He was a man of some gravitas, and his gaze was acute – it was not possible to lie to him, the daughters found. He was tall, lean and not prone to laughter; in a film, the older daughter thought, he might play a knighted surgeon, or a secret agent in wartime. Deliberation seemed to precede everything he did; his voice was quiet and steeped in certainty. Spontaneous demonstrations of affection were rare; the younger daughter was favoured, to a small degree, perhaps because she more closely resembled her mother and was more docile, and less robust, than her sibling. His protection, Naomi knew, was one of life's few constants.

His work was a source of great satisfaction and pride to him, and he devoted long hours to it, often staying at his desk late into the evening. His duty to the company was like an officer's to his regiment. Leaving home on Thursday, November 19, 1987, he reminded his wife that she should not expect him home before ten o'clock. At eleven she went to bed, alone but unperturbed. This had happened before, many times. Less than an hour later, the doorbell rang; she opened the door to two police officers, male and female, who informed her that Mr Staunton had been injured in a traffic incident, and had been taken to the Royal Marsden. She drove to the hospital, where she stayed until the Saturday morning, when her husband, having never regained consciousness, died.

He had been found in Clive Road, West Dulwich, by a resident of that street, who, having heard what sounded like a large box being dropped, followed by the tyre squeal of a car departing at speed, looked out of his window and saw a man spreadeagled on the road. A stolen car, abandoned less than a mile away, had damage that was compatible with its having struck a pedestrian; a man named Nelson Tansley, aged 29, was promptly arrested, after a tip-off. At the trial, the defence contended that Mr Staunton, in conditions of poor visibility (it was dark, and the nearest streetlight was defective, and it was raining), had stepped into the road without looking, so close to the defendant's vehicle that a collision would have been unavoidable even in clear and dry conditions. It was denied that the vehicle was moving at an excessive speed, but was conceded that the defendant had stolen the car that had killed Mr Staunton, and had driven away from the scene of the accident – an unthinking reaction that the jury was invited to understand, if not condone. Nelson Tansley presented his evidence with the air of a man who expected to be disbelieved, because such was his fate; after the verdict it was learned that he had a number of thefts and assaults to his name. Coaxed by his counsel, Nelson Tansley expressed regret for what had happened. When sentenced, he raised an eyebrow and shrugged; leaving the dock, he patted the guard on the shoulder as though they were going off to do a job together. By Christmas of the following year he was free.

Before Nelson Tansley had left the courtroom, Kate conceived the idea of killing him on his release, or at least causing an accident that would break some major bones. Were it not for the fact that she would immediately have been one of the chief suspects, she would, she believed, have run him down without compunction. For several years, intermittently, she entertained this idea of retribution. Soon after the sentencing, however, the punishment of Nelson Tansley ceased to be her primary concern.

Richard Staunton had been crossing Clive Road to his car when Tansley drove into him. Why Richard Staunton should have parked in Clive Road, a road that no conceivable route between office and home would have taken him near, was a question that perplexed his family, and their perplexity was augmented by the quickly established fact that Richard Staunton had left his office no later than 7pm on the night of the accident. His elder daughter, then seventeen, took it upon herself to investigate: carrying a photograph of her father, she spent a Saturday knocking on every door in Clive Road and the adjoining streets. One woman thought she had seen the man in the picture, four or five months ago, getting into an expensive car, possibly an Audi. Richard Staunton drove an Audi. The next day, she canvassed a wider area; eventually, in Martell Road, she spoke to a woman who was certain that she'd passed the man in the photograph, only a few months earlier, in the early evening, as he was ringing the doorbell of a house further down the street. She stepped outside to point out the house in question. Nobody was at home; Kate returned the following weekend, to be confronted by a surly individual who begrudgingly regarded the picture for a couple of seconds, scowled, and muttered: 'Next door.'

Two minutes later Kate was talking to Janice Wilson, formerly an employee of the firm of which Richard Staunton had been a director. Tears came to Janice Wilson's eyes when she looked at the photograph; or rather, tears fell when she looked at it – the eyes had moistened moments after she'd opened the door to Kate. It was not necessary for Kate to introduce herself: Janice Wilson knew who Kate was and she knew about the accident that had killed Mr Staunton. 'Mr Staunton' she called him, not 'Richard', but Kate comprehended the situation at once. Janice Wilson invited her into the living room, and left her there while she went to make a pot of coffee. Floral motifs were strongly present in the décor; a glass-fronted cabinet contained a precisely disposed array of figurines and trinkets. Pink cushions augmented the armchairs and sofa; rose-patterned curtains, ruched, hung from a rose-patterned pelmet. Flowerpots stood on doilies of lace. It was like a doll's house, thought Kate; she could not imagine her father in this room.

Janice Wilson took a long time to prepare the coffee. When she reappeared, bearing pot, cups, milk and shortbread on a dish, she had recomposed herself. She seemed relieved to have been discovered. There was one thing, she told Kate, that she should understand above all: her father had been a good man. On her very first day with the company, her boss had told her that Richard Staunton was a good man, and by this he had meant more than that Mr Staunton was good for the company's bottom line. Some of the senior people wouldn't give a secretary the time of day, but not Kate's father: his office was across the corridor, so she'd see him every day and he would always give her a smile, and maybe a few words. He could be a little intimidating, but he was never stand-offish. It wasn't until she had her bad year, however, that his kindness became apparent. 'I don't offer this as an excuse,' she said, having steadied herself with a long breath and a dose of coffee. 'Please don't think that. But it was a dreadful time.'

She'd gone through a nasty divorce ('But aren't they all nasty?' she corrected herself, anticipating an objection that Kate had no intention of making), then both of her parents had died within the space of three months. 'We were close, very close,' she told Kate; the eyes remoistened. As if that weren't enough, just nine months later she had found a lump. 'The grand slam,' she stoically jested, puffing her cheeks. Surgery and chemotherapy had almost destroyed her, and for a long time she was depressed, very depressed. She had to leave her job. It was disappointing, how people reacted. So-called friends became too busy to visit. They seemed to think that you could catch cancer from someone who had it. Or they were worried that they wouldn't know what to say, and so let themselves be governed by their discomfiture. Of her former colleagues, few took the trouble to stay in touch. But Kate's father was better than all of them. He phoned her, even when she was too depressed to talk,

and his calls became very important to her. He was very
kind, and wise. One day, when she was feeling extremely
low, she asked Richard (now it was 'Richard') if she could
see him. She wanted it to be noted: it had been her idea,
not his. Nothing inappropriate occurred: they walked
and talked, and when Janice went home she felt that she
could, after all, go on with her life. But 'one thing led
to another', she sighed; again the water welled on the
eyelids. They had briefly ('very briefly', she insisted)
become too close. It had been her fault. This was the
important thing. She had taken advantage of Richard's
kindness; despair had done something strange to her.
Immediately they had regretted it, 'bitterly regretted it',
she said, with eyes downcast in plausible contrition and
her voice very small.

It pained her, she said, that Kate might now think ill
of her father. 'You must not,' she ordered, in a whisper.
'Judge me, but not him,' she said. They had made a
mistake, a mistake into which she had almost forced him,
and after the mistake had been made it had been impossible for him to extricate himself from the deception. 'I
am the guilty party,' she said. Watery remorse ensued.
When the apologies had expired, Kate took her leave.

Recounting the story to her mother, Kate omitted the
supposedly isolated incidence of sexual congress: in this
re-edited version of events, her father had been intimate
with Janice Wilson, but the intimacy – though of an
order that had made its disclosure inadvisable – had
been that of confidant and spiritual support. Kate was
adept at the construction of narratives that possessed
a viable quotient of credibility; a jury might have been
persuaded. Her mother listened until Kate had no more
to tell. 'My God,' she murmured. 'All that time, he had
a mistress.'

'I'm not sure that "mistress" is the right word,' suggested Kate.

'Oh, I'm sure it is,' her mother answered, in a sleep-walker's voice. She looked out of the window for a full minute, her gaze tethered to nothing. 'I think I might have met her, years ago, at a garden party,' she said. She thought she could remember the name, but no face came to mind. 'What is she like?' she asked, to the window. 'What does she look like, I mean.'

Janice Wilson, said Kate, had a face that you'd have difficulty bringing to mind a week after you'd spent a whole evening in its presence. It was the median face of middle-aged British womanhood, with no distinguishing characteristics whatsoever. Pressed for details, she described a thick-waisted woman, fifty-ish, five foot five or six, with mousy hair and a roundish face, and eyes that she assumed were a nondescript brown because no colour was suggesting itself to her. 'It's incomprehensible,' said Kate.

'It is,' her mother agreed, frowning hugely to maintain control.

Perplexity compounded the grief, and there was only one course of action that might in any way reduce her mother's bewilderment. 'I'll have to meet her,' she announced, within a week. Kate was of the opinion that the risks of this course of action outweighed all possible benefits; but days later, her mother wrote a letter to the inexplicable Janice. A reply came back on scalloped and scented paper. Janice Wilson declared herself surprised to have received the letter and even more surprised that it should have been so gracious. A date was proposed.

Janice Wilson welcomed the widow solemnly, as if greeting an estranged, older and more successful cousin at a funeral. Then she started crying, and half-raised her arms, in case an embrace might be acceptable. Well before the end of their conversation, Kate's mother had decided that this was an irredeemably stupid woman. Richard had been a very happily married man, Janice Wilson informed her, as if this might be consoling news. Her relationship with him had not been an affair, she stated; it was not about sex. (This much was easy enough to accept. The woman was as plain as a sock, and had the shape of a matryoshka doll.) But, Janice confessed, having steeled herself with a long intake of breath, it was true that she had loved him. He had not loved her; there was no question of that. But she had loved him. She had to be honest. His capacity for empathy, his authority, his intelligence – she recited his love-worthy qualities. Janice Wilson appeared to be complimenting the betrayed wife on the calibre of husband that she had achieved. It had begun to appear that Janice had conceived the idea that she and the widow might become friends, united in their loss.

For Leonor Staunton, nothing was clarified by this hour in Martell Road. Quite the reverse: why her husband had chosen to spend any time at all with this garrulous and dumpy dullard, never mind have sex with her, was now a mystery that would remain insoluble. Janice Wilson was so drab that hating her was too much of an effort. Every passing minute in the woman's house had simply made her feel more tired; her presence was like a stupefying gas. On the doorstep, she shook Janice Wilson's hand and told her that she had been born in Portugal, a circumstance for which Janice should perhaps feel grateful, because if she'd been born a few miles further east she would have been Spanish and then everything would have been different. 'I might have ripped your throat out,' she said, sweetly, with the first and last smile of the afternoon.

It is not known what else Kate's mother learned from Janice Wilson about her clandestine friendship, or whatever one should term it, with Kate's father. She shared no other details with her elder daughter. 'I cannot begin to fathom it,' she told Kate on coming home. 'She's just so thoroughly uninteresting. Had she been a glamorous floozie, I might have understood.' It was distressing that this nothingness of a woman should, in any way, have known her husband better than she had known him herself: Janice Wilson had known that he was a man with a wife and daughters, whereas the wife had never known that he was a man with a mistress. And a frumpy one at that. 'But let's not talk about her again,' she said, and after that day, for Kate's mother, the name of Janice Wilson was like the filthiest swearword, never to be uttered.

It was decided that no good could come of telling Naomi what had been discovered, but she had to be told something, as it would be obvious that the investigation had been productive. Kate devised a tale involving a former employee, living in Clive Road, who had fallen on hard times; their father had lent this man some money, but had said nothing about the loan, because their mother had never liked the man (he was a drinker) and would have disapproved of giving him a hand-out. The story was credible, and it cast their father in a favourable light; Naomi would not think any less of him for having heard it. So Kate told her sister what had been learned about the former employee, and Naomi listened without interrupting. She bowed her head when the story was over, and dabbed an eye, and whispered: 'Don't lie to me.' The following year, in May, a police car brought Naomi home; she had been standing by the roadside in Clive Road for hours, talking to herself, the policewoman said.

9.

Martin arrives as the table is being laid. He comes into the kitchen and sees Naomi; he greets her amiably, and as if it's been only a few days since they last saw each other. In any situation, Martin can dissemble perfectly. His effectiveness in court owes much to the fact that, no matter what the provocation, or temptation, he can maintain a demeanour of immaculate opacity; his customary style is refined, courteous, undemonstrative – the fatal question, when it comes, is like being suddenly stabbed by the well-mannered gentleman in a three-piece suit who's been chatting to you on the station platform for the past half-hour.

Naomi freights the moment with significance. She puts down the cutlery and advances towards her brother-in-law, arms held wide to receive him. The embrace is over-extended, so that he might understand it as an apology. As she detaches herself, she puts a light kiss on his cheek. Stepping back, she scrutinises him from a range of two paces. 'You could do with a drink,' she says, as if seeing someone who is badly out of sorts, instead of smiling Martin. She has been into town to buy a nice bottle; she lifts it from the table, inviting his verdict; he knows little more about wine than Naomi does, but nods his approval.

'I'll be with you in ten minutes,' says Martin. He gives Kate a kiss and goes upstairs.

At the sounds of his footfalls in the bedroom overhead, Naomi looks up at the ceiling and smiles, and turns the smile unchanged to her sister, as if to say that she can understand her sister's happiness in this life, with her husband, in this house. She puts out the glasses. 'Is Lulu allowed?' she asks.

'A small one,' says Kate.

Naomi positions each glass exactly in the centre of its coaster. Then she says: 'Something happened today.'

'Oh?' says Kate, thinking Naomi means that something happened to her when she went out to buy the bottle.

'I can tell,' says Naomi.

'Tell what?'

'That something happened.'

'I don't follow.'

'With Martin. I could tell from his eyes. Something really annoyed him today.'

'Something usually does. It goes with the job.'

'Or is it me?'

'You mean did you imagine it?'

'No, I mean is it me who's annoyed him?'

'How could it be?'

'Well, I'm here. That's enough,' says Naomi, and she looks at Kate, frowning, almost tearful at the thought that this might be so.

'He's not annoyed,' her sister assures her.

'Irked, then,' says Naomi, as Lulu comes in; she strokes her niece's hair as she passes.

It turns out that there was indeed an irksome incident this afternoon, involving a member of the jury. On the first day of the trial it had become evident that this woman was more interested in her fingernails than in what was happening in front of her; she was one of those, says Martin, who makes her mind up as soon as the defendant appears, and nothing that anyone says is going to make a blind bit of difference.

'There's a non-listening type?' asks Naomi.

'Not a type, but a category,' Martin answers. 'Some people aren't prepared to pay attention. Or it's too much for them.'

'The proles,' Lulu explains gravely, to her aunt.

'Not always,' says her father.

'But you can look at your fingernails and still be listening,' says Naomi. 'They aren't incompatible activities.'

'Believe me,' says Martin, 'this woman's mind was elsewhere.'

Naomi nods. 'OK,' she says, with a small smile, the smile that signifies that she has caught the scent of an argument.

A year ago, on the night of the last great falling-out, Naomi had smiled exactly in this way; Kate can hear her sister telling Martin that he was one of the latter-day priests, the wise ones without whose ministrations the world would be wrecked by the idiocy and wickedness of the ordinaries. She replenishes Naomi's glass of water, and draws a finger along the back of Naomi's hand as she does so, as if the touch might be a preventative.

'Proceed,' Lulu instructs her father.

'So, today the woman with the fascinating fingernails turns up with hair extensions: long, straight, jet-black. The Morticia Addams look. She can't keep her hands off her new head; every other minute a hand goes up for a stroke. Some fiddling occurs, as if she's checking that things are securely anchored. The nails are given some more admiration.'

'Should be shot,' Lulu comments, with a complicit smirk for her aunt. But Naomi does not respond; looking only at Martin, Naomi receptively awaits the conclusion.

After lunch, one of the jurors had reported that Ms Extensions had been exchanging text messages while the jury was waiting to be recalled, and she had a strong suspicion that the texts were about the defendant. Ms Extensions was summoned; her phone was confiscated and examined. Five minutes earlier she'd received a text from her boyfriend: *Gilty???* Martin spells it out: 'G-I-L-T-Y.

And she'd replied: *As fuck!!!!!!!* Seven exclamation marks.'

'And then?' asks Naomi.

'Juror reprimanded; juror dismissed.'

'Christ, the public,' sighs Lulu. 'Can't spell. Can't think. They really are the weakest link.'

Again, Naomi misses the cue; she gathers some pasta carefully on her fork, thinking; but she does not seem to be plotting an attack.

'It's not a perfect system,' Martin says to Lulu, 'but it's better than the alternatives.'

'And he is guilty, right?' says Lulu.

'That's what I'm endeavouring to prove.'

'Sure. But he is anyway, yes?'

'I believe so,' says Martin.

Naomi eats the forkload of pasta, overchewing it, as though she thinks there might be small bones inside it, then she remarks, to Martin: 'I bet you made up your mind about Katie straight away.' The tone is accusatory, and she is not smiling. 'You liked her, and that was that,' she says, as if talking about someone who is not in the room, someone who should not be liked.

'Of course I liked her,' Martin answers. 'Who wouldn't?'

'More than liked, I'd say,' Naomi goes on. 'You knew right away that this was the one,' she says, and she looks at her sister with a gaze that is objective and almost stern, like a collector giving her verdict on an artefact of high value.

'I had a hunch,' Martin concedes. 'But I needed evidence,' he says, with a grin for his wife.

'The evidence comes after the verdict,' Naomi states, unyielding. 'You knew. The evidence just confirmed that you were right. That's what happens, nine times out of ten: within a few seconds we know, and all the rest, all the evidence, just falls into place,' she says. 'So maybe this woman knew. You saw right away that Katie was a good one, and Morticia saw right away that your defendant was a bad one.'

'The courtroom is not the place for intuition,' Martin tells her. 'Proof is all that matters. People have to be tested. You cannot go by impressions. People lie to you in court, and some of them are extremely good at it.'

'There's an incentive, after all,' Kate contributes. 'There's a lot riding on it.'

'And I've come across people who might have fooled almost anyone, at first,' Martin goes on. 'Very plausible; the picture of wounded innocence. I can think of one woman: a cuddly little grandmother, distraught that her own grandchildren should be telling such lies about her. If you'd asked for a vote on first sight, the jury would have acquitted.'

'But she didn't fool you,' says Naomi.

'She didn't fool the court.'

'And you're sure the court was right?'

'Absolutely,' says Martin. 'Of course. I was there to secure a conviction; they convicted.'

For three or four seconds Naomi holds Martin's gaze; one eyebrow tightens, in the slightest of frowns; it is as though Martin has made a statement of such subtlety that she is not at all sure how to take it. She looks down at her empty plate. Then, with a quick smile and a widening of the eyes, she seems to give the problem up. 'So how's school?' she asks Lulu, and for half an hour she is the perfect aunt: she remembers the names of Lulu's friends and teachers, she remembers the minor crises of the previous year, the music that Lulu used to like, everything. She is sympathetic, amusing – ebullient, even.

Lulu has attracted the attention of a boy named Otis, who is the school's best cross-country runner, and good-looking, but so boring that when he spoke to her last week, having cornered her in the library, Lulu started to panic and found herself struggling for breath; she has a feeling, though, that Otis misinterpreted the symptoms of panic as the symptoms of something entirely different. That's how stupid Otis is.

This predicament reminds her aunt of an episode from her schooldays, when she'd ended up going to the cinema with a boy called Billy, who had a nice enough face and could swim very well but was clearly destined for middle management and the chairmanship of his local golf club. She'd gone out with Billy, she thinks, as some sort of revenge against a skinny and short-sighted lad called Matthew, who wrote poetry but talked to Naomi only in order to talk about her sister, who was of course far too mature for him, and too refined. Kate has no recollection of this character; Naomi reminds her – he had very dark eyes, and a stare 'like a murderer'.

The boy with murderous eyes fails to take shape in Kate's mind, but clarification has to be postponed, because suddenly Naomi is overcome with tiredness, it seems. She closes her eyes as if steadying herself in a wave of dizziness; her head sways. 'I'm sorry,' she says, blinking quickly. She looks at her sister with deadened eyes. 'I need to go to bed,' she says. Getting up from the table, she gives Kate's hand a squeeze, strongly. 'Thank you all. It's been a lovely evening,' she says, like the guest of friends, not family.

When Kate goes up to bed, an hour later, she looks up the stairs to the guest room and sees a line of light under the door. She knocks. 'Hello,' Naomi calls out brightly, as if a visit at this hour were a delightful surprise. To Kate, it is almost the voice of twenty years ago. Lying in bed, with her knees drawn up, Naomi is reading a book. It seems that her exhaustion has been overcome. 'Was I all right?' she asks.

'What do you mean?'

'Earlier,' says Naomi. 'I felt I was boring.'

'You weren't boring.'

'I went on a bit,' she says. 'I think Lulu's frightened of me.'

'Why would she be frightened?'

'She thinks I'm ill. I mean, like cancer ill.'

'No she doesn't.'

'I'm perfectly healthy,' says Naomi, for the third or fourth time since yesterday. 'You'll make sure she knows I'm fine?'

'She knows you're fine.'

'No, I scare her,' she insists.

'I've told her everything's OK,' Kate assures her.

'She's tremendous,' says Naomi.

'Thank you.'

'And smart. As goes without saying. You and Martin – not going to produce a slow kid, are you?'

'She works hard.'

'I'm sure she does,' says Naomi, seriously.

'Are you going to come with me tomorrow?' Kate asks. A reminder appears to be necessary: 'To see Mum.'

Naomi is scanning the open pages of the book. 'Probably,' she answers, after a pause.

'You should,' says Kate. Receiving no answer, she asks: 'What are you reading?'

'Merton,' she replies, displaying the cover.

Kate moves closer to read it. The book is held in Naomi's left hand; in her right she holds the postcard that she is using as a bookmark. For a moment the message side of the postcard is facing Kate, and that moment is enough for her to see that the handwriting is unusually formal – nobody would write in this way nowadays except as some sort of exhibition or exercise.

Observing the direction of her sister's glance, Naomi asks: 'You want to see?'

'Can I?'

'Of course,' says Naomi, proffering the card. 'It's not what you think it is.'

But all that Kate is thinking is that the writing must be Bernát's, which is indeed what it is. The script is extraordinarily graceful and compact; the vowels are of exactly the same size, and the spacing is as regular as typesetting; the ascenders are exquisitely curled. No letters have been amended; the writing is immaculate; it is also incomprehensible. 'Can you read this?' asks Kate, and Naomi recites, without looking at the card:

Nincsen apám, se anyám,
se istenem, se hazám,
se bölcsóm, se szemfedóm,
se csókom, se szeretóm.

The voice in which Naomi recites is perhaps half an octave lower than her normal voice, and huskier. It is impressive that Naomi can do this, but Kate feels some embarrassment too, the sort of embarrassment that amateur dramatics can create. 'Meaning?' she asks.

'"I have neither father, nor mother, nor God, nor country, nor cradle, nor coffin, nor mistress, nor kisses,"' Naomi answers, solemnly quiet, as if repeating the words of a vow. 'A poem. A favourite of Bernát's.'

'You can read Hungarian now?'

'I'm getting there.'

Kate returns the card. 'Lovely handwriting,' she says.

Naomi nods; the remark is too banal to merit a response, it seems. She scrutinises the little manuscript, but as if it were a mirror in her hand.

'He must have worked at it,' says Kate.

'Of course,' Naomi answers, then the consideration of the card produces a smile.

'Tell,' says Kate.

Bernát's penmanship was attributable to a failed relationship, Naomi explains. A girlfriend, on the brink of becoming an ex-girlfriend, had remarked that his handwriting was contemptuous, 'just like him'. There was some justice in the accusation, Bernát acknowledged, albeit not immediately. He was twenty years old and very clever – much cleverer than the girlfriend. But he was in love with her, and her accusation hurt him, and made him think. If his handwriting was the image of his character, he reasoned, perhaps the improvement of the former might bring about the improvement of the latter. And so, for hours each evening, for many months, says Naomi, Bernát had studied calligraphy. 'A spiritual exercise,' she says.

'And did it work?' asks Kate.

'Well, it half-worked, at the very least,' says Naomi, releasing a small laugh. As though replacing a relic in its container, Naomi inserts the card into the book and closes the book softly.

'I'll say goodnight,' says Kate.

Naomi places the book on the pillow, then swings her legs around, to place her feet on the floor; she smoothes the bedding, making a place for her sister. When Kate is sitting, she takes a hand and holds it in her lap. 'I like Martin,' she murmurs; the remark is toneless. 'You know that, don't you?'

'I do,' Kate duly answers.

'I don't know anybody quite like him.'

'Neither do I.'

'He's so thoroughly himself, all of the time,' she says, quietly, as if talking of a phenomenon that she cannot fully comprehend. Talking to him, sometimes, she 'feels like fog on a mountain', she says. 'His life fits him so perfectly,' she says, in pleasant perplexity. She is stroking the back of Kate's hand, as one would a cat's fur. 'Do you ever argue?' she asks; the question does not seem to be a criticism.

'Of course,' says Kate.

'It's an achievement,' says Naomi.

'What is?'

'I think I might envy him sometimes,' says Naomi. 'And you.'

'I don't think you do,' says Kate; her sister does not contradict her. For a minute more Kate sits with her sister; Naomi's hand continues its stroking. 'I'm turning in,' says Kate, at a yawn from Naomi.

When Kate is standing, Naomi lies down again, on top of the bedding; she closes her eyes. 'Goodnight,' says Kate, and she puts a kiss on her sister's brow; Naomi smiles weakly, in a way that is meant to signify gratitude, Kate assumes, but is also suggestive of condescension. At the door Kate turns off the main light. Naomi's hands are joined on the book, holding it lightly to her chest; she looks like a figure on a tomb.

Not ready to sleep, Kate goes to her room. She browses websites for information about Prague in the early years of the twentieth century. Some time later, realising that she has spent the best part of half an hour looking at pictures of the railway station, she goes to bed. Martin is already asleep. Kate lies awake, imagining an incident that happened a few years before: Naomi emerges from the bathroom and, seeing Martin, closes her eyes and raises her hands, as if submitting to a firing squad; the towel falls; she is naked; it was a joke, said Naomi.

III

10.

At breakfast Naomi unfurls her fingers to present a pair of small grey oval things that look like diseased toenails. 'Do you think Lulu might like these?' she asks. Three small red beads are attached to each oval, and a silver hook; they are earrings. She tips them into the cup of Kate's hand. They are more like plectrums than toenails, with a rougher patch of darker grey at the wider end; the red beads have a black spot, and are rather pretty, Kate thinks. Naomi sits down next to her, close; she straightens the earrings on her sister's palm. The beads are seeds, the male seeds of the Huayruro tree, she explains. They come from the Amazon, and they protect the wearer from 'negative energy'. And the grey ovals are from the Amazon too – they are scales, from a colossal fish called the *pirarucu*. Its tongue is so tough that the native people use it as a rasp, she says. 'What do you think?' she asks, eager to please.

The ethnic look is not Lulu's style at all, Kate knows. 'She'll be very touched. Thank you,' she says, giving her sister a kiss.

'Even if she doesn't like them, they're unusual,' says Naomi. 'And they have a story.'

The earrings had been a gift from Bernát, of course. Bernát has a brother, Oszkár, one year his senior. The Kalmár boys were raised in the West Midlands, as far from the coast as it is possible to be in England, and Oszkár has often attributed the direction his career has taken to the fact that his home town was so deeply landlocked. Each summer the family had taken a holiday in Cornwall, always staying in the same clifftop chalet, overlooking a long beach. At the end of this beach rose an outcrop of rock, which would be wholly surrounded by water for at least an hour before and after high tide. Just before the incoming tide touched it, Oszkár would climb to the summit of this rock, where he would remain until the water had retreated from the landward side. He might take a book, but he rarely read more than a few pages of it; the spectacle of the sea was sufficient in itself. It was as fascinating as the night sky. The ever-changing constellations of the waves enchanted him. Nothing was more exciting for Oszkár than the annual voyage on a mackerel boat, to experience the dark immensity underneath him and all around. Once, an area of discoloured water, twenty feet from the boat, revealed itself to be the back of basking shark; the fish was as big as a canoe, and some of the other children on board the boat were terrified. For Oszkár, the encounter was akin to an annunciation.

A few years before Naomi met Bernát, Oszkár Kalmár was on sabbatical from his university, and was undertaking research in Brazil, studying the migration of Amazonian catfish; his first publication had been a study of the Indo-Pacific striped eel catfish, *Plotosus lineatus* and he had become, apparently, a modestly renowned authority on siluroids. Oszkár's activities in Brazil were focused on the Mamirauá reserve and he was based in a place called Tefé, a town that cannot be reached by road. Its isolation was perhaps the crucial factor for Bernát: he decided he would visit his brother. He spent three or four days in Manaus, which was like a tropical Croydon, Bernát reported, says Naomi, perhaps worried she might have given her sister the impression that the great man lacked a sense of humour. In Manaus he did the things that every tourist must do. At the Teatro Amazonas he admired the one hundred and ninety-eight chandeliers, the Carrara marble staircase, the rosewood seats. Outside the theatre, he inspected the rubber-coated bricks that had been laid to muffle the noise of the carriage wheels. He went to the fish market, where he saw very many varieties of catfish. He went back to his room, for the air conditioning. Traffic droned ceaselessly in front of the building and behind. He could have been in a motel beside a British motorway, had it not been for the finger-length insect that was gradually traversing the ceiling. A fourteen-hour boat journey took him to Oszkár.

Tefé was founded by missionaries in the eighteenth century and missionaries were still at work in the area. Oszkár had befriended one, a man named Walter Doniphan, from Virginia, who had been struggling to translate the Gospel into the language that was spoken in a cluster of villages upstream from the town. For several years Walter had lived among these people, and in all that time he had found no evidence that they had any idea of history or of myth. Indeed, they seemed to lack all forms of fiction. The story of Jesus did not engage them, once Walter had admitted that Jesus was not someone he had actually met. They asked him: why did his God give us this life if this life was not enough for us? Why did he need to test us? Why did he need to create us? Why did he need to create anything? To amuse himself? In the six months before Oszkár met him, Walter had made a single convert: a man who had been stung in the foot by a stingray. To cleanse the wound quickly a woman had urinated on his leg, but the woman was a prostitute, with diseases, and the man had been infected by her urine. It was more than possible, Walter conceded, that the man had thought that baptism would cure him. At times, in the small hours of the night, Walter had to battle against discouragement.

He had, however, met a remarkable man in Tefé, a man by the name of Afonso. It would be truer to say that Afonso's story, rather than the man himself, was remarkable. Afonso was a difficult character, it seems: abrasive, argumentative, and often drunk. Somewhere in Manaus lived a woman who had been his wife; she had gone away, with their son, because of his drinking, he admitted. He had been to jail for robbery. But Afonso's life had the makings of a book or a film, Walter told Oszkár.

Walter had first encountered him on the riverfront at Tefé. Strolling past a place where dozens of small boats were tethered, he heard a shout; in one of the boats, a man was kneeling, spanner in hand, over the components of a dismantled outboard motor; looking directly at Walter, he shouted again, as if summoning a slow-witted employee. An extra pair of hands was needed, it appeared. Despite the man's peremptory manner, Walter made his way to the boat, via the decks of several others. He was directed to pick up a spanner and tighten a certain nut, while the man held two wires in place; after ten seconds, his help was no longer required. Walter wished the man good day, to which the response was: 'Cigarette?' He mimed the action of smoking.

'Sorry, but I don't smoke,' Walter answered, in the language of the river traders.

The man squinted, as if not sure what to make of this reply. 'Where are you from?' he asked.

'Virginia,' said Walter. 'And you?'

He made a gesture as if flinging bait over the water, and laughed. 'Very far,' he replied. Terrible teeth were shown, like pieces of gravel wedged into the gums.

Intrigued, Walter enquired further, but he learned only that the man had been born in a distant village, by a river that had no name.

'The river is the river,' said the man. As for his own name: 'Here I am called Afonso,' he said. He had also been Abilio, but that was not the name he had first been given either. 'Here I am called Afonso,' he repeated, as if reciting an instruction that he had been given. Then he uttered a sound that Walter could not have transcribed; he repeated it, a little slower. 'My name,' he explained. Again he pronounced the word, and Walter tried to mimic the syllables. Laughing, Afonso put a hand on Walter's shoulder, in consolation for his failure. 'I am hungry,' he said; Walter understood that an exchange was being proposed.

They found a backstreet place with plastic tables and chairs, lighting as bright as an operating theatre, and a rotisserie in the window. Roast chicken, Afonso declared, was the best food. He ate an entire bird, and drank four beers in an hour. His story became difficult to follow in its latter stages. Whole sentences were unintelligible.

It was a miserable tale, but Afonso related it without self-pity or anger – or indeed any sentiment of any kind. 'My mother and father were not of the same blood,' he began, as though speaking of characters in a folk tale. 'When my mother was young,' he went on, 'her people started to die of an illness that could not be cured, so her family decided that they had to leave.' They took a boat, but after some days on the river the parents both fell ill, and they died. The children – Afonso's mother and two brothers – buried their mother and father in the riverbank and continued down the river. One of the brothers then died, but the two survivors at last came to a village. 'This is where I was born,' he said, dotting a fingertip into a line of beer that he had drawn across the tabletop.

On a map, Afonso could show where the village was, but not exactly. As for the people who lived there, the people of his father, they had a name that simply meant 'our people'. Afonso spoke the name and repeated it many times, for the American to repeat, comically. The name could not be written, because the language had no writing. Afonso could not write anything in any language.

At about the age at which her own mother had died, Afonso's mother died. How many years she had lived, Afonso could not say, just as he had no figure for his own age: when asked how old he was, he opened and closed a hand several times, in a gesture that signified nothing more precise than 'many years'. He would have been somewhere between ten and fifteen years of age, he thought, when his mother died. That was the point at which his life went bad, because his father took up with a bad-tempered woman who treated the children like slaves. There were arguments all the time: between the father and the children; between the woman and the children; between the adults; between the adults and the other adults. 'It is the same in the jungle as in the cities,' Afonso said, as if he thought the American might be in need of the lesson.

One night, Afonso and his sister ran away: they took a boat and set off down the river. They were on the water for many days, until they came to a place where there were river traders. Young Afonso was given work to do, first with these traders, then on another boat, and another, and another, and so he worked his way downstream, a very long way from his village. On the boats he started to learn his new language; for a long time, he said, it was 'like wearing clothes made of wood'. Eventually he and his sister came to Tefé; his sister, he believed, now lived in Manaus.

Several single-phrase answers were delivered, without emotion, as if they had been memorised for a test, before Afonso let slip an extraordinary item of information: his mother, he said, had understood a language that was not the language his father spoke, but was, as far as Afonso knew, a language spoken only by his mother's people, a people who, he assumed, had been eradicated by the disease from which she and her family had fled. In her new home she had, of course, been obliged to learn his father's language, but she had retained something of that original tongue for the rest of her life, though there was nobody other than her brother with whom she could speak it. She taught her children as much as she could, and they often used the old words when talking to each other. Even so, their knowledge of that first language, a knowledge that had been incomplete at the time of their removal from it, dwindled as their first memories faded, so what was passed to Afonso and his sister was but a tiny remnant of the language, a remnant that had decayed still further since Afonso's separation from his sibling. For all he knew, he and his sister were the last people on the planet who could comprehend anything of his mother's mother tongue.

Having intrigued Oszkár with the story, Walter Doniphan had taken him to the bar where Afonso was invariably to be found. The evening was something less than a success: Afonso had taken a lot of drink before they arrived, and was in a truculent frame of mind. In return for more alcohol, he had answered some questions from Oszkár, in the minimum number of words. Almost nothing was added to what Walter Doniphan already knew.

Nonetheless, when Bernát arrived Oszkár persuaded him with no difficulty that he would benefit from making the acquaintance of the remarkable Afonso. Accordingly, on Bernát's third evening in Tefé, he and his brother met up with Walter Doniphan and proceeded to Afonso's favoured dive. On the way, Walter told Bernát some of the things that Afonso had told him about the moribund language of his mother. It had no equivalents to north, south, east and west. The same was the case with left and right: orientation was achieved by reference to topography, to the position of hills, rivers, the village and so on. From Afonso's testimony, it seemed that abstractions of any sort were alien to this language. There were no nouns for units of weight or distance or time, nor any colour adjectives. The colour of an object was not a quality that could be considered apart from it: a pepper was a pepper and blood was blood; they were not instances of redness. None of these characteristics were unique, Walter knew, and he was also aware of other languages in which, as in Afonso's mother's language, different verb forms were employed when speaking of the past: one when talking of things of which one had direct knowledge; another to report things that had been inferred from direct evidence; a third for conjectures; a fourth for hearsay. But two aspects of the language of Afonso's mother surprised him greatly. Firstly: Object-Verb-Subject was the customary word order. Afonso was insistent on this point: whereas most people would say 'the man drinks the beer', in his mother's language one would say 'the beer drinks the man'. The second peculiarity was that it seemed to be the case that recursion was alien to it. In the language of Afonso's mother one would not say, for instance: 'I drank the beer that Walter paid for.' Instead, one would say: 'The beer drank I. The beer bought Walter.' Likewise, one wouldn't say: 'I am retelling the story that Walter told.' One would have to say something like: 'The story tell I. The story told Walter.'

A Dominican friar, writing about the Arawak language in the seventeenth century, had observed: 'There is no language poorer than this. They have no words for anything beyond what relates to our physical senses.' One might likewise be inclined to characterise the language of Afonso's mother as impoverished. This, said Walter, would be an error. The language of Afonso's mother, like the language of his father, possessed a superabundance of nouns. It had a specificity that makes English look under-stocked. So Afonso was amazed that a branch of a tree in Portuguese is always just a branch, regardless of its size; in his mother's language there was, for example, a word – something like *uxchâ* – for branches that were thicker than a man's wrist but thinner than a thigh. It was strange to him that the sun, in Portuguese, is labelled always with the same word, whether it be seen at dawn, noon or sunset, through cloud or uncovered. The Portuguese language had too few words for rivers, Afonso thought, and for varieties of shadow and shade. His mother's language had at least three different words for dusk, and three for what we call dawn, as did his father's. Why should he have to make do with only one word for 'we'? In his mother's language, there were two forms of the word, one meaning 'all of us, including you', the other signifying 'we but not you'. *Uxchâ*, Walter repeated, as if the word were magical. The tone of the last syllable was all-important. *Uxchà* meant something entirely different, and *uxchá* meant something else again.

They came to the bar. Men were playing cards at half a dozen tables; none of them was Afonso. The barman had not seen him that evening, but there was still time – it was not yet ten o'clock. The trio decided to wait, and they soon had their reward. Afonso appeared in the doorway, surveying the assembled drinkers with the air of a man fulfilling the last of the day's many and onerous obligations. Walter had failed to provide a description of Afonso's appearance, so there was some disappointment: he was an unimposing specimen. Not more than five feet tall, Afonso had legs that were disproportionately short, and bowed, and too thin for his torso. His upper body was almost cylindrical, with wide shoulders sloping into a sturdy neck. His hair, straight and dark as carbon fibre, came down to jaw level and was the same length all around; his skin was dark, and his cheekbones high and wide; the nose too was broad; his eyes were small, and the whites were pale amber. He wore a Brazil football shirt and capacious white shorts, heavily stained.

Smiling as if at the arrival of a long-time friend, Walter waved a hand to beckon him. At the same time, in a far corner of the bar, a man with the face of a long-retired and frequently beaten boxer was beckoning Afonso to join his card game. The latter, it appeared, was the more attractive proposition, but Afonso nevertheless made a detour to the table of Walter, Oszkár and Bernát. A bottle was brought for him, as an inducement. He sat down. It could not have been clearer that he was in no mood to be exhibited. The reluctance to linger was so palpable, as Bernát described it, that it was as if the seat were the north pole of a magnet and his shorts were another north. Introduced by Walter, Afonso shook hands with Bernát and gave him a grimace-smile, revealing the wreckage of his teeth; Oszkár received a fleeting grip and a semi-second of eye contact. There was an exchange between Walter and Afonso, in which ninety per cent of the talking was done by Walter. Afonso nodded as he listened, and glanced at Bernát a few times, and applied himself to the emptying of his bottle. This bottle, evidently, was far from being his first of the evening. It seemed that Walter had problems in making sense of what Afonso muttered at him. The gist of one extended grumble was that Afonso was very tired. Bernát said something to the effect that he had heard Afonso's story, and that it had made a strong impression on him; Walter translated the remark; Afonso nodded, drawing a finger through the little puddle that his bottle had left on the tabletop. Now the ex-boxer was signalling again, impatiently. Afonso glanced in his direction and shrugged, as if to say that the matter was out of his hands. He spoke to Walter at some length, and Walter, with a sympathetic smile, responded in a whisper; their hands briefly clasped; another bottle arrived.

After a deep swig, Afonso gathered himself for the effort of congeniality. He threw his arms wide, embracing the air that the foreigners occupied, and made a statement that Walter translated as a question: 'You would like to hear something?' He closed his eyes and released a long murmur, a sort of melodious gargling, a flow of vowel sounds and soft glottal stops. It lasted for perhaps twenty seconds.

'What was that?' Oszkár asked.

'A rhyme about a fish,' said Afonso, through Walter. 'A big fish.'

Oszkár looked to Walter for further elucidation. Walter spoke to Afonso, whose response, given with a show of apology, was: 'Portuguese doesn't have the words. Europe doesn't have this fish.'

An encore of the rhyme was respectfully requested. Afonso did not seem to be averse to the idea. He pondered; he drank some more beer; he spoke. What he had said turned out to be: 'London is a very large city.'

Bernát confirmed that this was the case.

In London, Afonso believed, there were buildings a hundred times higher than anything in Tefé, and everyone owned a car, and in a single week a man would be paid as much as a year's work in Tefé would bring him.

'But it's cold,' Bernát added.

'But there is work, and money,' countered Afonso. Suddenly thrusting his face close to Bernát's, he demanded: 'Why are you here?'

'To see my brother,' answered Bernát.

'Brazilian women are the most beautiful in the world,' said Afonso, slumping back. 'Are you here for the women?'

'I'm here for my brother,' Bernát told him.

'You are here for the men,' said Afonso; this amused him hugely; his laugh was like the bark of a small dog. 'How are the women in England?' he asked Oszkár.

'Some nice, some not,' said Oszkár.

'I think I will see the English women for myself,' said Afonso. Something in Oszkár's reaction both amused and antagonised him. 'You think I cannot want to see England?' he demanded. 'You think I am in heaven here?'

'Finding work in England is hard,' Oszkár warned. 'People sleep on the streets. There are hungry people in England.'

Afonso was incredulous. 'In London there are hungry people?' he shouted.

'Yes,' said Oszkár.

'You see them?'

'My brother lives in London. I live in a different city, where there are also people who have no money.'

Afonso's metallic eyes were trained on Oszkár for ten seconds; there was no discernible thought behind them. Then he turned to Bernát and, abruptly as a soldier speaking to a civilian of an occupied territory, demanded: 'Give me your phone number.' Gratified by the surprise he had caused, he laughed loudly, displaying every one of the shattered teeth. 'You live in London. You can help me,' he said.

Bernát recited a string of digits; he was so taken aback by the man's aggressiveness, he gave his true number. In English, Afonso repeated it perfectly. 'I will call you,' he stated, putting out a hand to conclude the agreement. That done, he stood up. He smacked the emptied bottle on the table like a gavel, before shaking the hands of Walter and the two Englishmen, as if he had bested the team of foreigners in negotiation. 'I am happy to have met you,' he said, in Walter's translation, then veered across the room to the card players. And thus ended the interview with Afonso – 'Walter's saint of the authentic', as Bernát called him.

Two days later, at the waterfront, Bernát encountered Afonso again: he was sitting on a rusted oil drum, behind a counter made from a cardboard box, on which various souvenirs were displayed for sale. He was threading beads into fish scales as Bernát approached; he gave no sign of recognition. Some sort of exchange was conducted, primarily by means of mime. At no point was there the slightest hint that the vendor had met his customer only two days before. Bernát bought six pairs of earrings, and added a substantial tip to the payment, as goes without saying. 'Goodbye,' said Afonso, in English, then he recited the London phone number, correctly, and laughed, aiming a finger-pistol at Bernát's face.

11.

There is potential in the character of Afonso, it seems to Kate. She lies on the recliner in her room, imagining him. A continuation of the story soon offers itself. Perhaps a year after the scene in Tefé, the phone of the Englishman rings, and a voice says, in accented English: 'I am in London.' Kate takes a notebook from the desk to jot down the words: *voice on phone – I am in London.* The caller identifies himself: it is Afonso. 'Things are not good with me,' he says. He seems to be implying that the Englishman had omitted to warn him that London was not a land of prosperity for all. They arrange to meet at the statue in Piccadilly Circus, the following evening. *Afonso & xxxx – Piccadilly – rain – café – women (tourists?)*, Kate writes.

Afonso appears, twenty minutes late. His hair is pulled back into a ponytail and he is wearing a bin liner with armholes cut into it, over a sweatshirt and jeans. His trainers make a squelching noise on the wet pavement. 'Good to see you again,' says the Englishman, or words to that effect. Afonso informs him that he wants a coffee. His skin has shrivelled around the eyes. He asks for a cigarette, but the Englishman does not smoke. Grimly, head down, Afonso follows him to a café.

'English coffee is bad,' he comments, on the first taste. Nothing in London is good: it is dark and dirty, and the people are hostile. He is working at a restaurant. 'They call it a restaurant, but it is not a restaurant,' says Afonso. '*It is a place where people go to stop feeling hungry,' says Afonso*, Kate writes. His job was a job that English people do not do, he tells the Englishman. All day he cleans floors, cleans toilets, empties bins, digs grease out of drains, unpacks boxes of burgers that look as if someone has painted them to look like meat. The

boss is English but the people Afonso works with are
not. *'We are the ones you do not see,'* he says, swivel-
ling his gaze *to encompass everyone in the indictment.*
At night he sleeps in a garage, many miles away. He
walks to work, because the buses cost too much money.
But sometimes, it occurs to Kate, Afonso rides on the
Underground trains, because on the Underground it is
easy to steal. 'Some days I steal a lot,' he announces,
loudly. Some teeth have been lost since the Englishman
last saw him. Afonso eyes a handbag that is hanging on
the back of a nearby chair, then laughs. One day soon he
was going to get caught by the police, he said, because
then he would be sent back home. 'I hate England,' he
says. *'But it is not so easy to be sent home,'* he complains.
One of the men at the restaurant where Afonso worked
had been arrested for taking things from a car, and had
been to prison, but they did not send him home when he
came out. 'Why is that?' he demands. The Englishman
confesses that he does not know; *his ignorance is what
Afonso was expecting*, it seems, Kate writes. *'Do you
have money?'* he asks. *'I must eat, and today I have
no money.'* A twenty-pound note is pocketed immediately, *like a debt belatedly repaid.* Abruptly he stands
up. 'I am working tonight,' he announces; he shakes the
Englishman's hand with a single downward motion, *as
though throwing a lever.* 'Thank you,' he says. By the
door he stops to ask a young Japanese woman for a
cigarette; she shrinks from him in fear; he bows low to
her, then flings open the door and runs into the rain.
And here the scene evaporates. *Where does this go?*
Kate writes. *Does it go nowhere? A short story? Two
locations: Brazil & London. Perhaps not Brazil? Lisbon?
Afonso encountered in Lisbon? Whole story in Lisbon?
Englishman speaks Portuguese???*

An hour later, she has relinquished the story of Afonso and the Englishman. She is now in Prague, with Dorota; this name has been fixed, as has the location. A scene is being sketched: walking home at dusk, Dorota is passed by a tram, which slows almost to a halt a few yards beyond her; at one of the windows, a face has turned to look at her; the reflections on the glass make it hard to make out the features at first, but as she comes alongside the tram she sees that the face is the face of Jakub, her dead husband. He has aged since he left her, and he has a beard, but there is no doubting that this is Jakub. She mouths his name; her voice is trapped within her throat. He smiles at her, but the smile has no recognition in it: it is the smile of a man who has gained the attention of an attractive stranger. The tram gathers speed, and the man at the window smirks, knowing that he has made an impression; it is an unattractive expression, and unlike Jakub.

She is writing – *the tram turns: flash of sunlight on the glass, then the face has gone??* – when she becomes aware of an intermittent rumbling sound: Naomi's voice, from the room above. The pitch of her voice rises briefly, as does the volume: a phrase is uttered with force, with anger, but no words are audible. The rumbling resumes, and stops after half a minute. Kate goes upstairs and knocks.

'Do come in,' Naomi calls out, with strained gaiety. She is sitting on the floor, holding her phone; she pulls herself up onto the bed. 'Sorry about the disturbance,' she says.

'Everything all right?' asks Kate.

'Gabriel,' Naomi answers.

'Oh?'

'He thinks we have things to discuss.'

'And you don't?'

'I'm all discussed out.'

'He cares about you,' says Kate.

'He's seeing a new woman,' says Naomi; she might be referring to an incorrigible brother. 'Another one off the internet. Edwina.'

'And how's that going?'

'Going OK. Nice-looking, apparently. Reads Tolstoy. Fan of Tarkovsky. Ticks a lot of boxes.'

'But—?'

'Well, for one thing, she loves Tchaikovsky. Really really loves Tchaikovsky.'

'That's a problem?'

'For Gabriel, yes.'

'Seriously?'

'Oh yes. And I think there are bedroom complications too,' she says, with a squeamish wince. 'I get the impression that Edwina is a bit too ...' – she pretends to search for the word – 'dynamic.'

'I don't want to know any more.'

'It's OK – I don't have the details,' says Naomi. 'But I hope he gives Edwina a bit more time. Maybe she'll do him some good. Widen his horizons. And give him a kick up the backside. He got one from me, obviously, in the end. But evidently it wasn't strong enough. Edwina might be just what's required. Get him out of his comfort zone, as we say nowadays. You never know.'

Before, it always appeared that Gabriel's inertia was fundamental to his appeal; he was gentle and cultured, and he knew how to cook, but above all he 'refused to play the game'; Kate remembers her sister saying this – nearing forty, but talking like a teenager. 'So you think he needs a kick up the backside now?' Kate asks.

'Very much so.'

'Because?'

'He's in a rut. A neck-high rut,' Naomi pronounces.

Previously Naomi had wanted her sister to believe that Gabriel's dead-end jobs were chosen deliberately, to 'cultivate boredom', as she once put it; in boredom there was freedom; in boredom he could think. He was in the world of retailing, but not of it. 'Is this news?' says Kate. 'I thought the rut was meant to be a good place.'

'He's been in that bookshop far too long,' says Naomi. Resentment is becoming Gabriel's dominant tone, she says; he is no longer suffering silently in the desert of commerce. 'He needs to do something instead of feeling sorry for himself,' she says.

'Like what?' asks Kate.

'I've no idea. His brother thinks he should write his gypsy book.'

'Is that such a terrible idea?'

'He's missed the boat on that one, I reckon,' says Naomi. 'Besides, he doesn't have your stamina.' As she says this, her phone buzzes; exasperated, she directs the call to voicemail, then laughs.

'What's funny?'

'For a man with no stamina he's bloody persistent,' says Naomi. She looks at her phone as if at the photo of a dead friend.

'He's very attached to you,' says Kate.

'So it appears,' says Naomi. 'But God knows why. I'm awful,' she states.

'Why do you say that?'

'Because it's true. I'm hard work, for little reward.'

'I don't think that. Gabriel doesn't think that.'

Naomi turns to squint at her sister, as though the compliment has taken her by surprise, and is opaque. Her gaze returns to the phone. 'It's odd, what's happened with Gabriel,' she says. She withdraws into a brief reminiscence, then elucidates: 'The first thing he said to me was: "I'm not desperate." Within a minute of sitting down. "I'm not desperate." And I said to him: "That's good. Because neither am I."' She was not one of those women who do this sort of thing because the clock is ticking; the ticking of her clock did not worry her, she had told him. And Gabriel wanted her to know, right at the outset, that he was not hoping for 'consequence-free sex'; nearly all of the other women he had met in this way had been hoping that the evening was going to end in bed; some of them, even after meeting him, had thought that the bedroom was the inevitable destination. Naomi assured him that she was an exception. 'I find lightness difficult,' Gabriel had said; it was nothing like an admission; he might have been informing her of his blood group. It had been the most peculiar conversation: more like an interview than a date – 'a mutual interview', says Naomi. When he was in his twenties, Gabriel disclosed, he had lived with a woman; he had decided that he would never live with a woman again; he did not go into the reasons for this decision, but Naomi understood that possessiveness had been the crucial issue. Gabriel was not a possessive person, he said; Naomi, who had never lived with anyone, felt herself to be in accord with this strange and forthright man. 'But now—' she laments, and she points to the phone as evidence of the change that has come over Gabriel.

Before Kate can suggest that something other than possessiveness might be at work here, the phone buzzes again – a text this time. Naomi reads it, with a rueful frown, and drops the phone on the bed; she looks out of the window, uncertain as to what she should do. 'What time are you going to see Mum?' she asks.

'Twelve.'

Naomi considers for ten seconds. 'I think it would be too much for her, seeing us together,' she decides.

Kate refrains from the observation that Naomi has not seen her mother for many months, and is therefore in no position to judge what would or would not be too much for her.

'I'll go tomorrow,' says Naomi. 'If you don't mind dropping me off. Or I could walk.'

'It's too far,' says Kate; Naomi knows this.

'I do care about him,' says Naomi, picking up her phone, 'but this has to stop.'

On the stairs Kate can hear her sister's voice, mollifying.

12.

Leonor had lived with her daughter and Martin and Lulu for a year, until it became clear that the arrangement was unsustainable. Incidents were frequent in the later months, and often involved the granddaughter. 'You never know what you're going to get from one hour to the next,' said Lulu, in tears; her grandmother, unable to find something that she had misplaced, yet again, had accused her of stealing. More than once Lulu came home to find her room in disarray. Under the misapprehension that the house in which she was living was her own, Leonor announced one evening that it might be best if Lulu were to find somewhere else to stay. In a moment of tenderness, she put her arms around her granddaughter and called her Daniela; Daniela, it was learned, had been a friend of Leonor's, when they were Lulu's age. At night Leonor sometimes wandered into Lulu's room, weeping, not fully awake. At the table she would stare at her, as if trying to determine who this child might be;

she might suddenly press Lulu's hand in a paroxysm of affection. Lulu's friends stopped coming to the house; her schoolwork suffered; she could no longer sleep properly. Something had to be done.

So now Leonor lives in a place called The Willowes. It is on the outskirts of a village four miles away, with a large garden and views of the Downs, and Kate visits her three times a week, sometimes more. The accommodation is the best that could be found nearby; the staff are professional and pleasant, and the residents are treated with respect and delicacy. A wide range of activities is on offer. 'We are here to make their lives not just comfortable but stimulating too,' the director told Kate and Martin. A woman named Tamae gives a flower-arranging class every week, which Leonor enjoyed for a while. The rooms are spacious and the best ones are arranged around a sort of cloister, which has a carp pond in the middle, surrounded by benches. Every room has a beech-veneered chest of drawers and matching wardrobe. A table is set by the window, with two chairs; there is an armchair too. Not every room looks out on the garden, but Leonor's does. A cherry tree stands ten yards away; in May the blossom gives a pale pink cast to the light in her room.

Residents are permitted to make some modifications to their private environment, by way of distraction from the reality of the situation. Leonor's lampshade, for example, came with her; the grooves of the frosted glass bowl are darkened by the dust of the living room at home. Over the armchair is hung a quilt that she made before she married. Between the bed and the window lies a rug that had occupied the equivalent space in the bedroom she had shared with her husband, many years ago. The carpet underneath is dark blue, with a pattern of broad waves, slightly lighter in hue; these colours, patterned in this way, Kate was told, help to foster feelings of tranquillity and wellbeing; every bedroom in The Willowes has this carpet; the curtains are of the same design.

Relics of her life, selected for reasons that have now been forgotten, are arrayed on the chest of drawers. Two photographs taken in Coimbra – young Leonor with her parents, at the river; the parents in old age, with their daughter, on a stone bench in the Jardim Botânico – stand beside a small blue porcelain jar that had once belonged to her mother. The management has hung, in every room, a framed reproduction of a famous landscape painting. Leonor's picture is a river scene by Alfred Sisley; there have been days on which Kate has arrived to find her mother gazing at it as if it were a second window. Above the bed hangs another picture, brought from home. It shows Saint Isabel, her head resplendent beneath halo and crown, with roses spilling from the scoop of her gown. Leonor's faith, quiescent during the years of her marriage, had resurged in her widowhood. One day, a few years after her father's death, Kate had suggested to her mother that she might visit her on the coming Sunday morning. Her mother told her that she would be at church, and that is how it was discovered that she had returned to the fold. It was ascertained that she had been attending Mass since the previous Easter. She had found a nice church and a priest she liked; this, more or less, was the extent of what Kate learned about her decision. It wasn't even a decision, her mother told her: one doesn't decide to become wiser with age, and this was the same thing. Perhaps life in England had buried some part of her spirit, she suggested. Her faith had not died – it had been in abeyance, weakened, deprived of the air and water of the Church. Her soul, she later proposed, was like one of those frogs that can live through long periods of drought by finding tiny pockets of moisture deep within the earth.

Today, on opening the door of her mother's room, Kate sees her in the wheelchair, gazing at the image of Saint Isabel, the patron saint of her birthplace, and of all victims of infidelity; Isabel's dissolute husband was the father of many illegitimate children.

'I don't like that thing,' her mother announces; these are the first words she utters. The vehemence would once have been startling. Before this phase of her life, mildness had been a defining quality of her temperament.

'What thing, Mum?' asks Kate. 'The picture?'

'It's horrible,' says her mother.

'Why do you say that, Mum?' asks Kate. The image of Saint Isabel has been there since the day her mother moved in; it was brought from home.

'Because it is,' her mother answers.

Kate does as she's told; she pretends to study the sentimental and clumsy portrait of Isabel. 'Do you want me to take it down?' she asks. 'I can do that. It'll take two seconds.' She moves closer to the picture, raising a hand to it.

Leonor frowns; she mashes her lips together; it is as if this situation were a problem of insurmountable complexity.

'I can take it down and if you change your mind I can put it back before I go,' suggests Kate.

After more consideration, Leonor decides: 'Better leave it. She'd be annoyed.'

'Who would be annoyed?' Kate asks. Her mother's gaze has meandered to the window. 'Mum. Who would be annoyed?'

'The Irish woman.'

'What Irish woman?'

Her mother does not know the Irish woman's name, but she knows she would be upset, because it was the Irish woman who had given her the picture and put it on the wall.

'It's your room,' Kate tells her mother. 'You can do what you like. We're not going to throw it away, are we? We can put it in a drawer for a while. She'll understand. Don't worry.'

For a few seconds, her mother seems to be thinking about what Kate has said, but then the thinking can be seen to dissipate. Her eyes are still directed at the picture, but she seems to be seeing only an arrangement of colours on a rectangle of card. They agree to leave Saint Isabel where she is, for the time being.

Kate kneels beside the wheelchair and takes a hand; it is cold and as hard as a puppet's. 'Mum,' she says, trying to get her mother's gaze to latch onto hers. 'Mum. Naomi is back. She's staying with us.' It appears that some elements of these statements do not make sense. 'She went away for a while,' Kate explains. 'But she's back now. Turns out she was in Scotland.'

'Scotland?' her mother repeats, as if Scotland were as extraordinary as Tasmania.

'Apparently. Not sure where, exactly. Up in the north somewhere, I think. Miles from anywhere.'

Her mother considers this information. 'When was she in Scotland?' she asks.

'In the summer. She came back a few days ago. She's staying with us,' says Kate, enclosing her mother's hand. 'She'll come and see you tomorrow. You'd like that, wouldn't you?'

For a minute her mother says nothing; her hand trembles within her daughter's. 'Naomi is living with you?' she asks.

'She's staying for a day or two, that's all. She'll come to see you tomorrow.'

'Why was she in Scotland?'

'She went with some friends.'

'A holiday?'

'I think so. I don't quite understand it. Naomi in hiking boots. I can't picture it. But she seems happier. And she's lost weight. A lot of weight. You'll see. She looks different.'

Her mother looks down at the carpet and scowls, perhaps from the effort of trying to summon the image of her younger daughter. 'What friends?' she murmurs.

'I don't know them. They seem to have stayed at a place belonging to someone called Bernát.'

'Bernard?'

'Bernát. He's Hungarian, but he grew up in England.'

'Naomi's been to Hungary?'

'Not as far as I'm aware, but you never know. Bernát lives in London. That's where she met him. He seems to be her new boyfriend. If that's the word. He's not a boy. Quite a bit older than Naomi.'

'Bernát?' her mother says again.

'That's right, Mum. Gabriel has been jettisoned.'

'Who?'

'Gabriel. The man in the bookshop.'

It appears that Gabriel's name has little resonance, if any, for her mother; her gaze roams the sky; panic is beginning to rise in her eyes.

'It's possible she never mentioned him,' says Kate. 'You know what she's like. Don't worry,' she says, pressing her mother's hand; her tone, she can hear, is patronising, but it is efficacious; the panic seems to have been halted.

'No, she talked about him,' says her mother, uncertainly. She is tracking the flight of a gull, as if it might lead to the meaning of Gabriel.

'Well, they seem to have called it a day. Or Naomi has.'

'Was he nice?' asks her mother.

'They went well together, I thought.'

The gull has flown out of sight. 'Oh well,' her mother sighs. 'What about Bernard?'

'I don't know, Mum. I haven't met him. He sounds unusual. A reformed banker, apparently. Knows a lot about music. More than Naomi, if you can imagine such a thing.'

'He's a musician?'

'No, he just knows a lot about it. And maths. Music, money and maths. His brother knows everything there is to know about catfish. Quite a family.'

'Naomi isn't interested in money,' says her mother, as if to correct an error and thereby make the story collapse.

'Neither is Bernát nowadays, it seems. He improved himself.'

'Is he staying with you?'

'No, Mum. We haven't met him yet.'

'Oh.'

'And I'm not sure when we'll get to meet him. It seems they're going back to Scotland together.'

Her mother purses her lips and looks at Kate; she seems lost in perplexity.

'To tell you the truth, Mum, I don't really understand what's going on,' Kate says, giving her mother a smile of unconcerned puzzlement. 'But we'll find out more, in good time.'

Leonor looks again at the picture of Saint Isabel, purely, it appears, as somewhere to anchor her gaze; there is no telling what is in her mind. After half a minute she announces that she wants to go into the garden.

'It's not terribly warm out,' says Kate; her dissuasion is ignored. She folds the quilt and smoothes it over her mother's lap, tucking it into the sides of the wheelchair.

The garden has a pond, with a small concrete island at its centre, on which sits a little stone boy, on a stone tree stump, inspecting the sole of one foot. Her mother wants to stop by the pond. The stone boy is frequently remarked upon. 'I hate that thing,' she often declares, as if this antipathy were newly conceived. Before she moved to this place, she never used that word, even of Janice Wilson; now she hates so many things, or so she says. Today, however, the stone boy seems not to offend. On the far side of the water, another wheelchair is parked. Its occupant is the oldest of the residents, a man named Cyril, who is ninety-eight years old and speaks in two-second gasps; few of the staff can comprehend much of what Cyril says, but a Trinidadian nurse named Vernita seems to hear every word, and it is she who is sitting beside Cyril, on a bench. She speaks to him, but he might be asleep; he usually is.

Kate positions the chair at a spot from which their view of the old man is obstructed by the stone boy, but no sooner has Kate applied the brakes than her mother starts to fidget. Grimacing, she leans to the left and to the right, then back to the left, stretching her neck as much as she can; she flaps a hand as if ordering the little statue to move. 'There,' she says, pointing a yard to the side. 'Put me there.' Kate moves the chair. Her mother sighs, like a busy woman who, having been delayed by the inefficiencies of fools, can at last get on with her business. One hand clasps the other in her lap; she aims her gaze at Cyril and Vernita, as if in the expectation of learning something.

In the distance, three paragliders are swerving above the scarp of the Downs. 'I could never do that,' Kate remarks; her mother, watching the old man and his nurse, does not respond. An observation about the weather likewise fails.

The old man stirs; his eyelids quiver; his head comes up, as though by a process of slow inflation. As Vernita takes a tissue from a pocket and wipes his mouth with it, Leonor's face softens into anguish.

'Mum—' says Kate.

Still looking across the pond, her mother states: 'I want to go home.'

This has been said before; it is a frequent ordeal, to have to explain that there is no longer a home to go to, that there has been no home for years. 'If you're not happy here, I can look for somewhere else,' says Kate, not for the first time; her dishonesty is nauseating.

Her mother glances at her: there is judgement in the glance, and perhaps dislike. 'I want to see John,' she says.

'Which John is that, Mum?' asks Kate. There is a nurse at The Willowes named John; the family's solicitor is a John as well.

'I want to see John,' her mother repeats, with emphasis, and she glances at her daughter again, to impart more force to the repetition.

Now Kate understands. This John is a man called John Jeavons, the only male companion of her mother's widowhood, or the only one known to Kate, which is tantamount to the same thing, she is sure. Twice in the past year her mother has spoken of him; this is twice more than she has made mention of her husband. More than fifteen years have passed since the end of that friendship, or whatever it was. He was a widower; they had met through the church; he was a civil servant of some kind, Kate seems to remember. On Sunday afternoons they went for walks together, or a drive. Her mother, as she recalls, used to speak of him as someone who had great responsibilities and many worries; there was a son who was the cause of concern, for reasons that cannot now be recalled and perhaps were never disclosed; the problematic offspring might have been the basis, or the source, of the relationship. Kate has not even seen a picture of John Jeavons. There had come a point at which she realised that it had been a while since her mother had made any reference to a Sunday walk. Mr Jeavons was no longer in London, she learned. Her mother had not appeared to be upset, as Kate remembers, yet now she is struck with guilt for her failure to ask the questions she should have asked, though she is not entirely certain that she had in fact failed to ask them. She knows so little of her mother, and now it is too late.

'Mr Jeavons?' she says.

'John,' her mother replies. 'I'd like to see him.' It is clear that she thinks this is something that her daughter has the power to make happen.

It is probable that John Jeavons is no longer alive; he was older than her mother, Kate is sure. She says: 'I don't know where he lives.'

'You can phone him,' her mother points out.

'I don't have his number.'

'Yes you do. I gave it to you. I remember writing it down.'

'I don't think you did, Mum.'

'I did. I know I did.'

'I don't have Mr Jeavons' number, I'm afraid.'

'Look it up then,' says her mother, exasperated. 'Use the directory.'

'Mum, I have no idea where he lives.'

'In London, of course.'

'I thought he went somewhere else.'

'Why would he do that?'

'For work?' Kate suggests.

'What work?'

'I don't know, Mum.'

'Why would he leave for work? That doesn't make sense,' her mother says. 'People come to London to work. They don't leave it,' she pronounces.

'That's usually the case,' Kate concedes.

'It doesn't make any sense,' her mother mutters. She examines the sky; there is nobody on whom she can depend, her eyes say.

'I'll look him up in the directory,' Kate promises, knowing that tomorrow, or in an hour, this conversation will have been forgotten.

The old man is mumbling into Vernita's ear. Her mother's gaze returns to him. In a voice that is suddenly clear and strong, she says: 'This is horrible. Take me back to my room. I'm tired.'

Kate helps her mother onto the bed; she curves a hand behind her head to ease her onto the pillows; the hair is as insubstantial as a veil of muslin. She is draping the quilt when her mother looks directly at her, and says: 'Bless you.'

That said, her mother closes her eyes, decisively. She smiles, perhaps in relief, now that the ordeal of conversation is over. 'Thank you,' she whispers, and within a minute she is asleep.

For a while Kate watches over her. Her mother's mouth makes a shape like a gasp of surprise, then does not move; her breath makes the sound of air being drawn through a wooden pipe. Kate looks at the face on the pillow, in its nimbus of white hair, and then she looks at the face of Leonor in the later Coimbra photo, in which she stands beside the old woman whom she has come to resemble more closely than she resembles her younger self. Is it possible, Kate wonders, that in her sleep her mother goes back to Coimbra, or some version of Coimbra, and sees it clearly, as it was?

13.

The sisters meet for lunch at the café-delicatessen by the bridge. Naomi arrives late, of course, but within ten minutes of the agreed time. 'I'm so sorry,' she gasps. 'Another five rounds with Gabriel. Sorry. Sorry sorry.' The beaker of water is drained in five seconds. With a napkin she dabs sweat from her temples and neck; she fans her face with a coaster. This performance is noted by a small boy at an adjacent table; she smiles at him, but the smile is not reciprocated.

'So,' says Naomi, having composed herself, 'how's Mum?'

'Been better; been worse,' Kate answers. She gives Naomi a report. 'She's looking forward to seeing you,' she tells her, and Naomi nods, but says nothing. A good-looking young man puts menus on the table, and directs their attention to the blackboard.

As the waiter answers a query from Kate, Naomi regards him, as one would a statue. He is wearing a long tight apron, and a white shirt with a black tie. 'Surprised they don't make the poor lad do a French accent,' she says, when the waiter has left them. The ersatz rusticity of the décor is remarked upon, as is the fragility of the seats: they are folding metal items, with wooden slats; the sort of seats you might find under the plane trees, beside the *pétanque* area. 'A few months ago, this thing would have collapsed if I'd sat on it,' she says, doing a small squirm and smiling as if overjoyed to be able to occupy so delicate a piece of furniture without risk. Reading the menu, she is appalled by the prices, but jovially so. Many things here appal and amuse her: the preserves and condiments on the shelves behind her, positioned with all the labels precisely aligned, like exhibits in a museum of good taste; the fruit displayed in wicker baskets, on beds of straw, as if they were made of blown glass; the huge loaves of artisanal bread, each of which cost more than the waiter earns in an hour, Naomi surmises. She orders a bowl of soup and a glass of fruit juice; the juice, she remarks, is more expensive than wine.

'I'm paying,' says Kate.

'No, it's on me,' says Naomi, with the look that will brook no argument. 'It's the least I can do,' she says, and she raises her sister's hands to her lips for a kiss. 'My God,' she whispers, 'look at her.'

An exquisite Japanese girl, a year or two older than Lulu, is sitting at a nearby table, with a boy who must be her boyfriend. The symmetry of her face is unimprovable and her skin is as smooth as a jar; she has a gorgeous little plum of a mouth, by which the boyfriend appears to be transfixed. Her lips are moving, but she does not seem to be speaking; the movement is like that of someone who's asleep. She is more interested in her phone than in her companion, but he is captivated. Now, stroking the phone, she says something, and her remark makes him smile; she glances at him, as if to check that the smile is there, then resumes her work on the phone. The boyfriend's gaze grazes her chest. The chest is that of a twelve-year-old boy. But she is wearing an interesting T-shirt: very tight, and bright pink, with writing in the centre, in complicated lettering, Gothic style.

Naomi, reading the T-shirt, recites: '*The Dave Breat Intervence – Remember the Ambition*'.

'Don't stare,' her sister tells her.

'I'm not staring,' Naomi answers, staring.

'Naomi, you might as well be shoving a camera in their faces.'

'They haven't noticed. In a world of their own,' she says, as the waiter delivers the dishes to the young couple's table. 'Who's Dave Breat?'

'No idea.'

'Maybe Lulu will know,' says Naomi. 'I thought it said *Dave Breast*. Which would have been amusing.'

'Please stop gawping.'

Naomi glances at her sister. 'And what's an *intervence*?' she asks.

'I haven't the faintest,' says Kate, as her sister's head swivels back. 'Naomi—'

'Did she just take a picture of her food?' she asks, in high consternation. 'I think she did. I think she just took a picture of her salad.'

'I believe she did, yes.'

The girl is performing a complicated procedure on her phone, at speed, with great concentration. 'Now she's uploading it, isn't she?' says Naomi. 'The salad is going online. All over the country, people will soon be looking at those tomatoes.'

'I would not be surprised. Now please stop staring.'

'What's the point?' says Naomi. 'Who wants to see a photo of a salad?'

'I'm sure she has many friends.'

'But a salad?' she moans.

'It's all about sharing,' says Kate. 'We're too old to understand. You should see the things that appear on Lulu's phone.'

'Such as?'

'Last week, a toilet.' At last her sister's attention has been secured.

'Really?'

'Really.'

'Why?'

'One of her friends went to a club in Liverpool and had to share the horror of the facilities. She's had pictures of food as well. Gigantic pizzas, huge ice creams. Funny vegetables. Carrots with willies. That kind of thing.'

Naomi glances again at the Japanese girl, who is now taking photos of her boyfriend as he eats. 'God, we're doomed,' Naomi sighs, and she presses her face into the bowl of her hands. The extravagance of her despair attracts the attention of the small boy, and his mother, and the mother's friend. Coming up for air, Naomi makes eye contact with the boy and tries another smile on him, this time with a wave as well, wiggling her fingers so that the rings – four of them on the one hand, each of them bold – perform a little dance for him; he shrinks against his mother's arm.

The sisters talk about Lulu; Kate tells her sister about things that occurred during the summer and in the months before, when the sisters were not speaking, and Naomi listens with interest, with concern, with amusement, and neither of them makes any allusion to their argument. At Naomi's instigation, Martin's workload is discussed; Naomi is sympathetic to the proposition that most members of the public have absolutely no idea of the amount of preparation that's required for a day in court. They move on to Kate's plans for next Easter's holiday – Lulu has always wanted to go diving, so they are considering Kuredu, in the Maldives. In the past, this topic might have caused some resentment, imperfectly masked, but today there is none, it seems. 'Sounds great,' says Naomi. They are talking about Kuredu when Naomi winces, as if the nerve of a tooth has suddenly fired. But it's not a tooth that's caused the pain – it's the noise from the group that has taken over the long table in the middle of the dining room. There are some excitable people in the group, and they keep talking over each other; one of the women is particularly loud and strident. 'Sounds like she's strangling kittens,' says Naomi, hitting the woman with a glance that only behaviour of supreme obnoxiousness would warrant. The woman, not noticing, shrieks again, making Naomi grimace. Her hearing is much more sensitive than it used to be, she tells Kate. Things that never used to be noise are noise to her now, and things that would always have been indisputably noise – 'Like her', with another assassinating glance – now cause her pain. 'We're going to have to leave,' she says. Though her sister has not quite finished her dish, Naomi goes up to the counter to pay.

'Shall we go up to the golf course?' Naomi suggests. It must be five years since they last took that path, a path so steep that Naomi had been forced to stop three or four times before turning back. She tucks a hand under Kate's arm to steer her in the direction of the hill.

At the junction the road is being relaid. The red and white barriers; the workmen, two of them, talking; the sunlight in the street; Naomi on her arm – Kate is reminded of another afternoon and an episode of alarm, as sudden as a stroke. Workmen in a trench were looking at her in a way that meant something, Naomi had insisted. They were not workmen, said Naomi, trembling, crushing her sister's wrist. They were not workmen and they knew something about her, she said. She was crying and could not move.

But in a moment the memory is broken: the pneumatic drill starts up, and Naomi flinches. 'God almighty,' she yells; clamping her hands over her ears, she hurries off. It's no more then twenty yards to the lane that leads up to the golf course, but she has to pause there for breath. In the crook of the lane, in the lee of the houses, the din is dampened a little. 'One moment, please,' she requests. She puts a hand to her chest and smiles, impressed by the speed of her own heartbeat. 'Like a wheel of feathers whirring in there,' she announces, then she takes her sister's arm again. Within a minute the gradient has become arduous, but Naomi strides on, stamping the tarmac as if pushing into the sand of a dune. Soon she is gasping. On the side of the road that's closer to the cliff, a path begins, on top of the high verge; having scaled the verge, Naomi stops, clutching the wire fence. 'A brief pause,' she says; which is as much as she can say in a single breath.

'We've come far enough,' says Kate.

'This is where we turned back last time,' Naomi reminds her. With half a dozen deep and slow draughts, she replenishes her lungs before resuming the ascent.

A hundred yards on, they halt again. They are far above the town now; from here, the sound of the drill is a purr. Naomi takes it all in, with a gaze that sweeps slowly from the river to the castle and on to the Downs, beyond the houses. Three swans are moving downstream, as bright as pearls on the brown water of the river; Naomi watches them, with concentration, as if it were of supreme importance that she should commit to memory everything that is to be seen here. Craning her neck, leaning forward, she peers over the fence; just a pace or two from her feet, the chalk cliff falls vertically; she has no head for heights, her sister knows; Kate recalls the high bridge over the river in Porto, and Naomi's fingers clamped on the railings like padlocks, her arms rigid with fright as the traffic shook the bridge's frame. Now Naomi takes a step back, her mouth agape in operatic terror. 'Let's go,' she announces, hands on hips, offering an arm like a wing. Kate's hand closes around a bicep; the arm feels like a cricket stump lagged with cotton wool.

Beyond the golf club, a gate opens out onto the hillside, where a broad track of close-cropped grass rises gently to the horizon. Arm in arm, the sisters amble up the slope. In the distance, silhouetted against the sky, three hikers are moving towards the next summit; these are the only people in sight; sheep are grazing on each side of the track; the rending of grass is the only sound, other than the sound of Naomi's breathing, which is as loud as a respirator. 'Let's stop here for a while,' she says, sitting down in the midst of knee-high tussocks. Arms outspread like a supplicant, she inhales through her nose, deeply, with deliberation, as if taking a prescribed dosage of the salubrious air. 'This is glorious,' she says; this has been a word of hers since she was young – music was often glorious; the heat in Provence was glorious, Kate remembers. Naomi closes her eyes, as though overwhelmed; her smile is blissful.

Kate gazes across the shallow valley. On the far side, the slope is topped by a crest of trees that resembles smoke; below them, the grass is pleated where the soil has slipped. The grass is bright there; huge cusps of shadow lie in the lee slopes; past the shoulder of the hill, blade-shaped pieces of the river glisten. Taking a notebook from her pocket, Kate writes: *river – blades of water – colour: tarnished steel.* She replaces the notebook stealthily, so as not to disturb her sister's apparent reverie. The shadow of a cloud slides up the valley floor and over the top of the hill. As the grass rebrightens, a bird becomes visible against the green: a hawk, teetering on the breeze, on stiff wings. And Kate recalls their father, holding the binoculars to his eyes, as serious as a general inspecting the field of battle. This might have been Glencoe; the bird was a hen harrier, a rarity. Its face is like an owl's, he explained, passing the binoculars so that Kate could see for herself, but she could not manage to hold the bird within the lenses, and she saw nothing but a flurry of feathers. She pretended she had seen the owlish face, then she handed the binoculars back. For as long as the harrier was in sight, it was not possible to leave the hill. The wind was very strong. She and Naomi and her mother stood side by side, leaning into it, with their arms out; the light, coursing across the heather, made the glen flash like a reef of coral.

Naomi, pointing, asks: 'Do you know what that is?'

'A red kite,' Kate answers. 'The tail is the giveaway.' She glances at her sister, and sees a frown that seems to have nothing to do with the hovering bird. 'I was just thinking of Glencoe,' she says; a nod is all the response she receives. 'You remember?'

'I know we went there, but that's about all.'

'You don't remember Dad and the harrier?' She makes binoculars of her hands and raises them to her eyes, clenching her face into a mask of intense vigilance.

Naomi looks into the grass; she closes her eyes, as if to consult the index of her memory. 'That wasn't Glencoe,' she decides.

'You sure?'

'Positive,' says Naomi. 'Glencoe was a washout. Rained all day. The harrier was Glenfinnan,' she states.

To Kate the name brings nothing with it, but it is probable that Naomi is correct.

'We thought we were going to be there all day,' adds Naomi.

'We did,' Kate concurs.

The red kite rises, veering towards the head of the valley; it comes up above the skyline and settles in the air, batting its wings against the wind that's up there; then down it comes, in a long low arc, to skim the grass of the slope on which the sisters are sitting, coming so close that Kate can see the black dashes on the plumage of its tail. She looks to Naomi, but Naomi is not watching the bird – she is squinting at a part of the sky that has nothing in it, and her lips are moving a little, as if she were reciting something under her breath. Kate waits, observing her sister askance; such distraction has been seen many times.

The silence is prolonged for a minute more, then Naomi turns, and from the slowness of the turn, and her smile, it is clear that she knows she has been under observation. 'I'm fine,' she says, with an affectionate smile.

'You were listening,' says Kate, as if – she hopes – referring to something like the exercising of a strange and special skill.

'I was.'

'Not just to the breeze.'

'No,' Naomi confirms; she seems pleased to be legible to her sister. A sheep has approached to within ten yards of her; having given the animal some scrutiny, she says: 'Mainly to myself. You know how it is. Thinking aloud in my head. The usual soundtrack. Nothing to worry about.'

'Thinking about what?'

'This and that. Good things.'

'Bernát?'

'Of course,' she says, gravely, as if thinking of Bernát were some sort of duty, like thinking of Jesus. She looks skyward and narrows her eyes, giving consideration to something. 'If you heard his voice,' she says, but the sentence is unfinished; words, it seems, cannot be found for the voice of Bernát.

'Well, I hope I will,' Kate responds, but the remark is squandered. She asks: 'That's what you were hearing? His voice?'

'I was remembering some things he'd said, yes,' she says, smiling at her sister.

'And are you hearing him now?'

'No, Katie, I am not hearing him now. It's OK. I'm not losing the plot.'

'I know, but—'

'Stop fretting. It's all right. Really. I'm absolutely fine, everything is fine,' she says, overdoing the soothing. 'My memory is peculiar, you know that. Our minds don't work in the same way. I can't invent things the way you can, but my brain is adhesive. I can play a whole opera in my head. *Parsifal*, start to finish. And I can play Bernát's voice, whenever I want to. It's the same thing,' she says. She shifts a little to the side, onto a more accommodating patch of turf; then, after checking the turf behind her, she lies back, lowering her head onto a tuft of long grass. She crosses her hands on her chest and gazes into the sky; she smiles as if the empty blue space were a scene of inexhaustible intricacy. 'This is wonderful. This is really wonderful,' she murmurs, and she closes her eyes.

Looking at her sister, Kate begins to see a day in Scotland, a warm day at a loch, and young Naomi drowsing. The name of the loch is unavailable, but she sees it; she presses her palms to her eyes and the scene becomes brighter: the yellow dinghy, water blazing in the sunlight; a small island, with a single small tree; a dark steep slope behind it. Their mother, on the shore, was waving to them, beckoning them back, calling, but barely anything of her voice reached the boat. Naomi withdrew the paddle, and the last ripple ran away without interruption, a very long distance. Kate waved back, and their mother stopped shouting. The loch was silent; its surface was a flawless replica of the sky. The sisters lay in the boat, their legs interlocked, their hands touching on the taut hot flanks of the inflatable, heads lolling on the cushion of air. Thirty, forty yards away, the snout of a fish came out of the water and they heard the sound it made. 'This is glorious,' Naomi would have said.

Now Naomi is smiling, as if remembering the same day, but she is listening again, Kate can tell; she is listening to Bernát. 'Anything you care to share?' asks Kate.

'By all means,' answers Naomi. Then for half an hour she talks, with barely a pause, staring into the sky all the while.

14.

One evening, Naomi and Bernát were sitting in the garden, on the bench that Bernát had placed in the farthest corner, between the magnolias, the one that Connor had been sitting on. The magnolias were in bloom; the air was cool and still, and some redness remained in the clouds. For a while they sat in silence, enjoying the sky, then they had begun to talk about their families, and Bernát had told her – almost as if he thought he owed her this clarification – that his trip to Brazil had not achieved what he had hoped it would. He had thought it might be possible to bring about an adjustment of his relationship with his brother, of whom he had seen too little in the preceding six or seven years. There had been no great falling-out, but a slow and inexorable 'erosion of sympathy', said Bernát, says Naomi.

His brother's marriage to Melissa had been the major cause of this separation, he said. According to Bernát, Melissa was a good-looking but unimaginative and selfish woman. He could never understand why his brother had fallen for her; he could only speculate that it had something to do with sex; her body was undeniably potent, said Bernát. Melissa worked in Human Resources, Naomi explains, as if this were an absurdity in itself. When her path crossed Oszkár's she was taking a break between jobs, having left a company that had not granted her the promotion that she believed to have been her entitlement. They met in Corsica, in a diving centre in Bonifacio; Melissa was twenty-three and already divorced; Oszkár, though ten years older, had never yet been in danger of marriage. Both were on holiday, though for Oszkár a holiday was never entirely without an element of research; later, this would be a cause of some friction between himself and his wife. They dived together. It must be assumed, said Bernát, that Melissa was seduced by Oszkár's knowledge of the submarine wildlife; maybe Oszkár had an air of incipient eminence, and Melissa imagined that life with an eminent marine biologist would entail plentiful weeks in the Caribbean and other exotic locales, and long sabbaticals, and the occasional posting to some luxurious Californian institution of scientific endeavour; who knows?

They married, and had two sons, and Melissa moved from job to job, serially underappreciated. In time she arrived at the conviction that the chief reason for the becalming of her career was that she had lost momentum in the years that had followed the birth of the boys. Oszkár was somehow implicated in this loss of momentum; he had been in some way insufficiently supportive. Sometimes Melissa would talk as though motherhood had been foisted on her, though in fact it had been virtually a condition of the marriage that Oszkár would impregnate her at the time of her choosing, and sooner rather than later. Oszkár had little understanding of the 'real world', Melissa regretfully told Bernát. It was not to Oszkár's advantage that he had Bernát for a brother: Bernát understood the real world and was a success in it; he had a car that seemed to impress her as much as a Nobel prize would have done. Once, Bernát told Naomi, his sister-in-law had asked him why he never talked about his girlfriends. 'You must have girlfriends,' she murmured to him; they were alone in the house. Bernát might have misunderstood the intention, but certainly Oszkár came to believe that Melissa admired his brother excessively. At times, it seemed possible that he suspected an affair.

Melissa eventually left Oszkár for an aerial photographer, a widower whose daughter was in the same class as Oszkár and Melissa's younger boy. It turned out that Melissa had been involved with him for more than a year. He was a qualified pilot and owned his own plane; when the boys met him, they thought he was cool; that's what Melissa told her husband, anyway. She had become bored, she told Oszkár. Or rather: Oszkár was at fault for becoming boring. But, said Bernát, Oszkár had not become boring. Oszkár had always been Oszkár: a moderate man; a man of decency and integrity; a fastidious scientist, devoted to the objects of his study. In the aftermath of Melissa's desertion, Oszkár's absorption in his studies seemed to have intensified. Never a voluble character, Oszkár now was clenched within himself; the adulterous Melissa could not be discussed. Oszkár would talk about his fish, and little else, but Oszkár's fish were of limited fascination for his brother. Another factor had to be taken into account, said Bernát, which was that Oszkár took much the same view of his brother's career as did their mother: Bernát had squandered his intelligence, for the sake of having enough money to fly to Paris or Milan for a night at the opera whenever the whim took him. An ethical investor was still a money man at heart, thought Oszkár.

The reunion in Brazil was not a great success. After two weeks in each other's company, they were no closer than they had been a fortnight earlier. But Bernát had gone to Brazil, he said, not solely in order to ameliorate his relationship with his brother. He had also travelled in the hope of amazement, he confessed to Naomi. London was suffocating him. He had taken to withdrawing to the countryside for days at a time, staying in remote guest houses, walking all day, whatever the weather. These retreats had a palliative effect, but the relief was transitory. Stronger medicine was required.

During those weeks in Brazil, he had seen some remarkable things, Bernát reported. He described some of the things he had seen. He had seen army ants flowing though the undergrowth like a stream of oil, and bats gushing from the trunk of a Kapok tree. He had peered into the maw of a *pirarucu* when it came up to the surface to breathe: it was like looking into a satchel of greasy white leather, said Bernát. He saw lilies that changed colour overnight and exuded a thick perfume of pineapple, and a trio of pink dolphins, near the seam in the river where the dark and tannin-rich waters of the Rio Negro flow alongside the pale and silty waters of the Solimões without mingling.

When Bernát spoke of what he had seen, says Naomi, it was like listening to a naturalist-explorer from a time before cameras. She cannot adequately describe the eloquence of Bernát in full flight, she tells her sister. He never fumbles for a word: it's as if his whole vast vocabulary is instantly at his disposal, and he simply has to reach in to extract the right words. But it isn't just a matter of fluency: it's the quality of his gaze when he seizes on a subject, and the way his hands, in constant motion, seemed to be giving form to objects that were elaborate and invisible. But the gestures were never actorly, Naomi insists; there was no element of performance. Rather, it was an act of transmission. Inspiration, she says, would not be an inappropriate word. Yet inspiration was not what Bernát had experienced. Even the spectacle of the skies had not been sufficient to dislodge the torpor that had settled in his mind. And the skies were wondrous. Daylight expired quickly on the river, he explained to her, and as the sun fell into the forest the sky was transfigured into galaxies of colour. All colours were in those sunsets, in a multitude of forms: quick-moving wisps of tangerine-tinted white; slow floes and slicks of crimson, magenta, saffron, cobalt; massifs of pale grey and graphite; diffuse expanses of cool gold and silver; purple and marigold mixed in huge moraines of cloud; iodine and buttermilk and tar; viscid messes of blood and egg yolk, which congealed into the colours of liver and old fat. Some sunsets were of an apocalyptic grandeur, said Bernát, and yet they did not stir him as he knew they should. He needed the sublime, and it eluded him. Instead, he merely registered that these arrays of coloured air were spectacular; he appreciated them; he watched the sunsets and found himself thinking of words.

Bernát was of course aware, says Naomi, that he should have been grateful for his good fortune. But being conscious of one's good fortune, she says, does not change the quality of the experience; one cannot force oneself into enjoying a meal by thinking of the starving millions. He was bored, still. The terrain was monotonous, offering nothing but foreground for hours at a time: reeds and bushes rising from the mud, in front of a wall of trees and vines and lianas, and only the sky beyond. Inside the forest, the sun is erased: you're in a dark green radiance that has no point of origin. 'North, south – you don't know which is which,' says Naomi, as if she had been there. It was not an environment to delight the senses. The smell of the forest is not the perfume of Eden: its scent, said Bernát, is the stink of formic acid. The climate was oppressive: he had overestimated his capacity for this type of discomfort. There was a bird that had a call like a wolf whistle, and it made its noise incessantly; others were like yapping puppies, or the squeal of rusty hinges; every day he heard them, for hours on end. At dawn and sunset the monkeys screamed.

When Europeans first saw the Amazon, said Bernát, they thought they had regained paradise: the forest was thronged with fabulous animals; the birds were as bright as stained glass; fruit dangled from every branch, inviting the hand. Soon they realised that this paradise was a false one, that the profusion was deceptive. The trees drew every drop of sustenance out of the earth, leaving soil that was no better than sand. No crops could be made to grow here. The waters seethed with fish that could kill a man; underfoot and in the air lived creatures that inflicted a pain as severe as the pain of an arrow. In a letter to King Philip II, the conquistador Lope de Aguirre wrote: 'There is nothing on that river but despair.' And despair did sometimes overcome Bernát on the river; in Manaus, watching the boats swarming on the water like a lethal virus in the bloodstream of the land, it was impossible to hold off feelings of doom, he said. But most of the time he was suffering trivially, from mere lassitude and dejection. He was dejected and bored – by himself, more than anything, he told Naomi, she says.

On the penultimate evening of his trip, in Manaus, Bernát went to a bar on Ponta Negra beach. The air was cool and clean, after rain. Lights from the tower blocks, quivering on the river, were conducive to contentment. Bernát sipped a beer and turned the pages of the book in which Lope de Aguirre's letter was quoted. It was impossible to read, however, because of the noise from a group that had taken over a nearby corner of the terrace. They were American and white and middle-aged, except for the loudest member of the party – a hefty and darker-skinned man, in a half-unbuttoned floral shirt. Evidently he was the host. He seemed to be employing a strategy of affable provocation to keep the evening lively. A small uproar arose, in which the big man's laughter was dominant. He declaimed: 'We've had enough of foreigners ruining our country. We can ruin it for ourselves, thank you.' Like a lord in a costume drama, he called for another pitcher of beer; glancing at Bernát, he raised his glass to him, before making a remark that provoked a screech of incredulity from one of the women. 'OK, OK, OK,' said the big man, raising his arms to quell the hubbub. 'Tell me this: why were the Jesuits expelled? Anyone know?' When a waitress brought another pitcher to the table, he put an arm around her hips and was not resisted. He saw Bernát looking his way, and smiled as if in recognition of a fellow aficionado of the female form. 'Come on over, lonely guy,' he shouted.

His name was Jack Taffarel; he ran river cruises on his boat, and these people had been his customers that day. Welcoming Bernát to the table, one of the group – a bristle-haired man in a sweaty pink polo shirt – warned him that the cruises were just a front: 'Turns out this guy's an agent of the Vatican,' he joked, with too much aggression. 'The Jesuits and the Vatican are not the same thing, not at all the same thing,' answered Jack, and he proceeded, with some wit, to summarise the issues on which the papacy and the Society of Jesus had not seen eye to eye. Bernát was intrigued, he told Naomi. Jack Taffarel looked as you might expect someone who worked on the water to look: the face was weathered, the arms powerful, the hands scarred. But he talked like a professional spokesman, and appeared to be peculiarly well informed on the subject of the Jesuits, particularly the Jesuits in South America. It would have been better, Jack Taffarel agreed with Mr Pink Shirt, if white people had never come across this country. But of all the white people, the Jesuits were often the best, he maintained. 'They provided protection against the worst,' he said. Though far from sober, he produced a succession of salient facts, or plausible pieces of information, to support this contention. Bernát was inclined to take his side, perhaps in a spirit of perversity, as he told Naomi. Regurgitating something he had recently read, Bernát told the group that the Jesuits in Paraguay had ensured that school lessons were taught in Guarani, the natives' language, rather than in Spanish. Jack confirmed that this had indeed been the case. In response to a woman who had 'a problem with the whole missionary thing', Jack had much to say on the topic of liberation theology. 'Sounds like communism to me,' commented Pink Shirt; the conviviality of the gathering was becoming fragile. Jack talked about the Fields of Man and the Fields of God. 'Forced labour,' someone remarked. 'There was no flogging and branding,' Jack countered. 'It wasn't like your cotton plantations.' Several took exception to this. Before long, Jack and Bernát were bidding the tourists goodnight.

The waitress joined them at the door; her name was Luciana. They strolled onto the beach, and Jack Taffarel told his story. His father, educated at a Jesuit school, had become a botanist, and at university had taught Jack's mother, who was American and had come to Brazil as a postgraduate. Now the parents were living in Florida, because in the end his mother couldn't live in Manaus any longer. Having given years of her life to the place, she thought it was only fair that her husband in turn should live in her country for a while. So his father had got a job in the States and the family – there were three children, including Jack – was transplanted to America, which is where they still were, except for Jack, who had been a teenager when they left Manaus and had found that he could not be happy anywhere else, though he had every sympathy with his mother, because Manaus was not an easy place. It was an ugly city, he knew. It was, however, the only place that Jack could live. He needed to have the river and the jungle.

At the water's edge they sat down. The water was as dark as engine oil, and made no sound as it trickled onto the sand. For a while nobody spoke, then Jack took an envelope from his pocket, and what appeared to be a pen. 'Anyone for fairy dust?' he asked. It was a herbal mixture, he explained – bark scrapings, with a bit of liana thrown in. 'Perfectly safe, in the right quantity,' he assured Bernát, 'and I know the right quantity. My education wasn't totally wasted.' He told Bernát that he would feel bad for a minute, but incredible things would soon happen. These things could not be described, he said. It would be like trying to explain sight to a blind man. Luciana dangled the envelope between her lovely eyes and Bernát's. At his nod, she knelt in front of him, her knees touching his. Into a palm she tipped a cone of powder; she sucked it up into the small pipe that he had mistaken for a pen. With a fingertip she pressed shut one of his nostrils, and to the other she raised the pipe. As it touched his skin she gave him a solemn look that compelled trust; she put her lips to the pipe and blew sharply. A violent bitterness rose into his mouth, and moments later it was if a hosepipe had been rammed into his gullet. He vomited. Pressure began to accumulate behind his eyes; in pain he closed them, and when his eyes were shut he saw an area that was like the beach except that it was indigo and there were movements in this indigo sand, as if in response to the pulsations of a vast object that was buried beneath it. When he opened his eyes the sky was also indigo and waves were travelling across it, mirroring the motion of the river. Then the river, a lighter shade of blue, began to change, and the wavelets became things like turtle shells, and there were bright green eyes, thousands of eyes, in the dips between them. He put out a hand towards the moon, and the hand seemed to be a hundred yards away, but every pore and hair was distinct, because his eyes had become telescopes. Removing his hand from the moon, he smeared white light across the sky, like car lights in a long-exposure photo.

It was a profound experience, an incidence of absolute vision, superior to any dream, he told Naomi. In dreams, he said, you see the same faces over and over again: your parents, your lovers, your boss, a miscellany of figures from your past. It's a nocturnal repertory company, performing dreary fantasias in settings that are nearly always nothing more than versions of places you've already seen. It's your life, but messed up, and messed up in a way that is rarely of interest. Visions like the vision at Ponta Negra, though, do not arise from the compost of daily life. They do not represent one's fears or desires or memories, suppressed or otherwise; the self plays no part in their creation; the self is overwhelmed, transfigured.

'Like being drunk,' Kate comments. The moisture of the grass can be felt through her clothes now; she stands up. Clouds are thickening over the horizon of the sea.

'The opposite,' says Naomi. 'When you're drunk you get smaller. Your brain slows down, you talk nonsense and then you fall asleep. What I'm talking about is an enlargement,' she pronounces. 'I'm talking about seeing beyond appearances.'

'Or, to put it another way, seeing things that weren't there,' says Kate, brushing pieces of grass from her jeans. 'I think we should be getting back,' she says. 'It'll be raining in half an hour.'

Naomi obediently stands up. 'But they were there,' she says.

'The river was not full of green eyes,' Kate points out.

'He saw them, so they were there,' says Naomi.

'No,' says Kate. 'There were no eyeballs in the river.'

'There were images of eyes, and the images were as real as anything,' says Naomi, as if her sister's objections were of a naivety that must be corrected with gentleness.

Walking side by side, the sisters retrace their steps, and Naomi endeavours to help Kate to understand. It is not disputed that the green-eyed things were not 'really there', in the sense that Kate is using the words. It was a vision, and Bernát knew that it was a vision, while it was happening. He knew that the things he was seeing could not be seen by anyone else. They could not be touched. They were made in his brain – he understood that, of course. This did not mean, however, that the experience was not 'real'. The world we inhabit is fabricated in our brains, says Naomi. Our senses are not the passive recipients of what is 'really there': when excited, our ears and our eyes and our skin send signals to different parts of the brain and the brain somehow puts them all together to make something that feels solid and predictable, something in which we can live. 'Colours are in here,' she informs her sister, knocking her brow with a knuckle, 'not out there,' she declares, offering the hillside.

'Yes. I know,' says Kate.

But Naomi cannot be brought to a pause. Soon she is going on about parallel universes. Physicists know that parallel worlds are a reality, she asserts. Experiments have proved it. There's a thing called the double-slit experiment, a very elegant and simple experiment which proves that light is both a wave and a particle and that there is more than one universe. Bernát, of course, explained it to her, and Naomi can explain it to Kate, but not now. For now it's enough to know that these are the facts. What we take to be reality is but an environment that we construct for ourselves. True reality is of too great a complexity for our brains to manage. 'We can cope only with what we make of the world,' Naomi states. The monologue continues, and Kate attends closely, with an appearance of thoughtfulness, though there is little sense in what Naomi is saying. Kate smiles whenever a smile might not be inappropriate, but she is unsettled by what she is hearing – not so much by the incoherence of it, as by its vehemence. In the past, such urgency has been an indicator of imminent crisis.

But suddenly, as if attuned to her sister's anxiety, Naomi interrupts herself, in the midst of a tortuous paraphrase of some semi-understood item of science. 'OK,' she says, stopping, making a clamping motion with both hands. 'I've lost the plot a bit here. Sorry,' she says. They are back on the steep path, overlooking the town. Naomi scans the buildings, as if in search of the visual cue that will bring her thoughts to order. This takes half a minute, then she nods and walks on.

Enthralled by his experience of the 'chemical sublime', Naomi resumes, Bernát had embarked on some research. After reading 'dozens of books and hundreds of articles', he had succeeded in concocting his own magical mixture, brewed from plants that he had gathered on his weekends in the wilds. 'It was amazing,' says Naomi. 'The taste was pretty grim, to be honest. You drink it like tea,' she explains. 'But the outcome was amazing,' she repeats, drawing the adjective out.

Kate does not provide the reaction that Naomi wants; she does not say anything.

'Are you shocked?' Naomi asks.

'Not at all,' Kate answers, which is true; the end of the story has come as no surprise. Her sister is reckless; it is disappointing, nonetheless, that she should have been so foolish.

'It was perfectly safe,' says Naomi. 'He'd tried it himself, lots of times.'

'Doesn't mean it was safe.'

'And I only tried it once. Or twice.'

'Glad to hear it,' says Kate, more primly than intended.

'But it really was wonderful,' says Naomi. Again the bait is not taken, yet she proceeds without encouragement. What she saw in Bernát's garden, at first, was the foliage starting to slip off the trees and bushes sliding into the air, like green-black lava. The lawn became a shining plate of emerald, then flames stood up from it, huge pale green flames that extended skyward, following the flow of the lava-leaves. Though the flames were moving towards her she was not afraid, because the fire had no heat; it moved over her, and as soon as she was inside the flames she began to rise. She became aware of figures in the distance, far above her – human figures, barely visible, disappearing into the light. For hours, it seemed, she was carried on the heatless flames; the joy, the tranquillity, was like nothing she had ever experienced. The colours that she saw were of a preternatural vividness – supercharged hues that no painter could mix. 'Blues that made the best summer sky seem insipid,' she says.

'Sounds like quite a ride,' says Kate. There was a time, she recalls, when Naomi would recount her dreams, in exorbitant detail, simply to share the extravagance of them; and Kate, required to reciprocate, could never offer anything of the same magnitude of invention.

'You would never have been tempted, would you?' says Naomi; her smile has commiseration in it.

For an instant Kate has an urge to step out of character. But what she says is: 'Need you ask?'

'Gabriel thought it was stupid, too,' says Naomi.

'And illegal.'

'It's a grey area.'

'I doubt it.'

'No, it is. Bernát checked.'

'We could ask Martin.'

'The offer is appreciated. But no need,' says Naomi, hooking a hand under her sister's arm. 'We'll not be doing any funny stuff up at the farm. Worry not. Bees and routine vegetables – that's the lot. No magic mushrooms,' she promises; she smiles, and squeezes the arm as one might squeeze the arm of someone elderly and beloved.

They are now at the foot of the slope that rises to the High Street. Waiting for a gap in the traffic, Naomi is apparently struck by an idea. 'Know what I'd like to do?' she says eagerly, with another squeeze. 'I'd like to see Martin.'

'Martin's in court.'

'That's what I mean. I've never seen him in action. There's a public gallery, isn't there?'

'Well, yes.'

'Come on,' she urges. '*Carpe diem* and all that. If not now, when? I'll be going back to London on Monday.'

'Oh. Really? I didn't—'

'Come on,' Naomi chivvies, tugging her sister off the pavement.

15.

Kate and Naomi are admitted to the public gallery as counsel for the prosecution – Martin – is cross-examining a man by the name of Peter Addison. It is alleged that on the night of Friday, May 2nd, Mr Addison set fire to a property belonging to a Mr Colin Simonsen, an erstwhile business partner and friend of Mr Keith Tranter and his brother, Mr Kevin Tranter, who are alleged to have commissioned Mr Addison to commit this act of arson. The Tranters allege that Mr Simonsen defrauded them of their rightful share of the profit from a resort development in Malta; they deny, however, that they had any involvement in the fire, as does Mr Addison.

Peter Addison is 35 years old and of jockey-like dimensions. He wears a shiny petrol-blue suit and radiantly white shirt, with a scarlet tie. He has astronaut-length hair, thinning on top; his eyes, deep-set below black brows, are as dark and cold as an otter's.

'Mr Addison,' the prosecutor resumes, 'the emergency services in Horsham were notified of the fire at Mr Simonsen's property shortly before 2.20am. As a witness will testify, at 1.30am a man bearing a close resemblance to yourself was observed removing an object from the boot of a Mazda sports car, less than a quarter of a mile from the scene of the fire. Yet you are adamant that this individual could not have been you. Is that correct?'

'Yes.'

'You drive a Mazda sports car, do you not?'

'Not any more.'

'But at the time of the fire you were the owner of a Mazda sports car?'

'Yes.'

'Silver?'

'I'd call it grey.'

'The same colour as the car that was seen in Horsham.'

'It wasn't me.'

'You were nowhere near Horsham?'

'No.'

'So would you be so kind as to tell us where you were?'

'Fishing.'

'In the small hours of the morning of May 2nd you were fishing?'

'That's right.'

'Where?'

'Tide Mills.'

'And where would we find Tide Mills?'

'Newhaven. By the harbour.'

'On May 2nd you decided to go fishing by Newhaven harbour in the middle of the night?'

'That's what I said.'

'Is this a frequent activity of yours, Mr Addison? Fishing at an hour when most people are asleep in their beds?'

'Fish don't sleep.'

The prosecuting counsel smiles. 'A nice point, Mr Addison,' he concedes. 'Nonetheless,' he continues, 'it might strike the members of the jury as a somewhat strange pastime, angling in the dark, on your own.'

'I like it. Clears your head. Gives you time to think.'

'I'm sure it does, Mr Addison, I'm sure it does. And if your head was clear, you'll remember the night in question.'

'Yes,' states the defendant.

'At what time did you arrive at Tide Mills?'

'About half-twelve, I suppose.'

'You "suppose"?'

'I didn't check my watch when I got there. I set off at twelve. You can ask my girlfriend. She'll tell you.'

'Yes, we are aware of Ms Kelly's statement, Mr Addison, thank you. It is not disputed that you left your home at midnight. And I am fully prepared to accept that prior to your departure you loaded your fishing tackle into your car.'

'Well then.'

'Well then what, Mr Addison?'

'That's what I've been telling you.'

'No, Mr Addison. I do not dispute the circumstances of your departure. It's your destination that's at issue.'

'I went to Tide Mills,' Peter Addison repeats, raising a hand to his tie, as if the maintenance of his good temper, against the provocations of this patronising toff, was determined by the adjustment of the knot.

'How often do you go fishing at such an hour of the night, would you say? Once a week, once a month? Every two months?'

'Maybe every month. Depends.'

'Not more frequently than that?'

'Depends, like I say. More in summer, less in winter.'

'So on average, once a month, more or less?'

'Something like that.'

'And on the night of May 2nd you arrived at the beach at half-past twelve, approximately.'

'That's what I said. High tide was at half-one. So I'd have got there for half-twelve.'

The prosecutor consults a piece of paper. He nods, as if impressed. 'High tide was indeed at 1.40am,' he confirms.

'That's what I told you.'

'A remarkably convenient hour.'

'Is that a question?' says Peter Addison.

'An observation, Mr Addison. I am making the observation that you practise this nocturnal pursuit once a month, on average, and it just so happens that in the month of May you decided to go fishing at precisely the hour that Mr Simonsen's property went up in flames. Some might think this a remarkable coincidence.'

'Well, that's coincidences for you,' Peter Addison banters, smirking.

At this Naomi wipes her palms down her face and whispers to her sister, 'Oh no.'

As if examining a wall on which an illiterate graffito has been sprayed, counsel for the prosecution applies his gaze to the defendant's face. 'Tell me, Mr Addison, were any other anglers on the beach that night?'

'Two or three.'

'Did you speak to any of them?'

'No. We were spread out. There was no one near me.'

'I see. The other people were at some distance, but you could see them, even in the dark?'

'They had lanterns. You always take a lamp with you.'

'It's quite a long beach at Tide Mills, isn't it?'

'Fairly.'

'But you have an unobstructed view, I believe. It's flat shingle, all the way to Seaford Head.'

'Correct.'

'How long did you stay on the beach at Tide Mills, Mr Addison?'

'Three hours, give or take a bit. An hour before high tide, two hours after.'

'Catch anything?'

'Nothing much.'

'Not a remarkable night, then?'

'Par for the course.'

At this point a pause is taken and papers are consulted,

papers in which, the barrister's expression implies, an incriminating detail is recorded. 'And it was definitely the night of May 2nd?' he asks quietly, turning a page.

'It was.'

'The Friday night? There is no possibility that your fishing expedition in fact took place on the Saturday?' His manner is that of a man of infinite patience, who is requesting assistance in the resolution of a minor difficulty.

'No.'

At a gesture of agitation from the defence counsel, the judge intervenes: 'I do hope that the conclusion of this line of questioning is within sight.'

'It is, your honour.'

'We'd be grateful if you could take us there without undue delay.'

'I shall, your honour,' replies the prosecutor, with an unctuous bow. The papers are put aside. 'Would you say that you have a good memory, Mr Addison?' he asks.

The defendant narrows his eyes, hesitates. 'Same as most people,' he replies.

'A very good memory, I should say. Exceptionally good.'

Peter Addison shrugs; he says nothing.

'I say this because you managed to give the police a verbatim account of a conversation that took place more than a year ago, in a crowded and noisy pub. I'm not at all sure that I would be capable of such a feat. I am impressed.' A single sheet of paper is picked up and read, so that something may be verified. 'I shall not detain you for much longer, Mr Addison,' says the prosecutor.

'Good news,' mutters his prey.

'Oh God,' Naomi whispers. 'You really should not have said that.' Her sister has had the same thought.

Counsel gives his document one last glance. To the witness he offers a smile, thinly compassionate – it could be the smile of a boss about to impose redundancy on an employee of whom he's wanted to rid himself for years. 'Tell us about the weather, Mr Addison,' he says.

'What weather?'

'The weather at Tide Mills, on Friday, May 2nd, between twelve-thirty and three-thirty in the morning.'

'How do you mean?' asks Peter Addison, apprehensive of a snare.

'Was there anything at all notable about the weather?'

'No.'

'A pleasant spring night,' the barrister muses. 'Mild, I assume?'

'Fairly. What you'd expect.'

'And the moon?'

'You what?'

'Do you remember how the moon looked that night?'

'No, I don't.'

'Isn't the moon important to anglers? Doesn't it have some influence on the proceedings?'

'I just felt like going out. I wasn't bothered about what the moon was doing.'

'You surprise me.'

'Well, there you go.'

'There was a waxing crescent moon on the night of the second of May, and it set at 11.42pm. So there would have been no moonlight. Moonlight would be an incon-venience, I should imagine, were one up to no good in the small hours, in the open air, in an area of housing. But let's move on. A clear night, was it?'

'Clearish.'

'Meaning what? Partial cloud?'

'If you like.'

'No, Mr Addison, it is not a question of what I like. It's a question of what you observed. I was not there. You were, or so you would have us believe. So: are you telling us that there was some cloud but not much?'

'I suppose.'

'Are you saying that you can't remember?'

'There were some clouds.'

'Good. There were some clouds. Now: did you get wet?'

'Pardon?'

'Did it rain?'

Peter Addison looks to his co-accused; Keith Tranter stares back with some force, as if to transmit information by telepathy; Kevin Tranter seems to be inspecting the floor. 'Might have been a spot or two,' he decides.

'You don't seem altogether sure, Mr Addison.' Martin gives his victim one second to respond, then goes on: 'Your memory for conversation is extraordinary, but now your recollection of the weather on this particular evening – this rather significant evening – seems a trifle insecure. This is strange, some may think.'

'I said there was a spot or two.'

'Yes, you did,' says the toff, firing a glance in the direction of the co-accused.

'And you were there until approximately three-thirty. That's what you said, correct?'

'Yes.'

'Windy, was it?

'Not as I recall.'

'So the sea would not have been rough, in that case.'

'No.'

'All was quiet at Tide Mills.'

'Yes.'

'A calm night in early May. Three or four fishermen on the beach, minding their own business.'

'I'm not hearing a question.'

'Just setting the scene, Mr Addison. But I do have a question, and my question is this. Let us suppose that there was a disurbance on the beach that night, you would have heard it, wouldn't you?'

'I don't follow you.'

'If there had been, let's say, a party on the beach at Tide Mills that night, with a bonfire and drinking and music, you would have heard it, would you not? You would have heard it and you would have seen the bonfire. You saw the fishermen's lanterns, after all.'

A momentary consternation opens Peter Addison's mouth by a millimetre; he glances at the Tranters.

'It's all right, Mr Addison,' says Martin. 'There is no need to say anything. Your reaction has been noted, thank you. For your information, there was no party on the beach that night, as far as I am aware. I was talking hypothetically. But I find it interesting – as I'm sure we all do – that you did not instantly put me right. Why, if you were where you claim to have been, did you not tell me immediately that there was no such party? But let's move on. We have other fish to fry.'

16.

'It was gruesome,' says Naomi, beaming at Martin as if she were an ardent admirer. 'Like watching a bullfight.'

'Except that nobody was dead at the end of it,' Martin points out.

'Well, he didn't seem to have much life left in him by the time you'd finished,' says Naomi.

'I don't think he deserves much sympathy,' says Kate.

'Not a great deal,' Naomi agrees. 'But a bit.'

'He's not a nice man,' says Martin.

'No doubt.'

'Nastier than he looks.'

'It must be exciting,' Naomi suggests. The cross-examination was a bullfight, she says again: the questions were the flourishes of the matador's cape, making the victim stumble, sapping his strength before the final blow. 'And there's the public to please as well,' she says.

'He has to convince them, not please them,' Kate points out.

'Is there a difference?'

'Of course there is.'

'And it's the public who will strike him down, not me,' says Martin.

'But it must be a thrill,' Naomi goes on, without a pause. 'Watching them going round and round in ever decreasing circles, getting weaker and weaker with every lie. That moment when they come to a standstill, the moment of truth – it must feel great. I know it does. I could see it,' she says, gently, encouraging him to admit that she's right. She smiles; she could be mimicking the smile of a therapist.

'It's satisfying,' says Martin.

Naomi mentions a film that she saw, many years ago, in which a character – an arsonist, as it happens – quotes his lawyer's own words back to him: 'Any time you try a decent crime you've got fifty ways you can fuck up. If you can think of twenty-five of them you're a genius.'

'And Peter Addison ain't no genius,' Martin responds, in a quasi-American growl.

Amazed, Naomi blinks. 'You know that film?' she asks, as pleased as a woman on a blind date that's suddenly taken an upturn.

'It would appear so,' says Martin.

Naomi scrutinises his face. One might think that he had deliberately kept this surprising aspect of his personality hidden from her, and that she is intrigued by the deception. A wry smile appears.

'And at this point I must make my excuses,' says Martin, rising from the table. He needs to do some preparation, he explains.

His departure seems to disappoint Naomi, but slightly. The sisters clear up, then they go to the living room, where Lulu, recumbent on the sofa, is watching TV.

'May we join you?' asks her mother.

'Be my guest,' says Lulu, withdrawing her legs to make space; having taken the vacated spot, Naomi reaches for her niece's feet and puts them down on her lap.

On the screen, a young man in a well-cut suit and white shirt, tieless, is talking in a room that's not much smaller than a tennis court; he stands on a deep-pile white rug, beside a white leather armchair, in front of a white grand piano; several white vases, overcharged with white flowers, are arrayed in the background, by a wall of glass that gives a view of a swimming pool; a replica of the Medici Venus stands on the water's edge. The young man escorts the camera crew to another room; in the doorway he pauses, to allow the viewers to be astonished; we are at the kitchen, which is as well-equipped as the set of a cookery programme; in the distance, a woman of southeast Asian appearance is examining the contents of a wardrobe-sized fridge. 'Good, no?' says the young man; the accent is strong.

'He's worth billions, apparently,' Lulu explains. 'He found a way of making insulation from volcanic rock. They need a lot of insulation in Russia.'

'And where's the tasteful residence?' asks her mother.

'London. That's what it's about. Invasion of the Russian squillionaires.'

Naomi, leaning forward slightly, frowning, watches the television with concentration, as she had watched the proceedings in court. Her hands are massaging Lulu's feet, a treatment that Lulu accepts without remark, as if this were an intimacy of long habit.

Now the camera is looking over the shoulder of someone who is standing at the window of a high-altitude London office; the shoulder belongs to a slightly older man, who regards the swarming traffic with the gaze of one who has come to occupy a place far above the trivialities and chaos of ground-level life. He takes a call, and speaks to the caller in English; his sentences are terse and decisive; his accent is a medley of Moscow and New York. Mobile phones and jewellery shops have made his fortune, we learn. He intends to start a bank, and various other enterprises which cannot yet be disclosed. Sitting at his vast and bare desk, in his vast and minimally furnished office, he imparts some of the principles of his thinking. 'Siloed thinking' is something he deplores; siloed thinking is the bane of British business. He has a '360-degree understanding of how any product will resonate within the consumer's life'. Appliances are no longer mere tools: they must 'reflect the personalities' of their owners. His bank will have a modern personality, he promises.

With her chin propped on her thumbs and her elbows on her knees, Naomi stares effortfully at the self-bedazzled tycoon, as though listening to the confessions of an unrepentant killer.

'This guy's a 360-degree knobhead,' says Lulu, lifting the remote. 'Shall I zap him?'

'Please,' Naomi sighs.

Lulu scrolls through the menu and selects a documentary; small monkeys are leaping into a water trough from the top of a streetlamp, in slow motion. 'OK?' she asks.

'Fine with me,' answers Naomi.

'Mum?'

'I'll leave you to it,' answers Kate.

'Where are you going?' her sister asks.

'Upstairs. I have to put in some sort of shift, even if it's only an hour.'

'I'm sorry,' says Naomi.

'What for?'

'Taking up all your time.'

'Don't be silly,' says Kate.

'If she doesn't do at least a page she can't sleep,' Lulu explains to her aunt, as if talking about some sort of behavioural tic, like having to wear a fresh set of pink pyjamas every night.

Kate leaves them. In her room, she ponders what can be done with Dorota and Jakub, or tries to; Dorota and Jakub will not materialise for her this evening. Because she intends, one day, to write a novel that might be a thriller, or a police procedural, she writes out the court scene, with different names and altered dialogue. Ideas for a subsequent scene suggest themselves, as does a twist that could be useful; it is not yet clear who will be murdered, or why, but there will have to be a murder. Arson, in a book of this kind, could only be a preliminary. After two hours she stops; Dorota and Jakub remain where they were, but something has been done. The notes go into the file labelled 'Murder Book', with a dozen other fragmentary scenes and character sketches.

The fragrance of bath oil had reached her in her room, though the door was closed; on the landing the air is as densely scented as the cosmetics hall of a department store. The light in the bathroom is on, but there's no sound; standing within inches of the door, Kate hears nothing. She taps, and whispers: 'OK in there?'

A woozy singsong voice replies quietly: 'Hello darling.'

'Just checking you're all right.'

'Very much so, thank you. Have you done what you had to do?

'I have.'

'Come in, if you want,' says Naomi.

'Are you out?'

'I'm never getting out.'

Kate opens the door, releasing an immense quantity of overperfumed vapour.

It seems that half a bottle of oil has been poured into the bath; the water should be barely tinted, but it's almost ultramarine. Naomi lies back, with her hands on her thighs; saturated by steam, her hair droops over her head and neck like a ragged cloth; her eyes are closed and she is smiling in drowsy contentment. 'What time is it?' she murmurs.

'Half eleven.'

'I should stir myself,' says Naomi, but she does not move. Her smile falls away; she lies in the water as motionless as a woman in meditation.

It is apparent that Naomi is inviting inspection. Kate looks. Pleated with empty skin, her sister's belly looks like a decaying peach; her breasts resemble enormous dead tongues; her collarbones are as stark as the rim of a bucket. Kate sits on the edge of the bath and leans over to raise the plug. At the rush of the water Naomi opens her eyes; it is obvious that she has been crying.

'What's up?' Kate asks, stroking her sister's cheek once with the back of a finger.

'Nothing's up. I'm happy. Couldn't be happier. Honestly.'

'Good. But—'

'Just having a sentimental moment.'

'About what?'

Naomi takes her sister's hand; she opens it and presses her cheek into the palm. 'I'm extremely grateful,' she says. 'You do know that, don't you?'

'You're my sister. Gratitude shouldn't enter into it.'

'Well, it does.'

'You're my sister, Naomi. I love you.'

As if the verb were a gift that had surprised her, and could not be accepted without thought, Naomi looks at Kate uncertainly; she takes Kate's hand and touches her lips to it. 'Same,' she murmurs, letting go. The water has withdrawn from her breasts; her gaze moves along her body, with the minimal curiosity of someone examining a zoological specimen in a dull museum. Then she says: 'Do you think you would have made such a success of yourself if Dad hadn't died?'

'I'm not such a success.'

'Yes, Katie, you are,' Naomi states.

'I've written a few books. But that's—'

'Success.'

'If you say so.'

'I do,' she says.

'Is that what you've been thinking about? The stuff that happened with Dad?'

Squinting at her feet, as if they were ambiguous objects in the middle distance, Naomi frowns. 'It was terrible for all of us, of course,' she says, after a delay, 'but I think you came out of it best. More determined than ever. You were not going to waste a minute.'

'Maybe.'

'Whereas I wasted many minutes,' says Naomi, without regret or self-pity.

'I wouldn't say that,' says Kate.

'But perhaps now I'm benefitting too.'

'Benefitting from—?'

'From being a half-orphan.'

'I don't follow you.'

Continuing to squint at her feet, Naomi does not respond immediately. 'Bernát,' she then says; she pauses and the frown reappears. 'This friendship. It's possible it wouldn't have happened otherwise.'

More than possible, Kate is inclined to answer; and the same could be said of the relationship with Gabriel and with his predecessors, none of whom – or none of the ones of whom she is aware – were notable for their youthfulness. But all she says is: 'Because—?'

'Bernát knew,' says Naomi.

'Knew what?'

'He knew what the story would be.' When she had told him about her father, she says, it had confirmed what he had already known; he knew, without talking to her, just by looking, in the bookshop, that a parent had died when she was young; her father, he thought. There was something in her demeanour and bearing – an 'inflection', as Bernát put it – that was unmistakeable.

'But you told him what happened,' Kate points out.

'Yes. But that's not the point.'

'It—'

'No, it's not. He knew,' says Naomi, with an incontrovertible glance. All the water has drained away now; Kate lifts a towel from the rail; Naomi takes it and drapes it over her body like a blanket. 'You think he was trying to make an impression?'

'That's not so outrageous an idea.'

'I'm not stupid, Katie.'

'I know you're not. All—'

'He doesn't bluff. If you met him, you'd know that.'

'Well, I'd like to meet him.'

'Some people are more observant than others, that's all.

It's like looking at someone's hands or the way they walk and knowing what kind of work they do. He wasn't trying to make me think he had some sort of super-intuition.'

'OK,' says Kate. 'So he—'

'And he wasn't talking about any sort of scar or injury,' Naomi goes on, to forestall her sister's use of such banalities. What Bernát had observed was not the evidence of damage but the evidence of a certain cast of mind, of a particular kind of knowledge; it was, said Bernát, like recognising 'an initiate', says Naomi. This is what he had said to her one evening, in the garden of his house; they had listened to music, just herself and Bernát, then they had talked, for a long time. For both of them this was a conversation of significance, says Naomi, fixing her gaze on the ceiling, as if to concentrate on recalling precisely, for the benefit of her analyst. They had listened to some music by Morales, and then Bernát had told her about himself and Lizzie, his 'first love', says Naomi. 'Lizzie was the woman at the concert, the grey-haired woman with the red beret,' she explains, now turning to look at her sister, and smiling to see that this development had piqued. 'Are you tired?' she asks.

'I have another hour in me,' answers Kate.

'So would some more back story be of interest?'

17.

In the first few years of her life in the West Midlands, Bernát's mother, Anikó, had only one friend of her own, Bernát confided to Naomi; all other friends and acquaintances (not that there were many) were workmates of her husband and his brother. Anikó's friend was a young woman named Lizzie Salter, who worked as an assistant to a portrait photographer, who was Lizzie's paternal uncle. He was the town's only professional portrait photographer.

To mark Oszkár's first birthday in England, Anikó took the boys to Mr Salter to have their picture taken, for the people back home. Naomi has seen the photo that resulted, she tells Kate: it's a sepia-toned scene, in which the boys are crammed into the cockpit of a half-size wooden replica of a sports car, against a background of painted fields and clouds; they look thoroughly disgruntled, she says. But Lizzie was charming and elegant: his mother would never forget the fuchsia-red colour of the dress that Lizzie was wearing that afternoon, said Bernát, nor the sumptuous long wave of her hair. Anikó took an immediate liking to her, as did the boys, and vice versa. Lizzie understood the young mother's situation; she empathised. The following week, in her lunch hour, she called at the flat, knowing that Anikó might otherwise go through the whole day speaking to nobody but her sons and husband. Mr Salter's studio was only a hundred yards from the paint and wallpaper shop above which the Kalmárs were living, the shop in which Anikó would in time be employed. At least once a week Lizzie visited Anikó, sometimes in her lunch hour, sometimes on her way home. Thanks to Lizzie, Anikó's proficiency in English improved rapidly. Soon she was introduced to Zsiga, who invited her to eat with them, that very evening. She became the boys' honorary English aunt.

When Anikó first met her, Lizzie was unattached. She remained unattached for some time – or rather, there were boyfriends, but none of any duration. It was assumed that the local lads were too unpolished for so poised a young woman. Then came the day on which Lizzie accompanied her uncle to the local grammar school, to take the end-of-year photo – that is where and when she met Christopher

Vidal, the music teacher. He was the youngest member of staff, and by some margin the easiest on the eye. In the moment he introduced himself, Lizzie knew that this was the one. His name in itself was attractive, and it became more so when she learned that it was an old Venetian name. It turned out that Christopher had no Venetian ancestors, or none of whom he knew; he had been born and raised in humdrum Bedford. No matter: he was nonetheless exotic, because Christopher inhabited a world of which Lizzie had hitherto known very little, other than that it was inaccessible to her – the world of music, of serious music. The violin was Christopher's instrument, and he was a fine musician – not good enough to be a professional, but good enough to play in public, and to make Lizzie marvel. When he showed her the scores of the pieces that he played from memory, she found it hard to believe that anyone could make anything of these blizzards of notes, never mind remember them and play them at such speed. 'Every music college in Britain has a dozen violinists who are better than I will ever be,' said Christopher. His modesty was a further enhancement. And he seemed to be immune to regret and disappointment: he was content just to be earning a living in music, he told Lizzie. She attended the school's Christmas concert, for which Christopher conducted the pupils' band. The boys were desperate to please him, she could tell; parents lingered in the hall for a chance to talk to him.

Lizzie and Christopher were married in the spring of the following year. Not long afterwards, they moved to Birmingham when he was appointed head of music at a more prestigious school. Encouraged by her husband, Lizzie set up her own photographic studio, specialising in the type of work that her uncle had taught her. Their life, she would later say, had been almost perfect. They wanted children. There was some sort of problem, but they were told that it might not be insuperable; they had time. Every morning, when she emerged from sleep, she felt grateful to be where she was, Lizzie would later tell Bernát. But one morning she was awoken by the ringing of the alarm on Christopher's side of the bed; it rang for ten seconds or more, and he did not stir; she stroked his arm; his arm was cold. He was thirty-five years old, and they had been married for only four years. 'His heart simply stopped beating. It happens,' she told Bernát, as if talking of a terrible misfortune that had befallen someone other than herself. Bernát never saw her cry, though the loss of Christopher was a blow, as she said, from which she could never recover.

Though he had met Christopher several times, Bernát in adulthood had no precise memory of him. He remembered more strongly the aura that surrounded Christopher after he had died. The surname was an aspect of that aura, as it had been for Lizzie, and it was significant that Christopher had been a musician: young Bernát understood music to be a mystery that was far removed from everyday business, and was wholly dependent on that most elusive of qualities, talent. And one other consideration was of importance: Christopher Vidal was dead, and had died at an age at which most men are only halfway through their lives. For Bernát, Christopher's premature decease augmented the lustre of his name and expertise, just as Lizzie's charisma was enriched by her immediate experience of his death.

For a year or so, Lizzie did not visit the Kalmárs. Bernát's mother went to see her in Birmingham, and reported that Lizzie was coping as well as anyone could have hoped. She had returned to work, and was finding that she could maintain her composure as long as nobody mentioned her husband, though she often had moments when, as Lizzie put it, she felt as if she were an actress who was playing the role of herself, and kept forgetting her lines. The evenings, however, were unbearable; she wept for hours. Most nights, she would come awake three or four times, and the loneliness into which she awoke was terrible. Unable to live in the place where Christopher had died, she moved to a flat in a different part of the city, where she would not have to deal every day with people who had known him. A month or so later, she wrote to Bernát's mother, saying that she would come to see the family soon. Another four or five months went by; letters were exchanged, but the visit was repeatedly postponed. And then, when Bernát was eleven years old, Lizzie reappeared, transfigured.

This Lizzie Vidal, the first that Bernát could remember in any detail, was a woman of bold bearing and considerable glamour. Though not tall, she was a powerful presence, with curvatures that commanded attention: the waist was tight, the hips generous, the bosom assertive. She held herself upright, and the angle of her head suggested the image of someone looking over an invisible wall that came up to her nose. When she spoke, she often moved her hands as if she were putting things in their rightful places. She was never flustered, and made no remarks that were unconsidered. When she listened, she looked you in the eye, always; she compelled you to talk sense, said Bernát. Her hair was spectacular: multifarious tones of straw, pale brass and barley were in it, and it was usually worn in a complex chignon. Her dress sense was distinctive: she had a penchant for short jackets and pencil skirts, often black, combined with blouses of bright colour; she was partial to cashmere twinsets. The style of her wardrobe was not modern; it was some sort of declaration, as young Bernát dimly understood. Lizzie's hands – slender, with long fingers – were as sleek as a mannequin's, and the fingernails were perfectly tended ovals, never without varnish; deep red was the customary colour. In summer the toenails were likewise painted, and her shoes had high and sturdy heels, always. Her face was strong rather than winsome, said Bernát. The brow was heavy, the eyes deep-set and dark, the jaw squarish, the nose aquiline and robust. She wore lavish perfumes, bringing with her the air of a well-stocked florist's shop. Her voice was quietly forceful and rather low. In short, for the boy that Bernát was, Mrs Vidal was a figure of some bewitchment and mystique; he knew that she was a person who was not to be trifled with.

Though Bernát's father from time to time expressed a preference for Lizzie as she had been in earlier years, when she had been more 'natural', as he put it, he nonetheless liked her; he was grateful to her for all the help she had given Anikó; and he felt sorry for her. It might even have been his idea, thought Bernát, that Lizzie should join the family in Cornwall. She was persuaded to stay in a neighbouring chalet for one week of the holiday fortnight. Bernát was now twelve years old.

The week that Lizzie spent with the family in Cornwall – to be precise, one particular day in that week; or to be more precise still, one five-minute conversation within that day – was to be of huge importance to Bernát, he told Naomi. It marked the transformation of his relationship with Lizzie, he said, and Naomi understood that what was happening when Bernát told her about this day was the transformation of his friendship with her – by which she means, she wants Kate to understand, that their friendship became the truest form of friendship, an acknowledgement of the profoundest affinity. Bernát was not trying to seduce her, she insists; in fact, he explicitly told her that this was not his intention. She has never had sex with Bernát and never will, she says.

She sets the scene in Cornwall: a stunningly hot day, so hot that the beach was empty; parasols dotting the dunes; people huddled in the shadow of the cliffs; when the waves broke, the light on the curving water was as bright as a camera flash. Despite the temperature, Lizzie had gone for a walk; every day she took a walk on her own, for a couple of hours. Bernát had watched her disappear into the shimmer that was coming off the sand; she was walking towards the headland at the northern edge of the beach.

Some time later, he decided that he too would confront the beast of the heat; he would go beyond the headland, enduring the sun with the stoicism of an adventurer in the desert. The tide had been going out for a while. As Bernát neared the end of the bay he found in the smooth damp sand a track of footprints, narrow and small, with the toes turned out; he knew that these footprints were Lizzie's. He followed them as far as he could, to a buttress of rocks at the base of the cliffs. Only when the tide was at its lowest was it possible to walk around this obstacle, so he had to climb. This was a pleasing challenge, because the rocks were steep and the stone was sharp. From the high point of the buttress he could see the next bay – this must be where Lizzie had gone. He detoured in the direction of the sea, as the stone was flatter there, and less rugged, and there were rock pools to investigate. Picking a path between the pools, he approached a tiny cove, a slot of sand from which the sea had not yet withdrawn completely. A few more steps brought him to the edge of the rocks, near the narrowest part of the cove, and then he saw two things, a split second apart: Lizzie's sky-blue swimsuit, on the sand; and Lizzie herself, with nothing on, lying in a pool that had formed at the base of the rock.

The pool was like a bathtub with gently sloping sides, and she lay with her head resting on the sand and her left arm out of the water. Her eyes were closed and she was smiling faintly, as if remembering something; she had not heard him. He knew that he should not be looking at her, but the water that covered her body was as clear as air in the sunlight, and he could see everything. Of course, he had some notion of what a wholly naked woman might look like: he had seen illustrations in textbooks; from photographs of girls in bikinis, and from real girls at the swimming baths, he had extrapolated the vision of their bodies unclothed. He had seen statues. This, however, was his first exposure to the reality of the fully achieved female, and the diagrammatic forms of his imagination were now obliterated by the sublimity of the mature Mrs Vidal. His gaze slid to her breasts, of course: they were wide and discrepant in size, and their softness, he could see, would feel like no other softness; the nipples were as large as pine cones. The belly, a shallow dome, milk-pale, curved down to a clump of hair that was the colour of rain-soaked brick; it looked like lacy seaweed. For several seconds his attention was fixed there.

Lizzie now opened her eyes. In an instant an arm went across her chest. 'How long have you been there?' she asked; she did not seem angry.

'Only a second,' said Bernát.

'With catlike tread,' Lizzie commented; there was a cleverness in this which he could not fully appreciate, he knew; her wit, her composure – she was like nobody else, thought the boy.

'I didn't know you were there,' he apologised.

Lizzie regarded him, saying nothing; the curve of one eyebrow steepened, and her mouth formed the smallest of smiles.

'I'm sorry,' said Bernát.

She continued to look at him, and then she shrugged. 'Ah well,' she sighed, 'you've already seen everything.' The hand came down.

As if she were an object that he had five seconds to memorise for a test, Bernát scanned her body from feet to neck and back again. 'Now run along,' said Lizzie, closing her eyes. 'And I think we say nothing to anybody,' she added.

This phrase, Bernát told Naomi, was not delivered as a threat, even of the mildest kind; he heard it rather as the proof of an understanding. And he spoke not a word about this incident to anyone, for many years. Lizzie again became a regular visitor to the Kalmárs' flat, and when talking to Bernát she never made the slightest allusion to what had happened that afternoon on the beach. Nothing in her manner gave any indication that something was being hidden; there were no covert glances. Bernát and Lizzie shared their secret, he believed, as two adults share a secret – as if it did not exist. The stupendous female body had been revealed to him, and the prestige of that revelation was increased by his concealment of it. He congratulated himself on being as devious and self-controlled as a spy, he told Naomi.

In the presence of the family Lizzie remained, for a time, perfectly even-handed in her dealings with Bernát and his brother, her two quasi-nephews: praise was distributed equally; questions about school, friendships, interests, and so on, betrayed no preference. In moments alone with Bernát, however, there were signs, increasingly frequent, that her affection for him was of a different order – a quick remark, a smile, an enquiry as to his opinion. Gradually it became understood that Lizzie's sensibility was more closely attuned to that of the younger boy than to that of the older. Many years later, she admitted that she had for a long time found Oszkár too tightly focused, too single-minded. 'You need more than a single mind to get the most out of life,' she declared, said Bernát, as Naomi tells her sister.

According to Bernát, Lizzie's partiality caused no resentment: even more than his father, Oszkár had misgivings about what they were inclined to perceive as Lizzie Vidal's artificial qualities. 'She puts too much work into herself,' Oszkár once remarked. He thought she was pretentious. Bernát, however, was flattered that Lizzie – the most exciting person he knew – took such an interest in him. She began to educate him in areas that were overlooked by his schooling, to transmit some of the enthusiasms that she had acquired during her time with Christopher. Christopher had inspired her, she said, and he continued to inspire her – not to create but to learn. She knew her limitations: she was an artisan, not an artist. She was a professional picture-taker and picture-maker, with a solid grasp of the technicalities of her craft. She lacked the spark of creativity, but had a good eye and a good ear, and her curiosity was as keen as a child's. Almost everything that young Bernát knew about music, he learned from Lizzie. French music, especially the music of the Baroque era, had been one of Christopher's passions, and it became, via Lizzie, one of Bernát's. She took him to concerts and exhibitions and plays, sometimes with Oszkár, more often without. Lizzie and Bernát even travelled to London. Everything interested her, said Bernát: Japanese ceramics, Sicilian puppets, Turkish carpets – he learned something about them all through his friendship with Lizzie.

'I know what you're thinking,' says Naomi, interrupting the story. She tells her sister what her sister is thinking, and her guess is not inaccurate. But she wants it to be understood that Bernát's emotional and intellectual development was in no way warped by this relationship, a relationship that she acknowledges might be considered strange. It might be supposed, Naomi proposes, that young Bernát's choice of girlfriends would have been influenced, consciously or not, by the girls' resemblance to Mrs Vidal. This would be quite wrong, Naomi asserts. His first full sexual experience was with a girl named Melanie, Bernát had told her, and only in her femaleness did Melanie resemble Lizzie: she was underweight, nervous, bookish, taciturn, and opposed to all make-up on principle. The sex, Naomi reports, was less than wholly satisfactory, at first. Was this because the young man's mind and body had been corrupted by his infatuation with the older woman, his illicit and unattainable ideal? Naomi posits the question with the pomposity of a self-appointed expert in the subject of human relationships. Devoted to the forcefully ripe Mrs Vidal, was he unable to find excitement with the slender and girlish Melanie? No, said Bernát, says Naomi. They were young and inexperienced, that's all. They had not yet got the hang of the intricacies of copulation. But they soon improved, Naomi assures her sister.

'This is rather more information than I need,' says Kate.

'You never know,' says Naomi, and she smiles to encourage reconsideration. 'Can the mill have too much grist?' she asks. Without waiting for an answer she resumes the tale of Bernát's sentimental education.

One momentous day, in his seventeenth year, the year of Melanie, Bernát cycled to Lizzie's flat: she had bought a recording that she thought was startling, and she wanted him to hear it; it was a recording of the B Minor Mass, conducted by Nikolaus Harnoncourt, he remembered. This was the first time he had been to the place where Lizzie lived. Her style at home, he discovered, was a version of her holiday style: she was wearing jeans, a man's striped shirt and thin-strapped sandals. She looked more French than English, he thought, and her flat – occupying the lower floor of a large Victorian house – was not like any he had previously been in. A scent of lavender pervaded the rooms and the floors were bare wood, waxed, with a large azure and oatmeal rug in the centre of the living room. Blinds, not curtains, hung in the windows. It was brighter than any house he had ever seen. From the kitchen a door opened onto a garden that had a wide oval of gravel where one would have expected grass to grow, and there was a bench made of lengths of warped grey wood. The zinc of the kitchen table bore dozens of scratches and interlocking stains, some faded, some not; the blatancy of these stains, he knew, signified a kind of sophistication that was very subtle. Pictures – most of them photographs; none of them bought from shops – were in every room, the kitchen included.

One of the pictures was of Christopher. 'My favourite,' she said, drawing a thumb lightly over the surface, as if to clear dust from it. 'A looker, wasn't he?' she said. Bernát's parents had a wedding photograph of Lizzie and her husband, and he would not have known, at a glance, that the groom was the same person as the man in this photo. In the wedding picture he was wearing a buttoned-up suit, and his stance was so stiff it was as though the trousers were made of steel; his smile was the sort of smile you make in the mirror when you're brushing your teeth. The photo in Lizzie's flat showed him sitting against the trunk of a tree, in the shade of its foliage, with a smile that seemed to have been caught in the telling of a story; his shirt, white, was half undone and he had not shaved that day. Together young Bernát and the widow regarded the face of happy Christopher, and she smiled at his image as you might smile while reading a postcard from a close friend, in which he tells you of something good that has happened to him. And Bernát would never forget what Lizzie then said. 'Does it ever strike you,' she said, facing the picture of her husband, 'that you're never just in one place? That you're here, where your body is, but at the same time you're always elsewhere?' The riddle was garnished with a quick and almost teasing look, as Bernát described it. 'What I mean,' she went on, 'is that you exist here, in your body, and you exist in the mind of anyone who is thinking of you. You live in your body, but you also live in the wider world, in the ideas that people have of you, in their memories of you. While you're still alive you live in other people's memories, and for most of your waking life your mind is occupied by memories too. We live in memories more than we live in the present.' She looked at him again, and the look was that of someone who regarded him as an equal, said Bernát, says Naomi. 'Does that seem like gibberish to you?' she asked.

'No,' he answered.

'I thought it wouldn't,' she said, rewarding him with a smile of commendation. Her eyes, looking into the eyes of the dead man in the picture, now narrowed; she pressed her lips together, and sadness came into her face. 'But the thing is,' she said, 'despite everything, he's fading. Bit by bit, he's going away from me. I remember that certain things happened, but I don't see them as clearly as I used to. I know them as facts, which isn't the same thing. And there's nothing I can do about it,' she said, with a heavy shrug. He had an impulse to put an arm around her; he knew, however, that this was something that could not be done.

Bernát thought it could be said, he told Naomi, that he loved Lizzie Vidal as he had loved nobody else: he loved her for the loss that she had endured, for the fortitude with which she borne it, for her devotion to the dead man, whom she had loved so greatly that she had not been able, for a long time, to speak of him. He admired her and was improved by her, he said. They had a bond that he had never experienced with anyone else, until now, he confessed.

As the years passed and Lizzie remained single, Bernát's father talked with increasing frequency of the 'black cloud' that Lizzie, to his way of thinking, had elected to live under. Gloominess was not an attractive quality in a woman, he maintained. Bernát saw no black cloud: he saw a woman who was intelligent and self-reliant and imcomparably dignified; there was an undertow of melancholia, certainly, and this undertow was perhaps becoming stronger with time, but this only compounded her allure. As Lizzie passed her fortieth birthday, Bernát's father concluded that she was doomed to loneliness because her dead husband, though a decade deceased, blighted the chances of any new candidate; Lizzie could not settle for less than one hundred per cent, and only Christopher could ever hit that mark; her fidelity to the ghost had become morbid. For Bernát, of course, Lizzie's absolutism was magnificent.

Ever-curious Lizzie was a compulsive participant in evening classes: pottery; French cinema; Italian cinema; flower arranging, Japanese style; continental literature and more. Various men of varying degrees of eligibility were encountered at these classes, and with some of these men Lizzie had sex. Bernát in his twenties became a confidant; he knew about relationships of which his parents knew nothing. A man called Max, from the pottery class, secured Lizzie's interest for longer than any of his predecessors, but he too was soon found wanting. He was a cultured man, she told Bernát, and rather debonair, and considerate. One could not wish to meet a nicer man, she said, 'but you can have too much niceness. And he is totally incapable of surprising me.' Besides, she went on, a woman has to make too many compromises in order to maintain a relationship with a man. A woman has to make something of herself that she is not, so that she can be fitted into the life of someone who is making much less of an effort to fit more closely into hers. She would never marry again, she declared. Marriage, Lizzie believed, was a prison for women, reports unmarried Naomi to her married sister. It might be a well-appointed and sunny prison, with spacious grounds and comfortable cells and a fence around the perimeter that was barely visible, but it was nonetheless a prison, and 'sooner or later you need to get out,' said Lizzie. Perhaps, even with Christopher, marriage might have started to chafe; she doubted it, but the possibility had to be accepted. She was enjoying life as a single woman, she said to Bernát, as they sat in the sunshine, outside a London café; she exchanged a subtle smile with a waiter, in demonstration of her liberty, he remembered. Women, she wanted Bernát to know, are less in need of men than men are in need of women, and she didn't mean merely that men didn't know how to cook or do the laundry or generally look after themselves, though in many cases that was true. Her point was more a philo-sophical one: that men – 'most men', she clarified, making an exemption of the young man to whom she was talking – require a woman to be their audience, their mirror, 'to assure them that they are important', said Lizzie, says Naomi. It was odd, Lizzie thought, that it should be commonly believed that women require flattery, when in reality it was the other way round. Too many relation-ships, she pronounced, are based on the terror of being alone. 'Women, in my experience, are braver,' she said. 'Widows fare better than widowers.'

Lizzie was very capable of creating surprise: new interests would develop quickly, and be pursued with zeal; her opinions were unpredictable. Her mind, thought Bernát's father, lacked cohesion; her thoughts had no 'weight', he said. For Bernát, Lizzie in her late forties was as stimulating and entertaining a companion as any of his student friends. And then, on the brink of fifty, she produced her greatest surprise.

At a wine appreciation class, Lizzie came to know a man called Barry Tillotson, six years her junior, whose business involved the renovation and highly profitable resale of vintage sports cars. Barry was freshly divorced from a 'madwoman' who had become convinced that her irresistible husband was sleeping with a different trollop every week. Whenever he came back from a trip, she interrogated him for hours; she insisted on unpacking his bags, looking for evidence. She would turn up at his office without warning, to catch him *in flagrante*; she was in the habit of intercepting the postman, to check the mail that was coming in. After the divorce, she took to parking outside his flat at night, watching the windows; the campaign of harassment was ended by Lizzie, who confronted her in the street at 3am and ended up in the passenger seat, counselling the poor woman until dawn.

Barry's business was successful. He drove a pristine Maserati 3500 GT, a gorgeous and powerful vehicle of infuriating fragility; Barry possessed the skills to heal the machine whenever it developed an ailment. He was an accomplished cook, and never bought a bottle of wine that had any English words on the label. Before long, Barry Tillotson had seduced Mrs Vidal, or vice versa, to the surprise of the entire Kalmár family. Barry was not a catch, in their eyes: the physique was no better than average for a middle-aged Englishman, and the face lacked all distinction. More to the point, Lizzie Vidal was a reader, whereas Barry was not; Lizzie enjoyed serious music, whereas Barry, by Lizzie's admission, did not; Lizzie liked to visit galleries and museums, which was not at all Barry's idea of fun. The meeting of Bernát and Barry was much as Bernát had suspected it would be; the conversation was turgid, and soon expired. Some time afterwards, Lizzie said to him: 'You don't get it, do you? Myself and Barry. You're at a loss.' Bernát had to admit that this was the case. 'Well,' she said, 'to tell you the truth, I've had enough of living on my own. I'm fed up. Week in, week out, round and round – school photos, graduation photos, wedding photos, school photos, graduation photos.' They were in her garden; looking at the engagement ring on her finger, she began to smile. 'And the thing is,' she said, leaning closer, though they could not be overheard, 'he is tremendously good at sexual intercourse.'

'Tremendously good,' Naomi repeats, as though the words had a relishable flavour.

'And this was the old lady at the concert?'

'It was.'

'So everything worked out fine in the end.'

'Not quite,' says Naomi. The relationship between Bernát and Lizzie had weakened after the marriage to Barry, she tells her; it weakened to such an extent that when he went back to the Midlands to see his parents, he didn't always visit Lizzie; whenever he did call on her, though, she seemed happy, Bernát told Naomi. Lizzie's second marriage lasted more than six times longer than the first, and the distance that had grown between herself and Bernát in that quarter century could not be closed after Barry died. But though it was not possible to restore the intimacy that Lizzie and

Bernát had once enjoyed, they did, with no great effort, succeed in becoming companionable again. Many times Bernát drove up to Birmingham solely to talk to her; after a year or thereabouts, she came to London, and they went to an opera together; her expeditions to London became quite regular. The last time she came down, she surprised him again: she announced that she was going to Australia to live out her last years in the Gold Coast town where her brother and his wife were living. Her brother, a Ten Pound Pom, had emigrated in the Fifties and had gone on to set up a boatbuilding business, which had made him so much money that he'd been able to build a huge house for himself and his wife and four sons, overlooking the ocean. A few years after Christopher's death, Lizzie had flown to Brisbane to spend a fortnight with her successful brother and his beautiful wife and their four irrepressible boys; she'd found the place unbearably dull, Bernát reminded her; there had been nothing to do except stare at the sea. Staring at the sea was what she wanted to do now, she answered; and the idea of being warm, all the time, was powerfully enticing. She would take a book to the beach and lie in a rock pool all day, she said. 'But she never got to do it,' Naomi tells her sister, and her eyes begin to water, as if the loss were hers.

She presses the heel of a hand into one eye and then the other, and smiles at her foolishness. 'Tired,' she explains. 'More tomorrow. One more instalment should be enough. Maybe two,' she says, then she hugs her sister too tightly.

IV

18.

The air is fresh and moist and still, and a bright mist lies
over the houses and the Paddock. The leaves of the trees
and bushes around the Paddock are a pallid monochrome.
It is almost silent; attention is required to distinguish the
sound of the traffic in the centre of town. Kate looks at her
watch; it is almost eight thirty and she has been sitting here,
at the end of the terrace, for more than half an hour now.
Minute by minute the haze is lifting from the summit of
the castle; she watches the stone walls coming into focus.
Behind her, cutlery jangles in the drawer: Naomi has come
downstairs. For a few minutes more, Kate stays on the
terrace. She wanders to the end of the lawn and looks back
at the house. The kitchen lights are on, all of them, and
Naomi is standing below one of the spotlights, holding a
pot of honey; she raises the pot above her eyes and swivels
it slowly, examining it as if it were something marvellous.

In Kate's mind, a scene begins to coalesce: a village; she
is sauntering with Naomi; a street of plane trees; green
light under the leaves, and a fountain; they pass a bottle

of water back and forth without a word. A rack of honey jars stands at the door of a shop. Inside, on the counter, in a track of sunlight, stands an unlabelled flask, lidless; the honey that half fills the flask has the colour of mahogany. With a small wooden spatula, Naomi takes a scoop and dribbles it onto her tongue; she closes her eyes; the taste seems to require concentration. Delicately, as if placing a thermometer, Naomi puts the spatula into her sister's mouth; her forefinger brushes Kate's lower lip. The honey burns like a spice; there is a smokiness in it, like the air of the scorched hillside above the village. 'Strange,' says Naomi; her hair, struck by the sun, is a thicket of golden filaments; there is not a sound in the shop. Remembering, Kate experiences the faintest taste-echo, an instant of elusive smoky warmth.

She steps into the kitchen.

'Good morning,' says Naomi; she seems cheerful.

'Coffee?' Kate asks.

'I'm fine, thank you' Naomi answers. She watches her sister at the machine; for half a minute neither of them speaks. 'Having book thoughts?' she asks.

'Not yet.'

'Something else then.'

'Not really thoughts.'

'Tell,' Naomi commands.

'Just remembering something.'

'Tell.'

'The honey shop in France.'

'The obese cat,' Naomi responds.

Kate remembers no cat.

'There was a vast cat, on the opposite side of the road,' states Naomi. 'Grey. Shaggy. Yellow eyes. Horrible.'

Naomi's memory of that afternoon turns out to be more replete than Kate's. The waiter at the café under the plane trees had taken a shine to their mother, apparently; some one-sided flirtation had gone on when he brought the change; Naomi mimics the waiter's smarmy smile as he put the dish of coins on the table. Their father, says Naomi, was unamused, and reduced the tip in retribution. In a side street they had seen a man working on the engine of an ancient Citroën; he had been singing something operatic quietly to himself, and his voice was rather good. She recalls much else besides. There is no doubt, for Kate, that Naomi's recollection is exact.

'And when was the waterfall?' asks Kate. 'Before or after the honey shop?'

'After,' says Naomi, instantly. She has cut her toast into tiny strips; she dips them one by one in the honey and takes them between her teeth, as if it were imperative that the bread should not touch her lips.

'That was a terrific holiday,' says Kate; Naomi nods, inserting another tiny slice. 'I often think about it,' says Kate; this is not true.

'Why?' asks Naomi.

'Because it was terrific.'

'It was,' Naomi agrees, but no residue of pleasure is audible in her voice. She takes a sip of her juice, then another little slice. 'But a very long time ago.'

'Not a very long time.'

'Thirty years, more than,' says Naomi.

'Christ,' sighs Kate. 'Doesn't feel like it.'

'It does to me.'

'But you remember it so well. Better than I do.'

'Maybe, maybe not. Perhaps I'm getting it wrong.'

'You're not. When you remind me, I remember.'

'When I remind you, you think you remember,' Naomi corrects her. 'If you're relying on your brain alone, you can't know I'm right. And I can't know I'm right. I might be convinced I'm right, but I can't be certain, without evidence. It may feel right, but that's not the same thing.'

'I can see the man fixing his car,' says Kate.

'Really? You can see him?'

'Yes,' says Kate, shutting her eyes to see more clearly.

'OK. What colour is his shirt?'

'I don't know.'

'Is he wearing jeans?'

'I don't know. But I can see the car with the bonnet up, and the man working on it.'

'You imagine him. You don't see him. He's not there to see.'

'I do see him,' answers Kate, looking at her sister. 'Just not as well as you.'

'I'm not seeing him. I don't know what colour his shirt is. I don't even know what colour the car is. Do you?'

'No.'

'There you are,' says Naomi. 'It's a mess. For all we know, some of the things I think were in that village were somewhere else entirely. I'm not observing the man and his car – I'm making him up. I can't observe him, because there's nothing outside of my brain to observe. The man with the car does not exist – he's a creation of our heads. It's not like an excavation – you're not digging up a picture. You create the picture when you look at it.'

'No, we're not making him up. He did exist. We know he existed because he appears in my head and he appears in yours. He's real. I might not see him like I'm seeing you, but I see him.'

'Fine,' says Naomi, to insert a pause. Meshing her hands on the tabletop, she leans forward; she looks at her hands and breathes deeply, as if deciding how to reformulate the facts in sentences that will be easy to comprehend. 'When you think of the honey shop, of us in the honey shop, as kids, do you think you're experiencing it again, as it was?'

'It's as if I'm there, for a moment, yes.'

'You become the girl in the honey shop?'

'For a second or two.'

'You're looking through her eyes?'

'Yes.'

Naomi regards her sister as if she were talking to someone likeable who is insisting that she has seen angels. 'But of course you're not there,' she says, 'because that place has gone. You're here.'

'I'm there and here at the same time,' says Kate. 'Put it another way: the girl is part of me. And young Naomi is part of you.'

'But she's not,' says Naomi. 'The kid who saw the cat in the street has gone. We go by the same name. And that's about as far as it goes.'

'That's not true, Naomi,' states Kate. 'You've changed. I've changed. Everyone does. But the girl is still here. Here is the only place she can be. Who else would she be if she weren't you?'

'Herself.'

'Which is inseparable from yourself.'

'No, it isn't.'

'You're saying she has no connection with you?'

'I didn't say that.'

'You remember what young Naomi saw, what she felt, what she thought.'

'I think I do, sometimes.'

'Because you're the same person. Your eyes are the same as hers.'

'I've inherited her equipment and some of the things she learned, that's true,' Naomi concedes.

'It's more than that,' says Kate. 'You're a continuation.'

'I can see continuities,' Naomi concedes; her smile suggests that she might be playing a game and is pleased that she has been able to take it this far.

'Thank you.'

'But maybe that's just hindsight,' suggests Naomi. 'We've arrived here,' Naomi goes on, 'and we can go back through the years and find a path that leads to where we are. We find a pattern in what we remember. Or perhaps we draw a pattern over it. But if you were somewhere else today, if you'd become a zoologist, a doctor, a meteorologist, a pilot, anything, you could look back and find incidents in which your destiny was evident for those with eyes to see.'

But it was odd, to say the least, Kate responds, to think about one's younger self as if she were another person. She could not imagine her life as some sort of relay race, with Kate Number Fifteen handing over to Kate Number Sixteen, who handed over to Kate Number Seventeen and so on. For how long did each Kate hold the baton? Was she to think of Kate in June of last year as someone distinct from Kate in July? Separating her life into episodes, each with its distinct Kate, was like trying to cut up a river, she tells her sister.

Naomi looks out at the garden; her lips form a shape as if touching the mouthpiece of an invisible trumpet; this was once a mannerism of hers, an endearing one. Still facing the garden, Naomi resumes: 'We don't think. To say that we think is to get it the wrong way round. Thoughts happen inside our brains, and they make us think that we made them happen. But we are not in charge; the thoughts are in charge. Everything comes afterwards. An idea happens, an emotion happens, a chemical reaction that feels like something, and then a reason is found for it, a justification. The brain makes everything seem to fit.

It makes us up.' She gives her sister a long and penetrative look, a look that is stern yet sympathetic; it says that their situation is worse than naive Kate believes, but not hopeless. 'When I've been mad,' she says, 'I—'

'Don't use that word. Please.'

Naomi returns her sister's gaze, but as if the interruption had been nothing but a noise from outside. She continues: 'When I've been mad, the voices in my head were saying things I would not say. They were invaders. The voices had invaded me. That's how I saw it. My mind had been hijacked. But this was a misunderstanding. I came to understand what had really been happening. The voices were the same substance as what I'd thought of as my thoughts, but in a different form. Like water and steam and ice. The same substance, but different forms. Do you see?'

'I understand water all right,' says Kate. 'But—'

'I hadn't been invaded – there was no I to invade. The invaders were what I was, as much as my regular thoughts had been. What I came to understand—'

'Exactly. What *you* had come to understand.'

'What had become clear,' Naomi revises, 'was that I was the product of the chemicals, of the reactions. I was the weather of this particular brain. I understood this, and I accepted it,' she says, placidly, as if talking of a religious conversion that had occurred many years ago. She takes Kate's hand, and raises it for a kiss. 'You think this is all terrible, don't you?' she says.

'No,' Kate answers, retaining her sister's hand. 'I don't think it's terrible. I think it's not right.'

'You think you have a wee woman inside your skull, pulling the levers? The Katie-essence? Mission control?'

'Of course not.'

'A soul?'

'The weather can't think about itself, Naomi.'

Her sister smiles; this objection is the obvious one, the smile tells her, and is easily refuted. 'The stuff out there can't think about itself,' says Naomi, pointing towards the garden. 'I grant you that. But the sky is simple stuff. Just water vapour and a few gases. In here,' – she raps a knuckle on her brow, with force – 'it's much more complicated. Billions and billions and billions of cells, fizzing away, day and night. So many chemicals and circuits. It's a universe in there,' she says, mock-boasting, and she laughs.

'Perhaps I'm out of my depth,' Kate suggests; Naomi does not contradict her. 'All I know,' Kate goes on, 'is that there is a person called Naomi, a person who thinks and talks and makes decisions, a person who is unique and herself, and always has been. It's not a vat of chemicals I'm talking to right now.'

'Oh, but it is,' Naomi replies, sorrowfully; the sorrow is for her innocent sister. She puts her glass on the plate; the toast has not been finished; she has eaten almost nothing.

'And Bernát?' says Kate. 'He's just a bag of chemicals that has achieved some sort of reaction with the bag of chemicals we call Naomi?'

Naomi stands up and kisses her sister on the top of her head. She carries the plate to the bin, then puts it into the dishwasher, in the wrong place. 'You get some work done,' she says, 'then I'll go to see Mum.'

'What are you going to do this morning?'

'Homework.'

'Homework?'

'Past tense, conditional mood,' says Naomi, with a teasing smile as she leaves.

Kate sits at the table. The lid of the honey jar is not straight; she removes it and replaces it. Idly she turns the jar on the tabletop; she tilts it, and watches the liquid slide; she gazes into it, as if impersonating a phony gypsy with her crystal ball. A memory duly rises.

At the waterfall in the Gorges de la Méouge, Kate remembers, Naomi was wearing a short dress, a yellow dress. She walked down to the lip of the rock. 'Be careful,' her mother called, and Naomi, mechanically obedient, took a couple of steps back. Now Kate can see more of the scene: the pool of green water; the smooth walls of limestone, streaked and curved; the deep blue sky, with one small cloud in it, a tattered globe of vapour, a small pretty stain on the vast plain of blue. At first the rock was too hot for bare feet. She found a ledge, shaded by a bush, on which she could sit and read; her parents were close, by a larger bush, and her father's head was resting on her mother's lap. It was noticed that Naomi had crept back to the edge; she stood motionless there, looking down into the churning water, her arms straight at her sides, with the fingers pointing stiffly down, like a soldier on the parade ground. Three or four boys in swimming trunks ran past her and leaped without stopping; one of them brushed her shoulder as he went by. 'Naomi,' her mother called, and Naomi turned and smiled and raised a hand in acknowledgement, but did not retreat; she turned back, and lowered her head to resume her examination of the water. Kate was sent to talk to her.

When Kate was ten yards away, Naomi raised her arms to the horizontal, brought her hands together and flexed her knees; she assumed an expression that was excited and fearful and prim, as if mimicking a Victorian girl on the brink of an extraordinary act of daring. 'Mum says—' was all Kate had time to say: Naomi sprang and plummeted, upright, her arms clamped to her ribs. Their mother screamed; the boys, bobbing in the pool, applauded and cheered. When Naomi emerged from the water, they gazed appreciatively at the butter-coloured form she offered; she would have been fourteen.

'It's perfectly safe,' Naomi assured her parents. Her mother, distraught at the close encounter with calamity, laid out the yellow dress on a rock with tremulous care, as if performing a ritual of thanks for her daughter's safe return. Admonishment was the job of the father, but his annoyance lacked force; thinking he was not observed, he winked at his younger daughter. The boys were preparing for a second jump; they disappeared from view; five minutes later they clambered back onto the ledge, uninjured. Now in her swimming costume, Naomi conducted her father to the precipice, so that the danger might be assessed. The judgement was in her favour. 'Come on,' she yelled to Kate, who was urged to comply by her mother, in the belief that the risk of mishap would thereby be reduced. Before Kate could reach her, Naomi jumped again, stiff-armed and stiff-legged, looking straight ahead as she stepped off, with the expression of someone facing down a challenge. Kate peered over, and saw her sister standing within the cascade, with her eyes tightly closed, aghast with pleasure as the water shattered on her head. When Kate called her name she waded out, and swam into the deepest part of the pool. Turning onto her back, she beckoned her sister to jump, but Kate stayed on the ledge; the warmth of the air was pleasurable; the water did not appeal, and neither did the leap. Naomi climbed back up and took her hand and hauled her to her feet. 'Together,' ordered Naomi, but Kate pulled her hand free. Naomi looked at her queryingly, then put her arms around her sister and pressed her against her cold wet body. 'Courage,' she whispered. Then she let go, turned sharply and marched to the launching point. Her palms slapped onto her thighs simultaneously, her chin went up, and into the air she stepped. It had to be done: Kate moved onto the sill of rock; she dithered there, watching her sister swimming into the waterfall; Naomi turned and shouted the order, and Kate went over, screaming. The smack of the water was exhilarating, and her face came up into the air in an instant. Naomi led the way back up and they jumped again, many times. Their legs went red from all the smacking of the water, she remembers.

Kate makes herself another cup of coffee, then goes up to her room and writes some notes about the afternoon at the waterfall.

19.

Alone in the house for two hours, Kate returns to Dorota and Jakub; or rather, they return to her, promptly, as if they had been awaiting her full attention. Of course Dorota cannot tell her husband that she has seen Jakub. (Might the second husband's name have the same initial as the first – Julius?) *Dorota no longer knows what her true feelings are*, Kate writes. Two days before Easter, the phantom of Jakub appears to her again, by the railway station. Dusk is falling. He is striding towards the station, very quickly – so quickly that his feet perform a little skip every four or five strides. At any moment, it seems, he might break into a run. Anxiety is evident in his posture; he glances from side to side frequently. Before the war, Jakub had worked in a factory, but this Jakub looks like a businessman or perhaps a clerk. He is smartly dressed, in a black suit, and he carries a briefcase. She sees him take a watch from a waistcoat pocket – and now, apparently in a panic, he starts to run. Dorota hurries, but she loses sight of him in the crowds on the concourse. Then a glimpse – Jakub is stepping onto a train. (Where is it going? This might compound the mystery, it occurs to Kate. Perhaps the train will pass through the town or village in which he was born? *Thread to be followed – Dorota & Jakub's parents*, Kate notes.) Dorota runs to the platform, but the guard is already blowing his whistle; seconds later, the train is in motion.

She needs to think about Dorota's relationship with her second husband. His name will be Julius, she decides; he is a bank clerk. Dorota has told Julius nothing about the apparitions, *but he has begun to wonder if she might be hiding something from him*, Kate writes, and in an instant, before she has written the last syllable, a development presents itself: Dorota catches sight of Jakub in an open carriage; the horses are being whipped by the driver to make them hurry, and Jakub is not alone – he is with a man whom Dorota knows, a former workmate. Dorota goes to the factory, where she is told that the man has not been seen since he went off to fight. She is given the man's address, and goes there; his wife opens the door, and Dorota understands immediately that this woman is a widow. She also understands that this woman cannot be told what Dorota has seen. *So what story does she tell the woman? Pretends was looking for someone else? Yes*, Kate writes.

20.

Kate drives back to The Willowes to collect her sister. There is still almost a mile to go when she sees her: Naomi is leaning against the gate of a field, looking at an ill-kempt horse which is cropping the grass only five yards from the gate, wholly indifferent to her scrutiny. 'A beautiful day, so I thought I'd take some exercise,' Naomi explains, stamping the soil off her shoes before getting in. The shoes are old moccasins, wholly unsuitable for gravel-strewn country lanes. 'Might have overdone it,' she says, putting fingers to her sweat-sodden hairline. She fusses with her coat before fastening herself in; she unbuckles it, having found a twist in the seatbelt; she unbuttons the coat, refastens the buckle. 'OK,' she at last announces, giving the dashboard a light tap; Kate turns the car round. 'Nice part of the world,' Naomi observes. Other remarks are made, none of them about their mother.

At the first pause, Kate asks: 'So, how was she?'

'OK. But she kept calling me Kate.'

'That happens with me. She jumbles up the names.'

'It was more than the names she was jumbling. Seemed to think I'm married to Martin.'

'She does get very confused. Did she think it was me she was talking to?'

'On the whole, no.'

'How long were you with her?'

'Forty minutes. Bit less,' says Naomi. 'She fell asleep,' she adds, defensively. She regards the passing countryside for a few moments, then says: 'She talked about Dad.'

'Really?'

'She called him John, but it was Dad she meant.'

'You sure?'

'She said "Your father". Seems safe to assume she had Dad in mind.'

'She never mentions him when I'm with her. Well, hardly ever. Was she upset?'

'Far from it,' says Naomi. 'Fond memories.'

'Gosh,' is all Kate says.

'Talking about a trip to the zoo, as far as I could make out. Or maybe a park. Some deer were involved, anyway.

Dad putting his hand out and a deer coming up to lick it. Ring any bells?'

'No.'

'Before our time, I suspect.'

'Must be,' says Kate. 'So she didn't get upset?'

'Not about Dad. But very peeved about her necklace.'

'What necklace?'

'I have no idea. Apparently I've broken one of her favourite necklaces.'

'When?'

'Maybe a crime of my youth.'

'I don't remember you breaking a necklace.'

'Perhaps it was you.'

'I don't think so.'

'Neither do I.'

'Maybe it was Daniela.'

'Could be.'

'Usually it's Lulu who gets mixed up with Daniela, but you never know.'

Facing away from her sister, Naomi puts her forehead to the glass. She mutters: 'That was terrible.'

'I did warn you.'

'She was extremely annoyed about that necklace.'

'She's often angry,' Kate tells her. 'Tells me to leave her alone sometimes. As if I'm persecuting her. It's hard. But you shouldn't take it personally.'

'I didn't break the necklace, but it's me she was angry with.'

'No, Naomi, you can't take it personally. We don't know what she was thinking about. It wasn't you who broke the necklace. Assuming there was a necklace, which—'

'It wasn't about the necklace,' Naomi interrupts.

'What do you mean?' asks Kate, fearing that she knows what is coming next.

'You know what I mean,' says Naomi.

'No I don't.'

'I'm always letting her down. That's what she feels.'

'No. She—'

'And she's right. I should visit her more often.'

'I live nearer.'

'I'm not good with her. I can't keep a grip on myself.'

'Well, it's not easy.'

'But I bet you manage it,' says Naomi. 'You're much better than me. You're a nicer person,' she says, looking at her sister.

'No I'm not,' says Kate, concentrating on the road.

'You are,' Naomi states. For half a minute she does not speak, then she says: 'I should go back.'

'Sure. I'll take you whenever you want.'

'I mean now. I should go back now.'

'There's no point, Naomi. We can come back tomorrow,' says Kate, opening the glove compartment to pass a packet of tissues.

Looking away from her sister, Naomi presses a tissue once, firmly, to each eye. She scans the fields and the sky with a dull gaze, like someone who is under arrest; then, after a minute of silence, she asks: 'Get anything done?'

'Not much,' says Kate. 'Some notes.'

Naomi glances at her, detecting an untruth. 'But good notes,' says Naomi. 'I can tell.'

'Something might develop,' Kate admits.

'But you don't want to talk about it,' says Naomi; there is no tone of complaint in the suggestion.

Kate says: 'I'm happy to talk about it. But there's not much to talk about at the moment.'

'I'd be happy with not much,' says Naomi.

So Kate tells Naomi about the widow Dorota and the day she sees her dead husband on the tram, and the scene at the railway station, and other possibilities that she has in mind. During the drive to The Willowes a scene had occurred to her: Julius spying on his wife. Julius might see Dorota looking across a street and suddenly reacting as if she had seen something terrifying, she tells Naomi; he could follow the direction of her gaze into the people who are walking on the opposite side of the street, and be unable to understand who among them might have caused her to react in this way.

'I like it,' says Naomi. 'Good stuff. Go with it.'

'You think so?' says Kate.

'I do. Definitely.'

'Thank you,' says Kate, though she knows that Naomi's interest is feigned; it always is, albeit impressively so. Naomi has read all of her sister's novels, and praised them, but they are the only novels she reads, and she reads them because she is obliged to. Fiction for Naomi is a pedestrian and encumbered art; this has been implied, if not stated in these terms.

'And how much of that did you come up with this morning?' asks Naomi.

'A couple of scenes.'

For ten seconds or more Naomi peruses her sister, as if in the presence of a great enigma.

'Only the outlines,' says Kate. 'There's nothing substantial yet.'

They have reached the junction with the main road into town. Leaning forward, Naomi looks to the right and to the left, as if there's a flotilla of hot-air balloons up there, and she says: 'Day in, day out. Such dedication. Every day, year after year.'

'Not every day.'

'As near as makes no difference,' says Naomi. 'How many did you write before the first one was published? Three?'

'Four.'

'Four. And you still kept going,' she says, as if such perseverance were heroic.

'Good for nothing else,' says Kate.

'No, Katie, that's not true,' says Naomi, to the window.

They are approaching a level crossing, and barriers are coming down. Kate stops the car and turns off the engine; there is no sound of any train and no other cars are waiting; the quietness, for Kate, has the quality of an incipient headache, but she finds that she is disinclined to talk. Her sister is staring at the flashing light on the barrier, but is seeing something else; she emits a sort of hiccup, an aborted laugh, and her mouth forms a rueful quarter-smile. 'What?' asks Kate.

Naomi continues to scrutinise the flashing light, as if there were something not quite right about it. There is some puzzlement in her voice when she says, at last: 'Dad and Mum.'

'What about them?'

Never taking her eyes off the flashing light, Naomi answers in a soft drone of a voice, as if recalling a dream. When their mother fell asleep, she says, she looked around the room, trying to decide what to do, and she picked up one of the photos on the chest of drawers, the picture of Leonor and her husband, taken a year or two before the first daughter was born, and she was shocked, as she is always shocked, she says, to see how bright and pretty her mother used to be. Then she remembered a day when her father had surprised her – 'surprised isn't a strong enough word', says Naomi – by talking about how he had courted his wife. Naomi was in the midst of a crisis at the time; she was on the point of abandoning music. This was not the first impasse, but it was the worst so far: she knew that she had reached the limit of her competence; all pleasure had gone from it. Many times her father had told her that she must not give up; the rewards, in the end, would be immense. 'Never give up – Dad's First Commandment,' says Naomi. He had encouraged her, several times, with the lesson of his own career: he had struggled for years with the complexities of actuarial science, and through sheer application had succeeded, overtaking others of more agile intellect. But now, with Naomi in the depths, the example of his career would not suffice; a different kind of story was needed. So he told her about the time he was in hospital, when he'd been smitten – 'his very word', Naomi remembers – by the lovely Portuguese nurse. She'd made a bout of pneumonia seem like a price worth paying, he told his daughter. A friend had visited him one afternoon and had seen Leonor: she was extremely nice, he agreed – and far too attractive to be bothering herself with a sickly number-cruncher like Richard. This was the consensus – he would not have a chance, friends told him. But he refused to accept that defeat was inevitable. It wasn't that he had too high an opinion of himself: he knew that he was not the best-looking man that Leonor would meet that month; he wasn't even the best-looking patient on the ward. He was prepared to be rebuffed, which he was, several times. In the end, though, he got his woman, he told Naomi. The relevance of this tale to Naomi's situation was not apparent to her, she tells her sister. Perhaps what her father was thinking was not so much that she'd be inspired by this example of his persistence, but rather that she would feel unable to let him down now that he had opened his heart to her in this way: 'I'd been made his confidante, so I would have to repay him with a bit more exertion,' she concludes, as the barriers start to rise.

'Well, it worked,' says Kate, restarting the car.

'I don't know about that,' says Naomi. 'Maybe I just snapped out of it anyway. I can't remember. But the chronology is interesting.'

'Because?' Kate asks.

'Well, he must have been seeing that Wilson woman at the time. Do you suppose he was persistent with her as well?' Naomi wonders airily, scanning the sky.

'I think we know the story of what happened with Janice Wilson,' says Kate. She glances at her sister, who is looking at her as though beguiled by her naivety. 'Nothing to be gained by revisiting that one.'

Naomi sustains the look for a few seconds more. Turning away, she sighs and says: 'You're right.' After a half-minute of silence, she resumes: 'Can't have been easy for her, coming to England on her own.'

'Who? Mum?'

'Maybe she recognised a kindred spirit in Dad. A fellow non-quitter.'

'Maybe.'

'And that's why she prefers you.'

'She doesn't prefer me, Naomi.'

'It's all right,' Naomi tells her, with a smile that seems genuinely tender. 'We don't have to pretend that the love has been spread around equally. It never is. How could it be? She prefers you and has done for a long time, and that's fine. In her situation I'd prefer you too. You're the better daughter.'

'I am not the—'

'But what's difficult – what has been difficult – is that she thinks that I've ended up doing what I do because I didn't make enough of an effort.'

'No, that's—'

'She would never say it, but it's what she thinks.'

'It's not.'

'Well, it's what she used to think. I don't know what she thinks now.'

'She's never thought that.'

'No, Katie, I'm right. If I'd stuck at it, I could have done better, but I don't have the drive or the backbone or whatever you want to call it. Practice makes perfect – that's all there is to it. Practice enough and Wigmore Hall is yours for the taking.'

'That's just—'

'No husband, no children, earning zilch. Failure on all fronts.'

'Your income is neither here nor there, Naomi,' Kate tells her.

'Mum has always had a healthy respect for the earners of the world,' Naomi insists. 'Another of Dad's attractions.'

'He wasn't much of an earner when they met,' Kate points out.

'True, true. But it would have been obvious that he was never going to be a pauper, don't you think?'

'I imagine so. That's not why she married him, though.'

'But it was a plus point, I'd say.'

'As it would have been for most people.'

'Maybe,' Naomi concedes, by way of putting the point aside. Her eyes are directed at the road, but her gaze has no power. She turns to the window beside her, and seems to notice now the faint reflection of her face in the glass; she looks at it, as though it were the face of someone on the other side of a two-way mirror, someone who is of no particular interest to her. Raking her brow with her fingertips, she closes her eyes and says: 'The thing is, she is a strong character.' The adjective is given a peculiar emphasis, as if it bore a private meaning. 'She's like you,' she says. 'Not crushable. Whereas I am. I've always been too fragile for her taste. Too delicate, too sensitive. An aptitude for music was the upside, but not as much of an upside as she'd hoped it would be. Primarily because I didn't put the work in. I allowed myself to be beaten. That's it, in a nutshell. She'd never—'

'No,' Kate interrupts, as softly as possible. 'Mum always—'

'And I can see her point of view. I could never have done what she used to do. Never. The things she must have seen. Every day, surrounded by the stricken. The ailing and the injured. And she just got on with it. She tended to the broken bodies. She helped them to endure. To keep despair at bay. Despair is a sin, and breaking down is a kind of self-indulgence. I know that's what she thought. People manage to live with terrible pain and disability, and there's nothing worse than that, so I should have been able to cope with a dose of unhappiness. Being bonkers – it was like choosing to step out of the real world. Fundamentally, she regarded it as a kind of weakness.'

Statements much like this one, and some even more extreme, have had to be corrected before, often. 'That's not true, Naomi,' she says. 'It simply isn't true.'

'I think it is.'

'She loves you.'

'It's not a question of love,' says Naomi gently, smiling as if there were no element of grievance in what she is saying. 'I know she loves me, in her way, and I love her, in mine. She has been a good mother, despite the fact that I have made life difficult for her. She had a tough time with Dad and all that business, a very tough time, but she came through it. And I made it worse for her, I know that. I know she loves me, but the fact remains: she is disappointed in me. And to tell you the truth,' she says, bowing her head, 'I've been a disappointment to myself. Until recently, that is. I couldn't accept that I had become what I'd become.

Another sin: pride,' she says, with a weak snort of a laugh, staring into the footwell. 'And envy too. I've often been envious,' Naomi tells her sister. This admission has no precedent, but it is uttered less as a confession than as a report, as if envy were a locality that she visited a long time ago.

'Of?' is all Kate says.

'People with talent.'

'But you have talent.'

'Not enough,' says Naomi. 'Sloth as well. I've been slothful,' she goes on, with the same impersonal frankness. 'I've imagined that I might have chosen a different road, and wallowed in regret for having taken the wrong one. I have been a first-class wallower.'

Kate shakes her head, and answers her sister with a sigh and a smile of helpless sympathy. 'You're too hard on yourself,' she says. In two minutes they will be home; there is some relief in the prospect of being able to retreat to her room, and some guilt at that relief.

'No. I'm not,' states Naomi. 'But it doesn't matter. Everything is different now,' she says, and she smiles at the view of the river and the meadows through the trees, as if seeing there the image of her new life.

'You talked to Mum about what you're doing?' Kate asks.

'Sort of. Didn't go into the details. Couldn't see any benefit in telling her I'm going to be at the other end of the country.'

Kate hesitates, then says: 'I've already told her.'

'Oh,' says Naomi; it is to be seen that she is suppressing her displeasure at this news. 'Well, she didn't let on.'

'Probably slipped her mind.'

Naomi turns to look through the trees again, and does not respond.

'Sorry,' says Kate.

'No harm done.'

'So what did she say?'

'About what?'

'You leaving London.'

'Nothing much,' says Naomi, as if the question were trivial. 'Not sure how much of London she remembers,' she says. She is looking closely at the reflected woman in the car window; she might be trying to ascertain the colour of her eyes. Then the tissue goes back up, for a single touch to the left and right.

'I know,' says Kate. 'It's difficult.'

'Yep,' answers Naomi. Not until they reach the house does she say anything more. Kate turns off the engine and opens her door; her sister stays in her seat, seatbelt still fastened, staring into the garage doors with the eyes of someone in the midst of a migraine. 'When she was falling asleep,' she says, 'she said something, but I have absolutely no idea what it was.'

'I often can't make out what she's saying.'

'No, I could make it out. She wasn't mumbling. I just couldn't understand what she was saying. It wasn't English. Portuguese, I assume. A couple of sentences, it sounded like. I don't know if she thought I was someone else, or was talking to herself. Maybe she knew who I was but thought I could understand her. I don't know,' Naomi murmurs. Turning to look at her sister, she asks: 'That ever happened with you?'

'Not that I can recall,' Kate answers.

Naomi describes what she had heard: two sentences, with a slight alteration in her mother's voice in the second sentence, as if it were a line of a poem or a saying. Her smile, after she had spoken, suggested the satisfaction one would get from hearing something well expressed.

'You didn't ask her what she'd said?' asks Kate.

'No,' answers Naomi, distractedly, immersed in the memory of the scene, it seems. 'No, I didn't,' she says, with greater firmness. 'That wouldn't have been a good thing to do. She was happy. Why bring her out of it?'

Kate waits for a few seconds, looking at Naomi, who stares at the garage doors. 'Let's go inside,' says Kate, but her sister does not answer, and she does not move. 'I'm going indoors,' Kate tells her.

Still Naomi does not move. Staring ahead, she says in a whisper: 'It really hit me: the things that are most important to her – perhaps we know nothing about them.'

'I think her family was the most important thing,' says Kate.

'She had a family before we came along,' says Naomi.

'And we met them.'

'We met the parents, yes. But that's all we did. We encountered them. But we couldn't speak to them.'

'Yes, but you can't say we know nothing about them.'

'Next to nothing.'

'No. We—'

'What if her early years, long before us, were the best of her life? That wouldn't be so unusual. Perhaps that's what she's going back to. Perhaps in her mind she's going home, and we don't know where that is.'

'Yes we do. We've been there.'

'We've walked along the streets, as kids, that's all.'

'And she talked to us. She told us stories. Lots of them.'

'True, but the stories were for our entertainment. Maybe stories aren't the essential stuff. And what about Daniela.'

'What about her?'

'She seems to have been important. But we know her name and that's about all. And we'd never heard of her until recently.'

'If she'd been really important, we would have heard of her a long time ago.'

'Is that what you think?' asks Naomi, with a grimace of incredulity.

'Yes,' says Kate, 'it is. Lulu knows about all the people who mattered to me when I was growing up.'

'Not the same situation, Katie. One very big difference: Mum grew up in a foreign language, a language that we don't speak.'

'She speaks ours.'

'Yes, but the situation is different when you have to translate. Explanation can only take you so far. When we stayed with her parents, when she showed us around, there were things we were never going to understand, because we're English. We could see, but we were looking through dirty windows.'

'We were just kids. Even if we'd spoken the language, we wouldn't have understood.'

'We'd have understood more. We'd have been more than tourists.'

'We weren't tourists, Naomi. That's an exaggeration.'

'Not much,' says Naomi. And now, at last, she unbuckles the seatbelt. 'But don't you wish she'd taught us to speak the language, at least a bit?' she asks.

'If we'd shown an interest, she would have done, I'm sure. But we didn't. And why would we have wanted to? What would have been the point? We were in Portugal for a few days, once a year. I don't recall either of us ever regretting that we couldn't understand what Jorge was grumbling about,' says Kate, getting out of the car. She hears a barely audible sound made by her sister, indicative of a modicum of amusement.

'I take your point,' says Naomi. 'Not understanding Jorge was a good thing.' Walking two paces behind, she follows her sister down the path to the front door. 'Odd, though,' she remarks, 'to be half-Portuguese but not Portuguese at all. Don't you think?'

'Can't say I do,' says Kate, putting the key in the lock. 'Born in England, raised in England: I'm English.' She steps into the hall, and without looking she knows, from the quality of the pause, that Naomi is going to start talking about Bernát.

Bernát's situation is very interesting, Naomi tells Kate, pursuing her into the kitchen. His parents had ensured that he did not become estranged from the mother tongue, but he had left Budapest when he was very young and so had heard and used Hungarian only at home, with his parents and his uncle and to a lesser extent with his brother, who hadn't been as keen as Bernát on keeping the link intact. And, though he was pushing forty when he returned to Budapest for the first time, Bernát had always felt a great attachment to the homeland. English, his second language, had become his first, yet he loved the music, the films, the literature of Hungary more than any native Englishman could, more than anything that England had produced. There was no writer he valued as highly as he valued Gyula Krúdy, no book he read with greater pleasure than *Napraforgó*, says Naomi, dropping the pitch of her voice for the exotic syllables. The point she wants to make is that when Bernát returned to Budapest, as a mid-life adult, it was not a case of getting in touch with his roots. (*Of course not*, thinks Kate, busying herself at the coffee machine. *Nothing so banal for Bernát.*) It was a hugely rewarding experience to be back in the city of his birth, the city of his parents and his ancestors, but it was not a homecoming for him. Budapest was as beautiful as he had expected it to be; it was not opaque to him, but there was a sense of distance. For almost a month he stayed there, and at the end of the month he still felt as if he were playing a part, a part for which he had done a vast amount of preparation, he told Naomi. He was in the city but not of it, he joked, reports Naomi. In Hungary he was an imperfect replica of a Hungarian; in England he was an imperfect replica of an Englishman, but a replica that was almost indistinguishable from the real thing. However, having been in Budapest, when he went back to England it was with a sense of being less English than he had been before. Every year he visits Budapest, says Naomi; with each visit he feels that he has moved a yard or two across a bridge that has no visible end.

'Interesting, as you say,' Kate comments. Unable to muster any worthwhile observations on the fable of rootless Bernát, she nods and tightens her brow, to imply that food for thought has been given. With unnecessary carefulness she settles her cup on its saucer.

Naomi peers at her sister's face. 'Interesting, but too much,' she diagnoses. 'You need a break from me,' she says, as if the last word did not refer to her.

'I need to finish what I was doing,' answers Kate. 'Give me a couple of hours and I'm all yours again.'

'Then I'll tell you about Bernát's book,' Naomi promises.

'OK,' says Kate, with a smile and a fleeting kiss to the cheek, but seized by something like foreboding.

21.

At her desk, Kate studies a photograph of the family in Coimbra. They are standing on a flight of chipped stone steps: Kate and Naomi at the top, squinting against the sun; their mother below, bright and pretty indeed, laughing, flanked by her parents. This is the last photograph of Jorge with his daughter and her children. His wife is smiling but he, as usual, is not; he looks like a man with a long-festering grudge. Kate regards the face of Jorge and tries to raise a memory of him. What comes to mind is approximate, and lacks warmth. She recalls a gnarled little man, with eyes like turtle beans, and a habit of mumbling in a manner that suggested that he was commenting, sourly, on what he had just seen or heard. Her mother rarely bothered to translate what Jorge had said. Almost every day, as Kate recalls, Jorge would leave the house at ten o'clock and return at one; he went to a café to talk to old workmates. The family's visit was no reason to adjust his routine. In the evenings he would watch the TV programmes that he always watched, and go to bed at his customary time. For his daughter there was an embrace upon arrival and another on departure, but otherwise almost nothing that an observer would interpret as evidence of love; much the same could be said of his dealings with his wife. When one has been married for so long, Kate's mother explained, one attains an intimacy so profound that mere gestures of fondness become superfluous; at some point this explanation was withdrawn from service. Had her mother, Kate came to wonder, offended Jorge irretrievably by leaving her home country? That was sometimes an interpretation that seemed persuasive. In his dealings with the girls and their father, Jorge was like a long-term resident at a hotel who was passing the time of day with some short-stay guests, as Kate once remarked to Naomi. It was hard to understand why Cíntia had married him, the girls agreed.

Cíntia had outlived her husband by four years, and is a more vivid presence: a nimble and energetic woman, with a scurrying stride and fidgety hands and a face as smooth as oiled wood. She seemed to be astute; she read every page of the newspaper, every morning, quickly, as if she had only a certain amount of time in which to process all this information, though all she had to do with her day was look after the house and her husband. Looking at the photograph, Kate can hear the sound of Cíntia's voice, a gentle patter of syllables in which nothing like an English word was ever caught by the granddaughters. Her doting gaze was turned upon the girls repeatedly, as if to transmit a spell to prevent their departure. She hugged them, stroked their hands, clasped their faces for intense inspection, as though to expend the surplus emotion that had accumulated since the previous visit. The attention came to be too vehement for Kate, however much she sympathised with her grandmother for having to live with joyless Jorge. And the world-view of Cíntia, as expressed in the décor of the house, became more oppressive as the years went on. Wherever you stood, you had Jesus, Mary or a saint in view. Mementoes of Lourdes were ranged on a shelf in the living room. A pope smiled at you from above the kitchen window, and a different pontiff emanated his sanctity at the top of the staircase. Even in the bathroom there was a Crucifix. 'I can't breathe in this place,' Kate complained to her sister. The whole house was gloomy. Its windows were small and the furniture was dark and heavy, like pieces in a museum, though it turned out that much of it had been bought when their mother was a girl. Hideous thick bowls and dishes, made in the factory where Jorge had worked, were displayed on shelves of black wood. Fat cushions of muddy hues adhered to the chairs like fungi.

Jorge did not seem to care greatly for his daughter's husband; but Jorge did not seem to care greatly for anyone other than the former workmates whose company appeared to be a daily requirement. Cíntia, on the other hand, respected her son-in-law: he was a successful and intelligent man; he had made her daughter happy and comfortable; he was the father of two fine young girls. The respect was reciprocated: one should of course respect the mother of one's wife. The conversations between them, mediated by Leonor, were exquisitely courteous; it was like a meeting of ambassadors, Kate came to think, with her father representing a large and powerful country and Cíntia a nation that was considerably smaller. There was deference in the way Cíntia listened to him; she seemed wary at times, perhaps because his mind worked in ways that were unfathomable to her. She found him interesting, even if, Kate thought, she could not love him as she might have loved a less analytical man or a man from her own country. But her father, Kate soon knew, was often bored in Coimbra. She understood that he did not greatly enjoy being there, and that their excursions from the city were as much for his benefit as for the children's, in compensation for the long days with the in-laws.

Driving towards a town that they had not yet explored, with miles of new road ahead of him, liberated from the house of Jorge and Cintía, her father became a different man, she remembers. Kate sees him as she writes: one hand is holding the steering wheel lightly, while the other dangles in the rushing air, or rests on his wife's hand, as it never did when he was driving in England. Gazing along an empty road, he smiled as though the tarmac were a splendid river. The family drove to Tomar and Viseu and to the coast; they drove to Porto, Braga, Barcelos, and on occasion even further. One day they drove to Fátima.

A scene presents itself.

Several dozen pilgrims were scattered across the plaza in front of the basilica. The plaza – grey and smooth and gently curved – put Kate in mind of the deck of an aircraft carrier. In the sunlight the basilica gleamed like lard. Later that day, in her diary, Kate wrote a description of the building. She was fourteen years old; her sister was thus twelve. It was a cool afternoon; it had been raining all morning. Long streaks of water lay on the pavement, and Kate saw, close to a streak that was as wide as a lane, a man whom she took to be a dwarf, walking hand in hand with a much taller woman. The woman wore a large and shapeless brown hat and a brown coat – an ensemble that made her look like a mushroom. Her companion, however, was dressed lightly for the weather; he wore a short-sleeved shirt, Kate recalls.

She took note of the mushroom attire and the short-sleeved shirt before realising that the man was not a dwarf: he was walking on his knees, and the woman – his wife, she assumed – was strolling beside him, her eyes browsing to left and right and up to the sky, as if there were nothing at all peculiar about what they were doing. They appeared to be heading for the column in the centre of the plaza; a golden figure of Jesus stood on top of it. Through the wide track of rainwater the man advanced; he emerged on the other side, leaving a trail of dampness behind him, like a gigantic snail; the woman released him and he toppled forward onto his palms, then spread his hands to bring his forehead into contact with the pavement.

Having told their parents that they wanted to take a look at the statue, Kate and Naomi walked towards the prostrate man and his wife. The sisters passed in front of the two pilgrims, at an unobtrusive distance. The man was weeping, and his mouth moved as if something gummy and disgusting were sticking his jaws together; the knees of his trousers were ripped. He reached for his wife's hand, and they moved on. Another man, Kate now noticed, was traversing the plaza from a different angle, also on his knees, with his eyes fixed on the basilica. Unlike the first, this man was moving quickly, hammering the ground with his kneecaps like a furious amputee; he had the face of someone maddened by thirst in the desert, hurrying towards an oasis in the desperate hope that it was not a mirage.

Their mother had not warned them that they might see such things. Fátima would be interesting, she had said; she had been to Fátima several times when she was young; she told them the story of the three young shepherds and the Miracle of the Sun, but said nothing about people walking on their knees and weeping. Kate found these people terrifying, and could not bear to watch them any more; but Naomi, standing below the golden Jesus, seemed transfixed by these lunatics, as if observing some rare wildlife.

Close to the column stood the chapel that had been built on the spot where the children had seen the Virgin. It was as busy as a weekend supermarket, and thirty or forty visitors – a coachload, all wearing yellow anoraks with a large red flower on the back – were taking photographs of the oak tree outside it. Kate, the designated custodian of the guidebook, read a sentence aloud, loudly enough to be overheard by the anoraks: this tree, she read, with heavily insincere regret, was a replacement for the original oak, which had been stripped bare by relic hunters many years ago. Her father, watching the deluded photographers, received this information with a small wry smile; her mother was walking towards the chapel, hand in hand with Naomi. Kate had another entertaining fact: the Second Secret of Fátima – a prediction of a great war – was not made public until 1941. 'So not much of a prediction,' she suggested, linking arms with her father.

Inside the basilica, he wandered off; this was what generally happened in churches and museums. With his head tilted upwards slightly and hands clasped behind his back, he scrutinised the building as if he were its architect, checking that everything had been carried out as planned. This church did not smell like a church should smell, thought Kate, she remembers. It lacked the fragrance of ritual and mystery, and was too bright and new. It had as little charisma as a sports hall.

She sat with her mother and sister, by one of the high arches. Small paintings were attached to the walls that separated these arches, one to each wall. At the end of a nearby pew, in front of a picture, a woman of her mother's age was praying. She was weeping too, but she was smiling as she cried. After a couple of minutes she stood up and then, as if a stopwatch were running, she hurried to the next painting, where she sat down and resumed her praying, and her crying, and her smiling. Kate wanted to leave; Naomi did not.

'What's that woman doing?' Naomi asked. Her mother explained what might have been going on in the woman's mind, and what might have been going in the minds of the men as they crawled across the plaza on their knees. Why, Kate wondered, did these people think it necessary to come to this specific church to show that they were sorry, if God could see them wherever they were in the world? Her mother endeavoured to make sense of it, as she had previously tried, to as little effect, to make sense of how Jesus could be both God and a man, and how He had washed away our sins by being nailed to a cross, including the sins of all the people who had conducted themselves decently, and all the millions of sins that had not happened yet.

For a few moments Naomi pondered; her face assumed its expression of precocious solemnity. She had a question: 'And what does this make you think?'

'I'm not sure what you mean,' her mother replied.

'This,' said Naomi, indicating everything.

Kate knew what their grandparents thought about this place: miracles had occurred here, and the site was sacred. Waving the family off for the day, her grandmother had smiled as if she thought the girls might return as converts. Something in her mother's face when Cíntia was talking about Fátima, however, had shown Kate that her mother did not regard the story of the miracles in quite the same light.

'The rolling sun and all that stuff,' Naomi clarified. 'What do you think about that? What do you think happened?'

'They saw something very unusual,' said her mother.

'But do you think the Virgin Mary was here?'

'I don't think the children made it up,' her mother answered.

The weeping-smiling woman had become even more agitated now; her hands went up to her face, and the fingers writhed like a nest of small snakes. 'I'm off,' announced Kate, unable to bear the sight of the woman's convulsions any longer. Her mother followed. Nearing the door, they looked back for Naomi. She had stayed in her seat, and was staring at the woman. She frowned with concentration. Then a smile appeared for a moment, and it was not a smile of amusement, as Kate remembers it.

22.

In the last light of the afternoon the sisters take a walk through the town and down to the river. 'We have a lot of ground to cover,' says Naomi, like a lecturer talking to a student in the corridor, on her way to the lecture theatre; she seems to be relishing the prospect.

About six months after Naomi's invitation to Bernát's house, and not long before she and Gabriel decided, as she says, to 'reassess their arrangement', she began to notice a change in Bernát. Gatherings were still held at his house, but sometimes, after the music, he would leave the room and not be seen for an hour. As before, he made a point of contributing to every conversation, but his contributions were becoming briefer. Other than Naomi, it seemed that the guest he found most congenial was Connor. Bernát was often to be found in the farthest niche of the garden, listening to what Connor had to say this week. Connor was a changed man, says Naomi. He had moved into a place of his own, and had not been in a fight for several months. Violence, he had come to understand, is the blight of humanity; it diminishes both the one who suffers it and the one who inflicts it. There had been too much violence in his life, he saw, and sometimes it had been his master. Amy, much taken with the new Connor, would often linger in the doorway, awaiting her opportunity.

One week, at short notice, the gathering was cancelled. Returning from a lesson, Naomi took a call from Bernát. This in itself was a surprise: like all of his guests, she had received messages from him, but never before had he spoken to her on the phone. Lizzie Vidal was very ill, he told her. 'In fact, Lizzie was dying,' says Naomi, dolorously, as if Lizzie has been established as a person whose demise should rouse a particular pity. More than a month passed before Bernát reappeared; in the interim, Lizzie had died, with Bernát at her bedside. It had been a good death, an exemplary death, Bernát told Naomi. Lizzie didn't believe that she was going to a better place, he said; she knew that this was the end of everything, and she was determined to depart in dignity, which she did. Until the penultimate morning, Lizzie was lucid; she was as bright and as fragile as a Christmas tree ball, said Bernát, and in her last hours she had said some remarkable things. But it would not be appropriate to share these things, not yet, he apologised.

It was after a concert that the death of Lizzie was recounted. Bernát had phoned Naomi and asked if she might be interested in going to a performance of Messiaen's quartet; this is when he told her that Lizzie had died, but he was not appealing for sympathy, says Naomi; he simply wanted to see her, he told her; and this also was something new. During the concert, his thoughts were elsewhere, it appeared. His calmness was unusual; he sat perfectly still, with the demeanour of a man hearing a pure silence rather than sounds. That night, Naomi stayed at Bernát's house. They did not sleep together; she has never slept with Bernát, Naomi tells her sister yet again. For hours they talked, and what Bernát talked about most, as Naomi remembers, was friendship. There were to be no more gatherings at the house, Bernát announced. He could no longer pretend that they were not, in large part, a manifestation of vanity. He had set out to obtain a circle of friends, and he had cultivated those friends, he admitted. They were people he liked and found interesting; he admired many of them, some of them immensely. But they had been acquired; the friendships had not arisen of themselves – they had been solicited. He had wished to augment himself, to divert himself, to entertain himself, as they in turn had wished to be entertained. 'To desire friendship is a fault,' Bernát pronounced. It could be said, of course, that the friendship with Naomi had been solicited; he had, after all, approached her. The friendship had developed in circumstances that he had brought about. But with Naomi, he insisted, it was not a recruitment. Rather, it was as if, encountering her again, he had known that it was necessary to speak; as he had said before, it was a recognition that he had experienced when he had first observed her, at the bookshop, a recognition that was confirmed at the concert; the third encounter, he had sensed, was an opportunity that demanded action.

'Love at first sight,' Kate remarks; no unkindness was intended, but she thinks she hears it.

'In a way,' Naomi concedes, almost bashfully. 'But without the element of romance.' Bernát had told her that he loved her; after Lizzie's death he had said this. 'But he did not have designs on me,' she says. When a man tells a woman that he loves her, Naomi tells her sister, it's nearly always to make her serve his pleasure, to put the woman in a place that he wants her to occupy.

Such as a shack in the middle of nowhere, Kate hears.

What Bernát meant by 'love', by contrast, was the 'ultimate form of friendship, if you like,' says Naomi. The word had become debased, said Bernát. Once, in Scotland, he had said something that had really made her think. '"To love someone truly is to consent to distance,"' she quotes, like a disciple.

So many words have become debased, said Bernát. Our minds have become clogged with polluted language. A person is valued according to the number of his 'friends', a label that now can signify people he has never met and never will. It is not sufficient to have an interest in something – one must have a 'passion' for it. Being upset is inadequate – one must be 'devastated' in order to be noticed. We are no longer citizens: we are 'customers' and 'consumers' in all things; even music and literature have become things we consume, Bernát lamented.

He found the city unbearable, he admitted, Naomi reports. To walk through the West End was to battle against a blizzard of inanity. On every street one was bludgeoned by advertising; it was impossible to get through a minute without hearing someone swearing loudly into a phone. Over and over again he heard the same words and phrases: *to be perfectly honest with you ... at the end of the day ... he's taking the piss ... no problem ... absolutely ... fuck off ... unbelievable.* They repeated in his head, uncontrollably: 'No problem, no problem, no problem, no problem, no problem, no problem,' Naomi recites, with glassy eyes and rigid jaw, like a ventriloquist's doll. Bernát's problem was one of which she had some experience, she reminds her sister superfluously.

There was too much noise for Bernát, she goes on, and his own voice had become a portion of that noise. He was tired of himself and tired of talking. Silence was what he needed – true silence, not the mere suppression of noise that could be produced by closing his door. He had bought a place in Scotland, he revealed one evening. Formerly a farmhouse, it was basic but inhabitable, and there was no other house within sight. He had decided to live there for a while; if the experiment proved to be successful, he might sell the London house. Some repairs were necessary, so Connor had gone there to do the work. This would take another month or so, and then Bernát would be leaving London. He showed her photographs of a plain block of a house, standing against an unspectacular hill. Inside, a bare wooden staircase rose to a landing where the walls, whitewashed, had lost large quantities of plaster. Doors opened on each side of the landing. One of the rooms to the left could be hers, should she wish to spend any time there, said Bernát. He had a picture of the room: it was spacious, with a large fireplace, and a narrow iron bedstead, and a large window in which the glass was broken; in the centre of the room was a long dark slot, where the boards had collapsed. The accommodation would not be luxurious, but neither would it be punitive, Bernát told her. He had installed a generator and solar panels, and water came from a spring above the house. Heat would come from the fireplaces and the kitchen range; there were ample supplies of firewood. Furnishing would be minimal, but there would be a library, 'as in any decent monastery'. He envisaged spending most of the day alone, either in his room or out on the hills; should she wish to join him, they would eat together, and talk in the evenings. Perhaps they could play music; he thought he would install a piano.

'An offer no girl could refuse,' Kate has to interject, deleting the words *in her right mind* as they arise.

Such facetiousness is inappropriate, says Naomi's glance. What Kate has to understand, she tells her, is that the offer was accepted not because Bernát's absence would have been hard for her – though she admits that he would have been missed – but because the retreat was what she needed. Had he offered her the use of the house for a month, on her own, she would have said yes, she claims. By the same token, had Bernát invited her to accompany him to New York, she would have stayed at home.

Connor had not travelled to Scotland alone. He had taken Amy with him, but she departed the day after Naomi and Bernát arrived. There was some shouting in the night, mainly from Amy, and at five o'clock in the morning she drove away. 'That girl is weird,' Connor told them, as he packed his bag; he deemed it necessary to follow her; there was no telling what she might do. The implication was that the full extent of Amy's weirdness had become apparent only when she'd been released into the wild. She was the neediest women he had ever met, said Connor; her father, evidently, had been a creep; there were issues, he said.

And the farm had been too spartan for her – at the very least, she had to have curtains on her window. At night the moon was like a spotlight in the room, and she had felt unsafe. There were inexplicable noises, at all hours.

For Naomi it was a joy to awake with the sun every morning. She would get out of bed to watch it rise above a saddle in the hills, and at the end of the day she would watch it fall; these became observances, she tells Kate. It was 'the right kind of routine', a regularity that was not monotony. No two dawns are the same, when you can see them properly, Naomi informs her sister. At first, Naomi admits, she had wondered, intermittently, how she would cope with the empty days ahead. The landscape around the farm offered no obvious excitements: there were no cliffs, ravines, waterfalls or torrents. It was a benign terrain, and it took time to become attuned to it, to see it in itself. When one looks and listens with true attention, every moment is full of sustenance: the slow passage of sunlight across grassland becomes enthralling; the sounds within the silence – a distant whirr of wings, the soft jostling of leaves – have an inexhaustible richness, says Naomi, as if bringing enlightenment to the benighted. At night she sat for hours outside, just looking. Below the farm there was a small loch, which looked like a pavement of perfect granite in the moonlight; the trees were like old silver; it was entrancing.

In the middle of the first week, Bernát told her that he was going to write a book, Naomi tells her sister.

For someone of Bernát's calibre, it is implied, writing a book is simply a matter of making the decision to write it. '*Walden* revisited, I assume,' says Kate.

It was an autobiography, of sorts, Bernát said, and he was going to write it in Hungarian. 'His mother's tongue, but not his mother tongue,' says Naomi.

It is obvious that the phrase has been rehearsed; the wordplay might be an instance of the wit of Bernát. 'Just for the hell of it?' Kate asks.

'To make it true,' answers her sister. Engulfed by the babble of English every day, he had become infected with its banalities and clichés. Hungarian, on the other hand, was a language that he had maintained through study and effort. With Hungarian, he would be in control. He would use the language, instead of the language using him. Distance would ensure exactitude, Naomi explains. He would be working with surgical instruments rather than the battered old tools from the shed.

And Hungarian is the most wonderful language, Naomi tells her sister, as if recommending a city known only to the cognoscenti. It's the most harmonious and flexible of languages, she says, with its endless suffixes and compound words, and its supple syntax. Every evening in Scotland, for an hour or two, Bernát had helped her with the grammar and vocabulary; studying Hungarian is the most rewarding thing she has done since she started to learn music, she says, and the most difficult; she seems to have an aptitude for it, she allows herself to say.

They have stopped at a stile; the sun will soon have gone; the river is very low, between wide banks of putty-coloured silt. Surveying the river, Naomi smiles at the prospect, and murmurs: 'In summer, towards the end of the day, the chestnut trees caught the sun in such a way that the leaves were turned to tangerine, and the grass beneath them was covered in shadows of various blues and greys, like the plumage of a pigeon.' She looks at her sister, as if the lines were quoted from a book that they had shared when they were younger; but the words are Bernát's, translated by herself, with his assistance of course, she reveals.

Kate pictures the master and his acolyte, at work together in the humble homestead: a simple table, a single lamp, fingers sliding over verb tables, touching; outside, the sun is setting beautifully on the heather; the wind makes natural music with the trees.

When she goes back to Scotland she is going to translate what Bernát has written, says Naomi. 'I'll send you a copy when it's done, if you like,' she says; the offer is made ingenuously, in the hope of giving pleasure.

'Of course,' says Kate.

'And don't worry – it's not really a book,' says Naomi.

'Why would I worry?'

'I think you'll like it,' says Naomi, ignoring the question. 'It's heartfelt. And short.' It's short because, having written just a portion of what he had envisaged when he began, and some pages of fragments, Bernát had put his book aside.

Only for a few seconds is Kate permitted to think that Bernát had realised, as do so many aspiring writers, that he did not after all have a book in him. No, Naomi clarifies, Bernát did not fail: he had decided to leave the book behind, as one might leave a path. Writing, for Bernát, had been part of 'a process of restoration', says Naomi. The chief reason for withdrawing to that place was to 'relinquish all artifice', she tells her sister, and by this Bernát had meant not merely the artifices of city life but the artifice of himself. Living in society, we learn ways to behave, ways to speak, ways to think. 'We become encrusted, year by year,' says Naomi. 'Layer builds upon layer, and the thing that is formed is what we come to think we are,' she instructs her sister. We are given masks, she says, and the masks turn into flesh, and then another mask is needed, and so it goes.

With effort, Kate refrains from comment.

Next, inevitably, Naomi tells her that Bernát was determined to strip away the masks. He wanted to cleanse his perception of the world, to rediscover what he called the 'gleam', says Naomi, as if the noun were a word of Bernát's invention.

'But the masks are what caught your attention,' Kate points out.

'Perhaps I could see through them,' Naomi answers quickly; it's like a proselytiser's programmed response to a cynic. Anticipating another objection, she hurries on: 'The simplicity of the retreat, the writing, the hours of walking, it was all to the same end,' she says. Then adds, as if this were a detail of no great consequence: 'As was the fasting.'

'And when you say "fasting", what do you mean? Skipping breakfast, an apple for lunch, or what?'

'Well, something a bit more purposeful than that. Obviously,' says Naomi, directing Kate's attention downward, to her over-reduced body.

'And you decided it was a good idea to follow suit?' says Kate.

'I didn't follow suit,' Naomi bridles. 'But I ate less than I've become accustomed to. Yes.'

'A lot less.'

'Yes. But more than Bernát.'

'Why?'

'Why more than Bernát?'

'No – why do it at all?'

'That's what I've been telling you,' says Naomi, perplexed that her sister should be so obtuse. 'It's a way of focusing. Of rejecting everything that's inessential. We live in a culture of surfeit,' she says.

'Food is not an inessential item.'

'Many people have done the same thing, for centuries. In every culture. Religious people, thinkers.'

Fanatics and the unwell, are the words that Kate hears in her head. To her sister she says: 'I can't see that this has anything to do with religion.'

'I didn't say it did. I'm just saying that it's not an unusual thing to do.'

'Did you think about the consequences?'

'The consequences were why we did it.'

'I mean in the long term. You might have wrecked your health.'

'Let's not be melodramatic, Katie. Actors have lost more weight than I have, in a shorter time, and they've not suffered in the long term.'

'And you know this for a fact?'

Another stile is imminent; the dusk is deepening. 'Shall we turn back?' Naomi proposes, so cheerfully it's as if the preceding minutes have already been forgotten.

They walk for twenty yards without speaking, then Kate says: 'You think it was a worthwhile experiment?'

'That's not the word I would use,' Naomi answers.

'What would you prefer?'

'Exercise.'

'OK. Do you think it was a worthwhile exercise?'

'Very much so.'

'Because—?'

'It made me see more clearly. Not literally,' she says, and she emits a shriek of a laugh, as if at someone she finds ridiculous. 'Things got a bit fuzzy at the end, to tell you the truth. But in the bigger sense, in the way that matters, I saw more clearly. In the sense of understanding. Accepting.'

'Accepting what?'

Naomi encompasses the river and the trees in a grandiloquent sweep of an arm, and says: 'Everything.'

'So you had problems with your eyes.'

'For a day or two. And a hum in the ears. Like a tuning fork. That's when I pulled back.'

'You were in pain?'

'Uncomfortable. But not in pain. Well, briefly. Which is when I reached my limit. I'm not as strong as Bernát.'

'Or you're more sensible.'

'No, not as strong,' Naomi states. Pain, for her, was a barrier through which she could not pass; for Bernát, it wasn't. 'On the contrary,' she says.

The comment is an invitation, which Kate pretends not to hear.

'Now I'm going to tell you something,' says Naomi, undeterred. 'You'll be appalled, I suspect. But I'm not going to keep anything from you. OK?'

'OK,' says Kate, in a faint nausea of dread.

She and Bernát had agreed a sort of 'pact of friendship', says Naomi: they would be 'absolutely honest and open', at all times. To this end, daily, they 'confessed' to each other, she tells her sister.

In the hiatus, the dread becomes heavier; Kate awaits Naomi's confession of what she had confessed to Bernát. It will be something, it seems certain, of which Kate would have preferred to remain unaware.

Naomi tells her that she had told Bernát about the various difficulties – psychological difficulties – that she has experienced over the years. None of it was a great surprise to him, she says, and none of it changed anything. And here Naomi wants there to be no misunderstanding about what she means by 'confession'. The sacramental sense of the word is to be disregarded, she insists. So when Bernát told her what he told her, he was not admitting to anything to which guilt or shame might be attached. In confessing, she says, he was not explaining or justifying; he was describing 'how it is with him'. She, likewise, was describing how it is with her.

Thinking it advisable to wait for the fog to clear, Kate responds minimally. 'I see,' she says, as if in thought.

The subject of pain is one to which she had never given much thought until Bernát talked to her about it, says Naomi. 'But it's an interesting question,' she says. 'What exactly is pain?'

'I think I know what pain is,' Kate answers, as required.

The question seems inane, Naomi agrees. We all know what pain is: it's a sensation that accompanies illness and injury; it is nasty, often intensely so, and any normal person would prefer not to be subjected to it. But pain is an experience, not a thing, says Naomi. It happens in the brain, not in the limb. A simple proof: people lose limbs and yet feel no immediate pain. Connor had witnessed this phenomenon, more than once. Conversely, having been maimed, they will feel pain in a limb that no longer exists. 'Pain is not an entity,' Naomi pronounces. 'Our brains create it, and our brains can use it.' She pauses, to allow this idea to settle. 'Now,' she goes on, coming to the crux, 'everybody accepts that our emotional states are often ambiguous. Horror can be cathartic; love is often not simply love.'

'Wouldn't argue with that,' Kate contributes.

'But the ambiguities of sensation are less acceptable,' she goes on. 'Sensation is regarded as a phenomenon of the flesh, and people become illogical when the flesh is the subject. Sensations are nothing but excitations of the body, and the body must be regulated, because the body is the arena of sin,' she proclaims, lowering the eyebrows to assume the glower of a joy-denying preacher. 'But the distinction is absurd,' Naomi declares. 'Emotion and sensation are indivisible. Both are events of the brain, and the brain is an organ of the body. Our emotions are irregular, volatile, paradoxical, et cetera; so are our senses. Yet our senses are policed and subjected to judgement,' she tells her sister.

'Is this you talking, or Bernát?' asks Kate.

'Both,' says Naomi. Then she repeats, in two or three sentences, what Bernát had told her about the relationship between himself and the woman he referred to as Una.

The bluntness of the disclosure is intended to enhance the impact, it seems; but Kate receives the information as if there were nothing remarkable about it. It had been foreseen, by half a minute. And the absurdity of the woman's name introduces an element of comedy.

Naomi gives her sister a mind-reader's squint and tells her that she can tell what she is picturing: a suburban dungeon; black walls; faux-medieval contraptions of restraint; a middle-aged man, spreadeagled flabbily to receive the attentions of a corseted Miss Whiplash; a tawdry scene.

This supposition is correct. 'I'm listening, not imagining,' Kate answers.

In certain respects, the situation was indeed tawdry, even risible, Bernát had conceded, Naomi concedes. He had made himself ridiculous, he knew. But self-respect was an irrelevance in this situation, because its purpose was to eradicate the self. And the unoriginality of the scenario was significant too. The equipment and techniques were not novel, because novelty would be inappropriate, says Naomi. The costume of the officiant, like a priest's attire, must be conventional, a costume specific to the ceremony: in this instance, a cladding that was both a vestment and an armour. It was more than that, says Naomi, as if what is being discussed is something of a more than private importance: covered in this perfect and artificial skin, the body was transformed into an ideal form.

'If you say so,' says Kate, envisioning the unideal form of her sister, compressed into an ensemble of latex.

Naomi wants to know why, if we revere the ideal bodies created by the sculptors of Greece and Rome, we should disdain someone who transforms her own body in this way. 'Imagination is at work here,' she says. 'You should approve.'

'It's not a question of disapproving,' says Kate.

'It obviously is.'

'No, I don't disapprove,' says Kate. 'Each to his own. It's just sex. And S&M is rather old hat, isn't it? Everyone's at it nowadays. Or pretending to be.'

'There's no such thing as S&M,' Naomi snaps, refusing to lighten the tone. In a relationship of the sort that existed between Bernát and Una, each partner plays a role. It's a contract – a contract of equals. In the majority of 'supposedly healthy relationships', on the other hand, there is an 'imbalance of power', Naomi ordains. Behind the charade of equality, there is always a dominant partner, and that dominant partner is the male, more often than not, she says; she seems to think that the point has some local applicability.

But Kate offers no visible reaction; this episode will pass more quickly if no objections are made to the teachings of Bernát.

Honesty and clarity were what defined the relationship of Bernát and Una, says Naomi. It was play-acting, yes, but serious play-acting. One partner consented to play the part that the other requested her to play, and he, her subject, consented to abnegate himself in the rituals that their contract governed.

'Mutual submission,' says Kate.

'Exactly,' Naomi answers, as if encouraging someone who is finally beginning to comprehend. 'Whereas the sadist, by definition, does not submit to anyone.'

'Therefore sado-masochism cannot exist,' says compliant Kate.

'Exactly,' Naomi repeats. Still, though, she has not finished. One has to think of it in spiritual terms, she says. When the pain commenced, all thought was abolished in the 'overwhelming consciousness of the flesh'. These were Bernát's very words. Everything was reduced, concentrated, to this: the body in pain. Each refreshment of the pain took the body further from itself. A transformation occurred – the pain became an experience that had no body. This seems to be a paradox, Naomi acknowledges, but paradoxes are entirely a creation of language. The flesh was 'etherealised'; the pain became itself alone, with no object and no subject. And then the apotheosis, as 'pain ceases to be pain'. One attained a 'blissful void', Bernát told Naomi, as she tells her sister, as if relating the passion of a saint. But Naomi is dissatisfied. It is impossible, she says, to translate into language the experience of which Bernát was speaking.

'Of course,' says Kate. 'Pain can't be shared. This we know.'

'Yes. But do you understand what I've been talking about?' Naomi demands, with some stridency.

'I think so,' says Kate. 'But I do have a question.'

'Ask anything,' says Naomi.

'Are you trying to tell me that you and Bernát—'

Naomi's laugh is a single loud expulsion of air that makes her head jolt back. 'No, Katie,' she says. 'Can you imagine? Me? My God.' With a downward sweep of each hand, she presents her body for inspection, as if it self-evidently disqualified her for such a role. She explains:

Una was not providing Bernát with a service. What she did for him was an act of love, and the love that Una had for Bernát, and vice versa, was of its own order. Their separation did not create a job vacancy. Bernát was not a 'type', and neither was Una, Naomi asserts, countering what she takes to be her sister's tacit judgement. Neither, of course, should either of them be regarded as being in any way deviant. Deviancy was a lazy concept, a creation of the unimaginative, of 'taxonomists', says Naomi.

Deep into the fast, after the book had been abandoned, she and Bernát had walked together to the loch – or rather, towards the loch, because Bernát was now somewhat weakened. It was a memorable day, says Naomi. He had made himself a walking stick, and as they descended the valley he pointed with it to right and left, naming the plants and trees and birds that they saw. He knew the names of everything, but his tone was one of parody. '*Calluna vulgaris*; *Fraxinus excelsior*; *Buteo buteo*,' Naomi intones, waving a hand from side to side, as though playing the part of a mad monarch, bestowing honours and titles upon vegetable matter and birds. '*Calluna vulgaris*; *Fraxinus excelsior*; *Buteo buteo*; *Calluna vulgaris*; *Fraxinus excelsior*; *Buteo buteo*; *Calluna vulgaris*; *Fraxinus excelsior*; *Buteo buteo*,' she repeats, making her voice a drumbeat of nonsense. 'But we are not essential to the order of nature,' Naomi proclaims, in lieu of Bernát. He was trying, he said, to rinse all names from his mind, to see the things of the world as they are in themselves, instead of projecting himself and his words upon them. It was difficult, he said, to use one's eyes as receptors rather than instruments of order. That was what he was attempting. He quoted a line about learning about a pine tree from a pine tree, and about grass from grass, Naomi reports. It's a pity, said Bernát, that we cannot do without words and simply sing to each other like birds.

Kate's tolerance for the wisdom of Bernát the investor-hermit-botanist-masochist-philosopher has almost expired. *Could this character be any more preposterous?* she manages not to say. Instead, restraining her disdain, she comments: 'Words are arbitrary things, Naomi. This is not an original idea.'

Her sister winces, as if this response had offended her taste buds. 'I never said it was an original idea,' she says. 'Obviously it's not an original idea. If it were original it wouldn't be true.' This too has the ring of a Bernát apophthegm. They are returning by a path parallel to the one they walked out along. In the vicinity of a straggling blackberry bush they move into air that stinks of rotted meat. Stooping at the edge of the bush, Naomi discovers the source – the remnants of a rabbit, eyeless and half-emptied of its innards. She crouches to peer at the carcass, and smiles, as if the thing were a gift.

The crouch and the smile are held for too long; a point is about to be made, Kate sees; the carcass will prove to be in some way pertinent to the teachings of Bernát. She imagines the instruction that will be drawn from the convenient little carcass. Perhaps: 'In the end, Katie, this is all we are.' It would be said in the voice with which Naomi had once informed her, as if she thought her sister was in need of disillusionment: 'In the end, Katie, we're all forgotten.'

But Naomi walks on, and for a full minute says nothing. Staying two paces ahead, she draws deep and sonorous breaths, demonstrably relishing the view. Then she turns, and she starts talking about Bernát again. He took himself to the brink, she tells Kate. He talked about 'peering over the wall'. There was a place near the house but out of sight of it, a small ridge, sheltered by trees, where he would sit for much of the day. This was as far as he could walk by then.

'And what about you?' Kate interrupts. 'You weren't in that state, were you?'

'No, I was not. I'm the sensible one,' she says, amused by her sister's alarm.

What Bernát experienced, Naomi continues, was related to what Lizzie Vidal had seen at the very end of her life, which Bernát now, at last, disclosed to Naomi. She had seen the boundaries between objects dissolving, said Lizzie. Perspective had become as strange as in a dream, she told him: things that she knew were near appeared to be far away and then close and then far away again; everything was in motion, in a perpetual slow flow. There was a vibration in every object, and she could hear the sound of this vibration, a soothing low white sound that had everything in it. It was wonderful, Lizzie told Bernát. And what happened to Bernát, as he sat watching the land and the air, was also wonderful, says Naomi, as tears begin to form in her eyes at the thought of what he had seen. Now, when he looked over the terrain around the house, at the grass and the trees and the heather, what he saw was not a landscape of discrete and solid elements but a 'constellation of energies'. The hills trembled in the light, as if releasing their energy as heat. He saw the horizon quiver and shrink, as it would shrink in the energy of the wind and the rain over thousands of years. The earth, like the clouds, was in motion, and he could sense that motion, says Naomi. His body was a minuscule element in the infinite exchange of energy between the earth and the air – he understood this, and he felt it, she says. He was aware as never before of the air moving into his body and out, taking particles of his body away with it. His nerves seemed to burn in the excitement of the light; he was conscious of the radiation of his skin. Having taken his body to its limit, Bernát was looking at death at close quarters, and he knew it for what it was: a translation, from one form of energy to another. 'That's all death is: a translation,' she repeats, as if making a presentation of the insight of all insights.

And it goes on, this nonsense. Calmly, in a tone of lucidity, she celebrates the mental and physical breakdown of Bernát – or rather, his attainment of grace. There is too much for Kate to remember; it becomes unendurable. *This is lunacy*, she wants to say. Instead, as Naomi is expatiating on vibrations and energies and ecstasy, she stops her with: 'If he'd died, you would have been in trouble.'

This is taken as a remark that might be insulting. 'What do you mean?' Naomi asks; her face undergoes a contortion of incredulity.

'There would have been questions to answer, if he'd died,' says Kate; she finds it impossible to use his name; the name itself is ludicrous.

'He was not going to die,' says Naomi.

'It can happen. When the body gets so weak—'

'He was not going to die,' she repeats. Bernát knew exactly what he was doing, she says; he had given her instructions for bringing him back; he had researched the procedure thoroughly, says Naomi.

'And now he's as right as rain?'

'He's recovering,' she says. 'He went further than me, so it's taking a little longer.'

They have reached the humpback footbridge that spans the river. The way home is to the right, away from the water, but Naomi turns left. 'One last look,' she says, and she strides with determination to the apex, where she stops; holding the handrail with both hands, straight-armed, as if bracing herself at the edge of a precipice, she surveys the river. Kate follows; standing beside Naomi, she can hear her sister's breathing; Naomi's hands are quivering with tension. 'Look at it,' she says in a whisper.

It's a drab scene: a featureless sky; a sluggish river, bordered with mudbanks and grasses; here and there, on the floodplain, a cow; a magpie; a pigeon; some crows, or rooks, in the thinning trees.

After half a minute of silence, Naomi says: 'I'm starving.' Then she laughs loudly; the laugh has no mirth in it.

23.

At the table, in the evening, Naomi barely says a word. The chief topic of conversation is Lulu's catastrophic new English teacher, a man for whom, Lulu complains, reading a book is a process akin to filleting a fish the wrong way round – he takes out the themes, as if extracting the bones, then throws the flesh away. 'He obviously doesn't enjoy teaching, and he doesn't seem to enjoy reading very much either,' she says. Her father makes some observations about the education system which on another evening might have roused Naomi to disagreement; instead, she smiles and shrugs. It appears that the afternoon's monologue has drained her. She clears her plate, however, as if to make a point; she even takes a little more. Then, twenty minutes later, she excuses herself; she goes upstairs to the bathroom, though she could have used the one downstairs; she's absent for a long time.

Restored, she returns to watch a programme that Lulu has recorded, a talent show. Without a word they arrange themselves on the sofa as before: Lulu at one end, Naomi at the other, with Lulu's feet on her lap.

Four teenaged boys are the first act. Starting in a cluster at the back of the stage, when the slow drumbeat starts they begin to move towards the front, separating. The camera turns on the best-looking boy, who slithers towards it, smouldering poutily.

'This is supposed to be sexy, I'm assuming,' Naomi comments.

'You're not the target audience, dear,' answers Lulu.

'Looks like he's checking for spots in the mirror.'

Lulu says nothing.

'Doesn't anyone know how to play a guitar any more?' Naomi asks.

'Wrong kind of gig,' Lulu tells her. 'And please don't comment on the hair, OK? That would be mega-boring.'

The warning is accepted without protest. For fifteen seconds Naomi manages not to intervene, then she says: 'Is there a lab somewhere, growing these boys in test tubes?'

'I believe there is.'

'Why do they all sing like that?'

'Like what?'

'Where are they from? Watford, was it?'

'I didn't hear.'

'I think they said Watford.'

'Well then, Watford it is.'

'So why put on those voices? They're from Hertfordshire. Why pretend to be from Los Angeles?'

'It's what they all do,' says Lulu.

'And that one can't hold a note.'

'Shush,' says Lulu sharply. 'He's cute. And he can dance.'

'He's flat.'

The four boys end their number with a synchronised four-way salute. Screaming erupts from every row. Girls are clawing at their faces in simulated ecstasy.

'Jesus Christ. It's not the bloody Beatles,' Naomi heckles.

'That's the format,' says Lulu.

'These people are not in their right minds.'

'Just doing what they're there to do.'

'But why do it? Are they paid?'

'Shush.'

'Are they?'

'Of course not. It's an honour to be part of the experience. And a thrill.'

'If you say so.'

'Wait till you see the next guy. You'll love him. He's terrible.'

'Bring him on,' says Naomi, and so the double-act patter goes on.

Kate withdraws, intending to read for an hour or so. But on the way to her room an idea occurs to her; on the landing she hesitates, though aware that the decision has already been taken, then silently, cloaked lightly with shame, she goes up to the guest room. Naomi's case lies open on the floor; it seems to have become her laundry basket. On the bedside table a small English–Hungarian dictionary rests on top of a notebook; some of Naomi's bracelets are scattered alongside; under one of the bracelets there's a book, a selection of essays by Simone Weil; underneath the book, Kate finds the phone. As carefully as a detective at a crime scene, having taken note of the precise alignment of bracelet and book, she extracts the phone, and finds that it has not been locked. She holds it in her palm, as if testing her motives by testing the weight of the thing. One consideration prevails: she must have corroboration of what her sister is telling her; and so she finds the number, memorises it, and descends to her room.

'Hello?' Gabriel answers. It is the voice of a man who receives few unscheduled calls. Behind him, a soprano is warbling.

'It's Kate,' she says. 'Kate Staunton.'

'Is everything all right?' he asks, preparing to be told that everything is not.

'Oh yes,' she assures him. 'But I just want to ask you something. Do you have a minute?'

'This is about Naomi, I assume.'

'It is. But if you'd rather not—'

'No. It's fine. Let me just turn this down,' he says, and the music fades away. 'Is she still with you?'

'She is. She's going back tomorrow.'

'And how's it going?'

'It's going OK. No rows. But have you seen her recently?'

'I have. Once. Diplomatic relations have now been broken off.'

'She looks awful, doesn't she?'

'Terrible.'

'And she told you about—'

'The transcendental crash diet? Yes, she told me.'

'It's idiotic.'

'It is.'

'And you know she's going back?' says Kate, in the faintest hope that this part of the story will not tally with what Gabriel knows.

But he answers: 'Yes.'

'And what do you think?'

'Same as you, I imagine, Kate. But what can we do? It's her life. Nothing I say is going to make any difference. I have a clear conflict of interest, you see,' he says, with a tone of downbeat irony that her sister used to find appealing.

Kate asks: 'You met this character?'

'Oh yes,' says Gabriel, over a grim chuckle.

'I don't like the sound of him.'

'Didn't much care for him myself, to tell you the truth,' says Gabriel. '"Bogus" is a word that springs to mind. "Pompous" and "smug" would also be applicable.'

Hearing some bitterness, Kate says: 'I understand if you want to stay off the subject. It's just—'

'Oh no,' says Gabriel. 'I'm happy to talk. It's therapeutic. What can I tell you?' he asks.

His account more or less matches what Kate has been told: the encounter in the bookshop; the sighting at the piano recital, with the elegant older woman; the meeting at the other concert, the 'purgatorial' one, followed by the walk to the Tube station with Bernát, whose pontifications about the music were like a recital from memory of some fantastically pretentious sleeve notes, says Gabriel. He recalls Bernát making a note for him – it was like being handed a presciption by some Harley Street bigwig. There had been an invitation to Bernát's house, he confirms. This had led to an argument with Naomi, who suggested that the reason Gabriel was disinclined to take up the invitation was that some jealousy had been kindled. But that wasn't the case, says Gabriel; he simply didn't much like the idea of being further patronised. And when Naomi reported back on proceedings, he was glad he'd stayed away; Naomi, however, seemed delighted to have been inducted into Bernát's suburban court. So they had argued again. He was so negative, Naomi complained; his 'negativity', as Gabriel pointed out, had not been a problem hitherto. And as Naomi knew, he had never liked parties of any kind.

At this, Kate recalls an arduous dinner party, with almost-mute Gabriel withering at Naomi's side; four strangers had been too much for him. 'She says she's not attracted to him,' she says.

'Clearly she is.'

'But not—'

'No. It's not about sex. I mean, sex isn't happening, and it won't be happening. I'm sure of that,' says Gabriel, with untypical force.

And Kate, quelling the impulse to disclose what she's been told about Bernát's proclivities, has to ask: 'Because?'

'Because Naomi has certain—'

'Insecurities?'

'I'd rather not go into it. I think we can be sure that sex will not be a feature of the rural idyll. Let's leave it at that.'

'You're talking about body image,' Kate proposes.

'One way of putting it. But we should move on.'

'OK,' Kate concedes. 'So, if there's no sexual attraction—'

'God knows. He has a nice house, I believe. And an outstanding CD collection. Perhaps that's what hooked her.'

'Seriously, Gabriel.'

'Seriously? I don't know. He has a hammy sort of presence, I suppose. I imagine he'd like to be described as "imposing". He puts a lot of work into it. You've never seen a beard so well groomed. Not a silky whisker out of place. And the way he talks. The phony precision. Always "I have not", never "I haven't". So I don't understand it, Katie. I really don't. Naomi has fits of enthusiasm, you know that. Some more understandable than others. With Naomi you're never on an even keel. That was what I liked. One of the things.'

'I think he's dangerous,' says Kate. 'For Naomi, I mean. He's dangerous for Naomi.'

'Not a good influence, I agree.'

'She's done damage to herself.'

'It's possible.'

'And what about the nonsense with the drugs? Unbelievably stupid.'

'You've lost me.'

'Bernát's magic mixture. The mind-bending tea.'

'No. I'm not with you.'

'Oh,' says Kate, for a moment uncertain of her memory. 'I thought you knew,' she says. She tells Gabriel about Bernát's adventure in Brazil and his psychotropic drink.

'So many strings to that man's bow,' Gabriel sighs.

'But someone like Naomi, especially, shouldn't be messing with things like that.'

'I completely agree,' he says.

'She says it was a one-off, but who knows?'

'If that's what she told you, I'd be inclined to believe her.'

'It's not really a question of believing her. It's what might happen when she's up there, with that person. Given what's already happened.'

'We don't know,' says Gabriel. 'But she's made her mind up. Nothing we can do.'

'I need to address this thing head-on,' says Kate. 'I have to be straight with her.'

'I was assuming you'd already done that.'

'I didn't get the full story till this afternoon. And you know what it's like with Naomi. Tiptoe tiptoe.'

'Indeed,' says Gabriel. 'Well, good luck.'

'Thank you. And thank you for talking to me.'

'My pleasure,' he says. Then, as if a brighter conclusion were needed: 'How's Martin?'

'He's fine.'

'And Lulu?'

'Doing well. And what about you? You're seeing someone, Naomi says.'

'For the time being,' he answers.

'Oh.'

'She's nice. But, you know—' he begins; he does not go on.

'OK,' says Kate; she has some affection for Gabriel.

'Anyway, nice talking to you,' he says.

'And you.'

'Take care, Katie,' he says, in his tone of resignation; it is like his favourite, most comfortable coat.

'And you,' she says.

Downstairs, Naomi and Lulu are watching a film, a high-cost thriller. Men in T-shirts are crashing through windows and walking away unbloodied. It's impossible to believe that Naomi is enjoying it, but she says that she and Lulu are having a laugh; the film has an hour to run, and they are staying to the end, says Naomi, as if she has intuited that her sister needs to talk to her, now. Another fight begins; each fighter takes half a dozen punches to the face, without bleeding; Kate goes to bed.

It is past eleven o'clock when Martin finishes what he has to do. Kate wakes up as he is undressing. 'I have to tell you the latest,' she says, and she gives him a summary of what Naomi had told her during their walk. And she has done some research: severe fasting, she has found, produces significant increases in depression and emotional distress, to say nothing of the damage to the body. 'So what do we do?' she asks, slipping into the cradle of his arm.

Martin's reading of the situation is much the same as Gabriel's: there is no evidence that Naomi's mind is unsound, and nothing that anyone says to her is likely to change her mind, other than to increase her determination to do what she has decided to do. They must try to stay in contact with her, he says, and hope that this infatuation, or whatever it is, will blow over. He recalls a troubling boyfriend of Naomi's from many years ago, Radomír, the 'staring Czech'; somewhere in the house there's a CD of Radomír's 'music', a single seventy-minute track that sounds like two tortoises ambling up and down the keyboard.

'God, he was awful,' Kate remembers, hearing Naomi on the stairs; it's too late to talk to her tonight.

'Wonder if he was into S&M too,' Martin murmurs. 'Wouldn't have been a big surprise, would it?'

'I see him more as a flogger than a floggee,' she says.

Martin's laugh is quiet and drowsy. 'Mind you,' he says, 'I can just picture you in a rubber catsuit.' She pulls back a little to look at him; he nips the tip of his tongue and curls an eyebrow. Nudging a strap aside, he kisses her shoulder.

'I'd look like a seal,' she says.

Closing his eyes, Martin whispers: 'Seals are sexy beasts.' A finger travels down her throat and crosses a breast.

'Tomorrow,' she says; but if Naomi were not upstairs, perhaps within hearing range, sex would be happening now.

Soon Martin is asleep. Kate is not. Memories and imaginings, none of them coherent, bloom and vanish in her mind; the figures of Naomi and their mother appear and reappear in places that have no substance; then she is in Córdoba.

24.

In the Museo Municipal Taurino, Kate recalls, she and her sister had stood before a squad of mannequin bullfighters. Each mannequin was kitted out in full regalia, with encrustations of sequins and beads on silk and satin of the gaudiest colours – cyclamen, cerise, gold and apricot side by side. The outfits were like something a Las Vegas showgirl might wear, their father remarked. Photos showed bullfighters in triumph, preening in front of slaughtered animals, as if making statues of themselves, to be worshipped. These men were fatuous, the girls agreed. 'The Portuguese are sad, but the Spanish are mad,' said their mother, not for the first time. Spain, she maintained, was a nation of hysterics. Fado is melancholic and philosophical, she said, but flamenco is childish melodrama. Religion in Spain is nothing but morbid saints and flagellation. Bullfighting provided another proof of the Spanish sickness. In Portugal the animal is fought by men who have no weapons – 'it is braver', she maintained, 'and not cruel'. In Spain the bull must always die and it must die for the audience: it must suffer and bleed, and the crowd has to see its suffering. In Portugal, a bull may fight and afterwards be freed to pasture, to breed; in Spain, the animal will always die, to amuse the people. 'Torture is the whole point,' she said, raising her voice for the benefit of the museum's other visitors.

In one photograph – Kate can picture it now – a bull with horns as thick as a man's forearm was arrested in mid-leap; the tip of one horn was no more than an inch from the matador's face. Had the matador not arched his back at precisely that moment his jaw would have been destroyed, yet he gave the appearance of examining the horn with relaxed curiosity, like a botanist on holiday, inspecting a branch of unusual blossom. Naomi was entranced; she examined the photograph minutely, as though it showed a momentous event in history. Another picture was given similar attention: a massive animal leaned into the matador as it veered to attack the cape; the matador was Manolete, the caption informed them. He was as slender as a twelve-year-old. It was hard to understand how so slight a man could have stayed on his feet when buffeted by this monster; harder still to fathom how he could have maintained this nonchalance – he seemed to be inspecting the crowd, as if idly wondering whether a certain acquaintance might be present that afternoon. With Naomi, the effect was the intended one: she admired the courage that was so histrionically on display. She directed her sister's attention to the obituaries on the walls. One misstep and a horn removes your guts, and you die like the great Joselito; one unexpected movement and a horn goes through an artery, and you bleed to death as Manolete did. She uttered the names as if she had long revered them; an hour earlier she had never heard of Joselito or Manolete.

These people are absurd, Kate told her sister. Naomi did not disagree, but said that there was also something superb in their courage. She envied their self-certainty, she confessed. Later, perhaps months later, she said that the face of Manolete, as he studied the bull that was about to charge at him, was like the face of the saints they had seen in so many paintings in Spain, the saints who held a skull into the light of a candle and gazed into the empty pits of the eye sockets. 'Look at this imbecile,' urged their mother, at a photograph in which a blood-smeared matador, holding aloft a severed ear, submitted himself to the torrential applause of the crowd. His grin, she thought, was that of a half-witted bully. 'All that, just to get people to like you,' she said. Naomi said nothing, because, as she told her sister, she knew that her mother was wrong – the adulation of the spectators was not the only reason; it was not even the main one. At the heart of the performance, she could believe, there was a moment in which the man became a solitary in the midst of a multitude. The fight became a spiritual exercise, she said. That is what she had said, Kate is sure. Naomi tried to imagine what Manolete would have been thinking as he faced the bull, the embodiment of death. *El momento de la verdad*

– the phrase, for Naomi, was more than bombast. Kate remembers her sister in the museum, standing beside the effigy of Manolete; above him, displayed like the relic of a martyr, hung the hide of the bull that had killed him; and Naomi stood there with her head bowed, as if in reverence. She was fifteen years old; before the end of the year, their father would be dead.

And a few days afterwards, in Toledo, Kate recalls, came the encounter with another saintly effigy, the miniature St Francis. Their father, always prepared, had a marked-up map of the city, with numbers signifying each of the things that had to be seen. He led them in procession to the cathedral, through debilitating heat. The streets were monochrome in the brutal light, but inside the cathedral there was succulent colour, in stained glass that glowed turquoise and gold and scarlet in the heights of the building. All were duly amazed by the immensity of the church, by the mighty larchwood altarpiece, by the famous *Transparente*, with its tumult of alabaster sculptures. In the Treasury they were amazed again, by the gilded monstrance of Juan del Arfe. 'It weighs five hundred pounds, and for the feast of Corpus Christi they carry it through the streets,' their father informed them, reading from his book. Nearby, in a glass cabinet, stood the idol of St Francis. Lips parted, pallid, he stared into the heavens. Kate assumed that the shock of his ecstasy was what had drained the blood from the holy face. It turned out that the deathly pallor was in fact the pallor of death: what the figure represented was the saint as he had appeared, uncorrupted, when his tomb was opened in the presence of Pope Nicholas V, in Assisi, in 1449, more than two centuries after Francis's death.

Kate had been bored by the El Greco paintings to which they had been compelled to pay homage within hours of arriving in Toledo – all those grey-faced starvelings, those wisps of the holy spirit, as indistinguishable as candles. The tiny St Francis, on the other hand, made her laugh. He was made of wood, mostly, but the dainty rope that hung down the front of the wooden cloak was made of hemp, and the eyes were painted glass; real hair had been used for the eyelashes; the teeth – irregular, with a gap both top and bottom – were tiny lozenges of ivory. The literal-mindedness of it was pitiful; it was the apotheosis of kitsch. She thought up phrases, and wrote them down: *apotheosis of kitsch*; *devotional dolly*; *hallowed homunculus*; *a perfectly preserved specimen of micro-saint*. She made a remark to Naomi, but was ignored. Naomi had put her face to the glass, and was staring at the little figure. The upturned eyes of St Francis were directed at something that no one else could have seen, like the eyes of a sleepwalker; Naomi put her own eyes into his line of sight, and kept them there, unblinking, as if to receive the transmission of its visionary gaze.

She was not the same person as she had been in Fátima, said Naomi afterwards, in response to teasing. In Fátima she had been intrigued by what those pilgrims appeared to be experiencing, and had wondered, despite her common sense, if what they believed might be true. The story of the Resurrection and everything else had seemed improbable, but could anything be more improbable than the idea that the universe had arisen out of nothing? For the girl at Fátima it had not been possible to dismiss everything that she had seen there as a manifestation of delusion. At Toledo, on the other hand, she had no doubts. In the interim there had been many conversations with her mother, about the stories in the Bible and the lives of the saints, and she had arrived at a certainty that could not be admitted to her mother, but was admitted to her sister: it was a fiction, but a fiction of marvellous complexity. There was no risk of conversion, she assured Kate. She could not say exactly why she had been so taken by the figurine of St Francis, but it had nothing to do with God, she insisted.

That night in Toledo, as Kate remembers, she and Naomi were allowed to roam the streets together, leaving their parents at the hotel. They came to a courtyard where the buildings were all unlit. The sky above the court-yard was like a roof of black granite, speckled with mica. Scrutinising a portion of the sky through the loop of a thumb and forefinger, Kate began to count the stars. She counted twenty, then counted again and saw forty. Like microbes of light they continued to proliferate; there was no end to the number of them. A scent of vanilla was in the air; somewhere high up, two loud televisions were tuned to different channels. Kate began to look for constel-lations; with a finger she traced a figure onto the blackness. She named it, for the instruction of her sister. Naomi said nothing. She was staring into the sky, and her mouth was open slightly, as if in mimicry of the expression of the little St Francis. 'You look like the village idiot,' Kate muttered, tapping the underside of her sister's chin; and Naomi laughed.

Unable to sleep, Kate lies beside her sleeping husband. She gazes into the ceiling, and imagines the night sky beyond it; it is like lying under the lid of an enormous tomb. Turning onto her side, she shelters against Martin. Sleep is still not possible. She flees to her room. With no purpose, she skims some of the notes that she has made. She can picture Afonso in the bar; she imagines a man who is Oszkár, sitting with a man who looks like Brahms, and an American in a linen jacket. While adding detail to the figure of Oszkár, she has a thought, and turns on the computer.

V

25.

From the stairs, Kate hears Lulu talking in the kitchen. An inaudible remark from Lulu elicits from Naomi a laugh which is loud and full-throated, and does not sound like Naomi's laugh. At the door, Kate stops to listen. Lulu is talking about her friend Taryn; evidently Taryn has dumped her boyfriend, Scott, after some misbehaviour at a party; Scott claims there were mitigating circumstances: he was pissed, but not as pissed as Belinda Sargent, who threw herself on him, according to Scott. 'And if Belinda Sargent throws herself at you,' says Lulu, 'you're really in trouble, she's a very big girl. A huge great pair of mitigating circumstances.' Again her aunt laughs, a little less loudly; it seems as though sustained hilarity has sapped her strength. 'And the other thing about Belinda Sargent—' Lulu resumes, as her mother comes in.

'Good morning,' Naomi sings, extending a hand to the side, for her sister to take. At the same time she looks at Lulu and nods her head slightly; this appears to be some sort of cue.

Turning to her mother, Lulu makes sounds that may or may not be words.

'I haven't the foggiest notion what you've just said,' Kate responds, as seems to have been the intention.

In the same voice as before, Lulu repeats: '*Jó reggelt, anya.*'

'"Good morning, mother,"' Naomi translates.

'*Lulu vagyok,*' says Lulu.

'"My name is Lulu."'

'*Nem—*' Lulu begins, but she has to look to her aunt for a prompt.

'*Tudok.*'

'*Nem tudok jól magyarul.*'

'"I cannot speak Hungarian well,"' Naomi explains. She leans back in her chair and, looking at Kate, directs an open hand towards Lulu, as if presenting a pupil for praise. 'Picked that up in a few seconds,' she says. 'Perfect pronunciation. Much quicker on the uptake than me.'

'One smart bitch,' says Lulu, glancing at the clock, as her mother sits down. 'Got to go,' she says, though it's some way short of the time at which she usually leaves. She goes to the fridge and takes a slug of apple juice from the carton.

In different circumstances, Kate would tell her to use a glass.

'Your daughter has been entertaining me,' says Naomi.

'Gossip,' says Lulu, after a second gulp. 'Friends and acquaintances,' she adds, to reassure her mother that the gossip had nothing to do with life at home.

'She knows how to tell a story,' Naomi tells Kate. 'Must get it from you.'

Lulu comes over to her mother and gives her a kiss on the brow. 'I go,' she says. She steps back and holds out her arms in a half-formed gesture of embrace, directed at her aunt. 'Well—' she says.

'OK,' says Naomi, standing. 'I'll come to the door.' She follows Lulu into the hall, where some quiet words are exhanged. Kate hears the front door open, then her sister calling up the path: 'Be impactful! Leverage those talents!' Finally, at higher volume: 'Remember: you don't have problems – you have challenges!' When she comes back into the kitchen, the smile suggests that she has just said goodbye to an incorrigible friend. She returns to the table, still smiling; she sits down, and says nothing.

'That appeared to be a parting,' Kate remarks.

'I have delighted you enough,' answers Naomi. She looks towards the door and says: 'You must be very proud of her.'

'You're going back to London?'

'I am,' says Naomi. 'I did tell you, Katie,' she says; the tone is apologetic, though it's clear that she thinks no apology is due.

'You said you'd be leaving soon, yes.'

'You need to have your house back,' Naomi tells her.

'What time train are you going for?'

'Don't know exactly. Mid-morning.'

'How about coming with me to see Mum?'

Naomi directs her gaze towards the garden. 'I don't think that's a great idea,' she says.

'You wanted to go back,' her sister reminds her.

'It would end in tears, one way or another. I'm not good for her.'

All visitors are good for her, Kate almost says, but she has no strong inclination to argue. 'If that's what you think,' she says.

Naomi continues to study the garden, perhaps reconsidering. 'What time are you going to see her?' she asks.

'Probably half nine or thereabouts. I need to do a couple of things first.'

For another half-minute Naomi's gaze moves back and forth, from bush to bush; at some point it becomes apparent that the thoughtfulness is for the sake of appearance. 'I'll come down again soon,' she says.

'Before you go to Scotland?'

'Yes. I promise,' she says, with a glance like an oath.

'Why don't you stay for lunch?' Kate suggests; her voice, almost wheedling, displeases her.

'You've been very kind to me, Katie,' says Naomi, 'but I don't want to outstay my welcome.' It is clear that Naomi has said everything she wants to say, and probable that she suspects that her sister has not.

'You won't be outstaying your welcome,' says Kate. 'That's not possible.'

The hyperbole is misjudged, says Naomi's smile. 'I'll leave when you leave,' she tells her sister. 'You have to get on with your work.'

It turns out that Naomi has not eaten anything yet. Kate assembles a breakfast for her: a sliced apple, honey, a glass of juice, a single slice of toast, unbuttered. For herself she makes a cup of coffee and reloads the toaster, while Naomi tells her how much she has enjoyed the last few days; Lulu is a delight, she says, and Martin is brilliant. 'It's done me good,' she says. Looking at her sister, Kate can believe that this is true: if nothing else, the appearance of exhaustion has gone.

The sisters sit on opposite sides of the table, and they talk easily, as if nothing of note had happened to either of them in the preceding months, and no significant change were imminent. It would be best, Kate almost decides, to leave certain things unsaid. But then Naomi turns aside, distracted by a squirrel on the garden terrace, and Kate looks at the skin of sister's cheek – it's like the surface of cold coffee. Watching the animal, Naomi bites into another slice of apple; a smear of blood is left on her front teeth.

'You're bleeding,' says Kate, tapping one of her own incisors to direct Naomi to the smear.

Naomi scowls, and wipes a finger briskly across her teeth. Having glanced at the stain on her skin, she rubs it out with a thumb.

'That's not a good sign,' says Kate.

'Getting better,' Naomi answers.

'I think it needs to be looked at.'

'It's nothing.'

'You should see a dentist,' Kate tells her.

'If it hasn't cleared up in a few weeks, I will.'

'You should do it now. In London. Is there a dentist anywhere near where you're going? I'm guessing there isn't.'

'I'll find a vet,' jokes Naomi.

'I'm being serious,' says Kate. 'That's not good, Naomi. Something's wrong there. And it'll get worse if you don't have it treated soon.'

'It's trivial,' Naomi tells her. 'Really. It'll clear up.'

'Says—?'

'Enough, all right? Let it go,' says Naomi. 'If my teeth start to wobble, I'll seek professional advice and submit to the recommended treatment. But believe me, it's getting better.' She takes a demure little bite from her piece of toast.

'And what are you going to be eating up there?' Kate asks. 'You can't live on honey and potatoes.'

'God, Katie, you're carrying on as if I'm emigrating to Siberia. We'll be in a temperate zone, same as here. Civilisation will be just a short drive away.

'OK. I'm only—'

'If we need to, we'll drive to a shop and buy stuff. We have a freezer. Don't concern yourself with our diet – we'll be eating more healthily than ninety percent of the UK population. That statistic is entirely arbitrary, but you get my point.'

'You're not eating enough, though.'

'I'm not eating much at the moment, I grant you. But I'm eating what I need to eat and what I can safely eat. You want me to be careful and that's what I'm doing. Taking it step by step. Being sensible. You should approve.'

'But have you had a check-up?'

'Why would I need a check-up?'

'Because you've put a huge amount of stress on your body. You might have done some serious damage to your heart. I've done some research. If your body—'

'I bet you have,' says Naomi, as if research were a peculiar and amusing compulsion. 'I have not damaged my heart. Feel,' she says, offering a wrist, with two fingers pressed to her pulse point.

'What sort of condition is Bernát in?'

'What do you mean?'

'Well, clearly he went too far. There could be all sorts—'

'He knows what he's doing,' says Naomi.

'So he's a medical expert too?'

Looking at her sister, Naomi blinks four or five times, quickly, as if this last remark were inexplicably aggressive.

With a sensation akin to that of moving out from the shelter of the harbour wall, Kate says: 'There is something I have to ask you.'

'About Bernát, I'm guessing,' says Naomi.

'His brother is called Oszkár, yes?'

'That's right.'

'And he's a marine biologist.'

'He is.'

'Expert on catfish.'

'Yes.'

'A world authority, in fact.'

'So I believe.'

'To be an authority one must have published several articles on the subject, I would assume.'

'Possibly. I don't know.'

'If you're an academic nowadays you're obliged to publish, at regular intervals. That's how the system works. You publish; the university gets the credit; you keep your job.'

'You may well be right.'

'I think I am,' says Kate, feeling the swell of the open water. 'So doesn't it strike you as rather odd, then, that you can spend hours searching the internet and find no trace of a marine biologist called Oszkár Kalmár?'

'You've spent hours searching for Bernát's brother?'

'Maybe not hours. But a thorough search, yes.'

'Why?' asks Naomi, as if Kate had confessed to something idiotic but inconsequential, like having her car resprayed with polka dots.

'I wanted to see what he looked like,' Kate answers. Naomi raises an eyebrow. 'That's not so strange, wanting to put a face to the story,' Kate tells her.

'So I assume you looked for Bernát too,' says Naomi.

'Of course.'

'Find anything?' Naomi asks. She might be an insouciant suspect, asking questions of the policewoman who has just ransacked her house.

'No, but I didn't expect to.'

'Because?'

'Given his line of work. But Oszkár – that's different, isn't it? You'd expect some sort of public profile. So why couldn't I find him?'

'Perhaps you were spelling his name wrong.'

'How do you spell it?'

'O-s-z-k-a-accent-r K-a-l-m-a-accent-r.'

'Tried that. He seems to be non-existent.'

'No – you couldn't find him on the internet. That's not the same thing.'

'There can't be many eminent scientists who have absolutely no presence online,' says Kate. 'Not a single mention. Doesn't that seem strange to you?'

Naomi rubs her face, as if it were middle of the night and the conversation were in its third hour. 'What's your point, Katie?' she asks.

'Can I be blunt?'

'I think you're going to be, whatever I say.'

'My point is, I'm concerned.'

'About what? Oszkár's low internet profile?'

'About shutting yourself off with this man.'

'Why? You think he might be dangerous?' says Naomi, clasping a hand on her mouth and doing horror-struck eyes.

'Well, what he did to himself was dangerous, wasn't it?'

'You want to interview him?'

'I'd like to meet him, certainly.'

'To put him through the vetting procedure?'

'To talk to him.'

'About his intentions towards the little sister?'

'No. To—'

'It's not going to happen.'

'Why not? I met Gabriel.'

'I thought you'd find Gabriel acceptable. You wouldn't like Bernát.'

'I don't know why you say that.'

'Because I know you wouldn't. You'd hate him. You'd find him pretentious.'

'And he might find me boring and bourgeois. But I'd still like to meet him. I met Gabriel, and he—'

'Katie, it's not going to happen,' Naomi states, with a percussive glance.

'Fine,' says Kate, hands raised an inch from the tabletop, in an incipient gesture of surrender. She stirs her coffee, though there is no reason to.

'There is nothing to worry about,' says Naomi. One might think that Kate rather than herself was the vulnerable one.

Kate gazes into the dregs. Perhaps from this position, she thinks, it would be possible to retreat. But she finds herself saying, quietly, as if in closing: 'But what do you know about him?'

'I don't understand you.'

'Seems a straightforward question to me.'

'I know a great deal about him. That's what I've been talking about for the past three days.'

'But I mean: what do you actually know about him? Not: what has he told you? What do you really know?'

'What do you know about me?' Naomi counters.

'Be serious, Naomi. This is important.'

'I am being serious. I've spent a lot of time with him. I know him very well. As well as anyone can know anyone else.'

'Well, that's—'

'But of course you know that I'm deluded. You—'

'I'm not saying that.'

'Yes you are.'

'I'm not. But I have my doubts, I have to say. The person you've described – he makes me uneasy.'

'Then that's my fault.'

'I don't think it is. The story of the brother – well, to be honest with you, I don't think he has a brother. Or not a brother of that name. I think it's a story.'

'Everyone tells stories,' replies Naomi in an instant; it might, thinks her sister, be a phrase from some vapid song.

'An invented story, I mean.'

'Everybody exaggerates. Everybody lies. Particularly people who know too much.'

'I have no idea what that is supposed to mean.'

'OK,' says Naomi, with an indifferent shrug.

'Please, don't be glib.'

'My apologies. I didn't think I was being glib. We can't all live up to your standard.'

'Naomi, please.'

'Please what?' says Naomi, presenting a sullen and ingenuous face.

'Are you saying that I might be right?'

'Right about what?'

'The brother.'

'No. I'm saying I don't care what you think,' says Naomi; she speaks with no apparent anger, but her lips are whitening.

'Naomi—'

'You think I'm a gullible idiot. That's what you're saying.'

'Of course not. I just—'

'Yes you do. You think I've been taken in by some sort of charlatan.'

'I don't know him. I've never met him.'

'But you have an opinion. You've arrived at a verdict.'

'No. I have my doubts. Some of the things you've told me, I—'

'You've not understood,' Naomi suggests, as if helping.

'Perhaps. But the person you've been telling me about – to me, sometimes, he sounds ...'. Leaving the sentence unfinished, she makes a hesitating grimace.

'Say it,' says Naomi. She flicks the empty coffee cup with a fingernail, five or six times, to provoke her with its tuneless ringing. 'Come on. Words are your thing. Don't beat around the bush. Finish the sentence – "he sounds ...". Go on.'

Kate confronts her sister's gaze, and sees contempt. 'Some of it strikes me as bogus,' she says, with a cringe of apology.

Closing her eyes, Naomi begins to rub her temples with paired fingertips, mechanically, as if turning small wheels. For a full ten seconds she does this, then she looks at Kate. She looks into her eyes as if peering through small apertures into a room in which something very small has been hidden. 'You've been talking to Gabriel, haven't you?' she says, smiling at the foolishness of the conspirators. 'How did you get his number?'

'He rang me.'

'No he didn't,' Naomi tells her. 'Why would he have done that?'

'It was some time ago. When you were together.'

'And how would he have known your number?'

'I gave it to him, when he was here.'

Naomi scrutinises her sister's face, assessing the plausibility of the explanation, then sits back, suddenly deciding that it's not worth the thought. 'Well, I'm sure you and Gabriel had a productive meeting of minds,' she says.

'He still cares about you.'

'So he says.'

'We all do.'

'But you're not happy that I'm happy,' says Naomi, not in protest, but as if simply drawing attention to a paradox.

'I do want you to be happy. Of course I do. But I'm not sure—'

'I understand: you think you know best,' Naomi interrupts. 'You think I need to be saved from myself, and from this charlatan. But I don't need to be saved. I know what

I'm doing. I know Bernát, and you don't,' she goes on, in a passionless near-monotone. 'There is nothing bogus about him. He is a mathematician, and there is no such thing as a bogus mathematician. But that's only part of who he is. You haven't heard him talk. You have to hear him to know how he thinks, to appreciate his mind. He's an original. His brain doesn't work like yours or mine. But it's not just a question of how he talks. Forget about the stories. What's most important is what he does. That's the main thing, for everybody, isn't it? Martin always says so. Your character and what you do are not separate things. You're not acting out of character when you get drunk and hit your girlfriend. That's what you are: you are a man who gets drunk and hits his girlfriend. You are what you do,' she says, seeming to believe that a point has been unanswerably made.

'I'm not following,' says Kate.

'It's a simple point,' says her sister. 'He gives money away. That's what he does. It's not a pose. And it does some good. Money is what gets things done in this world,' says Naomi, as if she thinks her sister would be inclined to disagree. 'And what happened in Scotland – that wasn't for my benefit. It wasn't a performance.'

'I never said it was.'

'It was very, very real, and true. And brave. Extremely brave. I couldn't have done what he did,' says Naomi.

'Thank God,' Kate cannot prevent herself from muttering.

Naomi pauses to consider her sister; there is some disappointment in her eyes. 'It's hard for you to understand,' she says, with sudden sympathy. Then she proceeds to tell Kate that Bernát is a deeply spiritual man. In three sentences she uses the adjective four times. It is to be inferred that the spiritual is for Kate an alien domain. Hearing Bernát play the piano, Kate would think that Bernát was unaccomplished, Naomi tells her. Kate would hear the mistakes and think that he was pretending to be able to play. But the wrong notes don't matter – the spirit of the music is what matters, and Bernát always understands the spirit. Kate needs everything to be in order, her sister tells her, as if commenting on something as neutral as her height. Kate is like Martin in this respect, says Naomi. They are both supremely reasonable. But Bernát knows that the rational can only take us so far. He cannot be put into a category, and that's why Kate is uneasy about him. 'You want explanations, but all I can give you is descriptions,' says Naomi. Her voice has a terrible calmness; anyone overhearing her from outside the room would think that point was following point in a way that was logical. She no longer seems to be trying to convince her sister of anything: it's more like a recitation of points that she has committed to memory and now needs to discharge, omitting nothing. Kate's problem, Naomi tells her, is that she thinks that living in isolation is irresponsible.

And here, at a slight hesitation, Kate can interrupt. 'No,' she says. 'But society is what makes us what we are. We are social animals. We need other people.'

'I don't,' says Naomi, with a rueful half-smile, suggesting that she wishes this were not the case.

The ruefulness is entirely for Kate's sake, Kate knows. 'You won't be alone in Scotland,' she points out.

'For most of the day I will be,' Naomi answers. 'We'll each have a cell,' she says, putting some humour into the phrase, by way of appeasement. Kate slides a hand towards her sister; it is taken, lightly, as if it were a globe of thin glass, and quickly released. 'I will be happy,' she says, and it sounds like a declaration of modest intent.

26.

Kate's mother is in the garden, by the pond. Her hair has been washed and teased into as full a form as it can support, and she is wearing the pink cashmere cardigan that Kate bought for her last year. The wheelchair has been set in the sunlight. Her mother's face is raised; her eyes are closed and she is smiling.

'Hello, Mum,' says Kate.

Her mother's eyes come open, as if from sleep, and her smile broadens. 'Hello, Katie,' she answers. She keeps her face angled into the light, as if the sun's rays were a medical treatment and she is under instruction not to move until told to do so.

Kate sits on the bench, and her mother puts a hand on her arm. There is strength in the fingers, and no tremor that Kate can feel. 'How are you today?' Kate asks.

'Well,' she replies. 'Very well.' She closes her eyes and restores the smile.

'You look it,' says Kate. Her mother's hand tightens for a moment, but the eyes stay closed and the smile does not change. 'You've had your hair done,' she says.

'Thank you. The German girl did it.'

'A professional job,' Kate tells her. 'Which German girl?'

Her mother opens her eyes to search the garden. 'Her,' she says, pointing towards the ramp that leads up to the conservatory; on the ramp, a nurse is steering a wheelchair; her name is Kornelia and she's Polish; and she must be at least thirty-five. The wheelchair is occupied by a tiny woman, swaddled in many blankets; she looks like a chrysalis.

Leonor surveys the garden with a benign gaze. 'A beautiful day,' she remarks. She strokes a sleeve of Kate's jacket. 'This is pretty,' she says. 'Is it new?'

'Fairly,' Kate answers; it's a couple of years old, and she's worn it to The Willowes several times.

'I thought so,' her mother says, gratified. 'A pretty colour. Petrol blue,' she remarks, then she recalls the pullover of the same colour that Kate had worn when she was a teenager; she recalls which Christmas it was bought for, and what Naomi received that year – an encyclopaedia of wildlife that had a fold-out panorama of an African rainforest, which Naomi had copied in crayon. 'It took her months,' her mother reminisces.

Kate remembers it: Naomi at the table every evening, proceeding inch by inch across the scroll of paper, matching every strand of fur, every leaf-vein; she can see the armoury of pencils, aligned in a spectrum along the table's edge; she has a glimpse of young Naomi, with her face close to the paper, concentrating like a lacemaker. Her mother, prompted by Kate, recalls the discipline with which Naomi went about the task: the ordering of the pencils; the sharpening of each one after use; the care taken not to crease or smudge the paper.

'You could see every single scale on that snake,' says her mother, with pride and wonder.

The drawing was remarkable, Kate agrees. But what's more remarkable is her mother's state of mind today. It's months since she was last so voluble, so cogent.

Kornelia and the tiny woman are passing. The tiny woman grins at them, as if this excursion were a treat that she is enjoying immensely.

'Good morning, Miss Grunberg,' Kate's mother says, like a grand chatelaine to a fee-paying visitor. Miss Grunberg chuckles, as if at a sly joke; the sound she makes is like the clicking of a plastic door catch.

'Hello, Mrs Staunton,' says Kornelia; the greeting, Kate is pleased to observe, is suggestive of respectful affection.

'This is my daughter,' answers her mother, placing a hand on her daughter's arm; and Kornelia plays her part perfectly, smiling at Kate as one would smile at a first introduction.

Miss Grunberg and Kornelia continue down the path, watched by Kate's mother, who watches them until they have turned out of sight, behind the laurel hedge. 'A good girl,' she remarks. 'Kornelia. A handsome name. It suits her,' she says, as though to herself, and she raises her face into the sunlight again, closing her eyes. 'Talk to me, Katie,' she murmurs. 'Are you writing a book?'

'Just starting one, I hope.'

'You don't know if you're starting one?'

'Early days,' Kate explains. 'It's like being pregnant. Things often go wrong in the first few weeks.'

Her mother's laugh is barely audible. 'What's it about?' she asks, smiling into the warmth of the sunlight.

'A woman called Dorota,' Kate replies; she recounts as much of the story as there is to tell.

Under the eyelids her mother's eyes are moving, as if scanning the figure of Dorota. 'People like ghost stories,' she says.

'They do.'

'But why not set it in London?'

'Prague just seemed the right place,' says Kate. It's like picking the location for a film, she explains.

'But have you ever been there?' her mother asks.

'We went a few years ago. It was special.' Kate describes some of the things that she saw during their week in Prague; her words flow away on the air.

After a pause, her mother says: 'Which ones have I read?'

'My books, you mean?'

'Yes.'

'All of them, I think.'

'What's the saucy one?'

'Gosh, I don't—'

'The one in Italy.'

'*Giulia the Beautiful.*'

'Yes,' she says. 'I remember. I liked that one.'

It seems that Naomi will not be mentioned if she doesn't raise the subject herself, so Kate says: 'So did Naomi tell you about her plans?'

'Not really. I don't think so,' she says.

'She didn't tell you about going to Scotland?'

'She might have done,' her mother answers placidly. 'But I forget things. You know that.'

'She didn't talk about Bernát?'

'Who?' she asks, and in the space of a second a furrow appears and disappears on her brow.

'Bernát.'

'She talked about a friend, but I don't think that was his name.'

'Was it Gabriel?'

'It could have been Gabriel, yes. And Martin. She talked about Martin.'

'My Martin?'

'Of course. Who else? She likes him,' says her mother, and now she opens her eyes and grins at Kate.

The mischief of this grin is horrible; this is not her mother. 'No, Mum,' Kate says, too sharply. 'He's not Naomi's cup of tea.'

'Why not? He's your cup of tea.'

'Exactly.'

'She likes him,' her mother repeats, turning back into the sunlight. She closes her eyes on her daughter, and sits at ease in silence.

'And how did she seem to you?' asks Kate, after a minute.

'What do you mean?' her mother replies, in a whisper in which Kate hears a sharpness of impatience.

'This thing with Bernát. It's worrying.'

'Why?'

'I don't think he's a good influence.'

'She's not a child.'

'I know that Mum. But look at her.'

'I don't know what you mean.'

'She looks terrible.'

'I thought she looked well.'

'She's lost so much weight.'

'You always said she was too big.'

'I said she should do some exercise. That's not quite the same thing.'

'It was very nice to see her,' says her mother, with a look that seems to accuse her daughter of a lack of kindness.

'Of course it was,' says Kate. 'Of course. But—'

'She said you're not getting along. She told me you had an argument.'

'An argument about what?'

'She didn't say,' her mother answers. 'Her fault though,' she adds, as if it were known that Kate resents any suggestion of culpability, in any situation.

'And when did this argument happen?'

'Recently, I suppose.'

'We had an argument last year. Maybe that's what she meant,' says Kate. 'But we were both at fault for that one.'

Her mother shrugs. She grimaces, but this seems to be because the sunlight has gone; clouds are sliding overhead, advancing from the ridge of the Downs.

Though she knows the question of the argument should be relinquished, Kate says: 'She told you this yesterday?'

'Last week,' is the immediate answer.

A week in her mother's world is a flexible unit of time, signifying the middle distance. 'Didn't you see her yesterday?' Kate asks, with the greatest gentleness.

The question provokes a glance that suggests offence has been taken. Turning away, Leonor examines the condition of the sky, surveying the whole extent of it.

'Well, we had a row this morning. A big one,' Kate admits. Receiving no response, she explains: 'About Bernát.'

Her mother sighs, in boredom, it seems. 'Naturally,' she says.

'She's left,' Kate tells her. 'I don't know when she'll be back.'

Still her mother watches the eventless sky. It might be that every word that has been spoken in the past ten minutes has already been extinguished.

'Perhaps we should go indoors?' Kate suggests.

'In a minute,' her mother answers. Her attention has become fixed on one cloud in particular; her gaze flickers across it, as though it were a vast and difficult painting. A hand rises onto the upper buttons of her cardigan and tightens there, gathering the material into her fist. Her mouth opens, takes a bite of air, and closes.

Kate puts a hand over the fist, and the touch makes her mother start, as if a nettle has brushed her skin. 'Let's go inside,' she says.

On the way out, she tells a lie to the receptionist, to ascertain that her sister had indeed been there the day before. In the car park she starts to weep.

27.

'Nice to have the place to ourselves again,' says Lulu, with a smile to show that she knows this is what her mother is thinking too. They are sitting in the kitchen, on the same side of the table, each looking out on the garden as though the view had changed slightly since this morning.

'I thought you two were getting along well,' says her mother.

'We were,' Lulu answers. 'But sometimes she can be a bit—'. And she mimes, briefly, with both hands outspread, the action of pressing down on a large soft ball.

'She can.'

'I mean, having music on your phone – not really a crime against civilisation, is it?'

'She said that?'

'More or less.'

'Naomi has her principles.'

'But I do like her,' says Lulu.

'I know.'

'Even if Dad's never going to love her.'

'He's fond of her.'

'OK,' says Lulu, raising a sceptical eyebrow.

'But she's not always been on her best behaviour with your father.'

'I know.'

'You don't know the half of it.'

'Half is enough,' says Lulu.

Kate strokes her daughter's arm, once, in thanks. A sudden sound makes her start – her phone is buzzing on the tabletop; the message is not from Naomi.

At a thought, Lulu smiles.

'What?' asks her mother.

'The earrings,' says Lulu.

'What about them?'

'It was nice of her.'

'It was.'

'But they're a bit creepy.'

'They are,' Kate agrees. Her gaze is following a blackbird as it bounces across the terrace; she is aware that Lulu is looking at her.

'You all right?' Lulu asks.

'Oh yes.'

'And how about Naomi? You think she's all right?'

'She says she is.'

Now Lulu's phone rings; she reads the message and in fifteen seconds sends a reply. After a small hesitation she says: 'When I looked out my window this morning she was standing in the garden. Talking to herself. Smiling, but talking to herself. And looking at the Paddock.'

'She's always talked to herself,' says Kate. 'I talk to myself. It's what I do all day.'

'Not really,' says Lulu.

'In a way.'

'So you think she's OK?'

'It would be better if she weren't going so far away.'

'Can't picture her on a farm,' says Lulu.

'I don't think it's quite a farm. More like an allotment with accommodation.'

'Can't picture her on an allotment either.'

'Same here.'

'It won't work. She'll be back soon.'

'Maybe,' says her mother.

As if to reassure, Lulu says: 'I think she enjoyed being here.'

'She enjoyed talking to you,' her mother tells her.

'She really does like to talk, doesn't she?'

'Not always,' says Kate.

Lulu gets up from the table. 'Homework awaits,' she announces, and she gives her mother a kiss on the cheek, with meaningful pressure.

For the fifth time since Naomi's departure, Kate calls her sister, and as before she hears only the voicemail message. She sends a text message: *Can we talk?* She sends other messages. In the evening, at last, a reply arrives, by text – *I'll be in touch. Thank you & M & L for the hospitality.* The following day it is the same: half a dozen messages sent, a single response received – *All fine. Same with you, I hope. Lots to do.* For two weeks this goes on. Naomi will not talk.

One afternoon, Kate is told by her mother that Naomi was recently at The Willowes. Her mother is surprised by Kate's surprise; she had been under the impression that Naomi had been staying at her sister's house. A man called Bernard had brought Naomi down, but he had stayed outside. The nurses confirm to Kate that her sister had been at The Willowes three days before, and that a man – 'elderly, with a grey beard', says Kornelia – had been driving; he had sat in the car, reading, throughout the two hours. Leaving, Kate calls her sister from the car park, and talks to the voicemail. 'You might have told me you were visiting,' she protests, with some anger. For a full minute she talks into the phone. No sooner has she hung up, already regretting having lost her temper, than she gets an answer: *I think we've said all that needs to be said.* It seems possible to Kate that she will never see her sister again.

VI

28.

The day's post includes an envelope that contains a photograph and a note. The photograph shows a white stone fountain, topped by the figure of a naked male archer, green with patina; in front of the fountain Naomi smiles, shielding her eyes with a hand; beside her a bearded man – in appearance not dissimilar to Brahms in later life – similarly shields his eyes; the shadow of the photographer rises from the bottom edge of the picture and tapers towards the feet of Naomi and the bearded man. The note reads: *Me & Oszkár. Have advised him he needs to do something about his web presence. He is grateful. Am well, and heading north. Shall write.* The shadow, it is to be assumed, is the shadow of Bernát. Naomi's hair is lank and unkempt, as if washed without shampoo shortly before the picture was taken; she's wearing a sack-like coat that seems to be lacking some buttons; she looks like a jolly tourist from some less favoured country, on the holiday of a lifetime. Kate rings her right away, but cannot get a connection.

29.

From the window of her room Kate sees a young man and a young woman walking up the sloping road. They are perfectly in step, but apart; their shoulders do not touch as they lean into the wind; his coat, unbuttoned, flails the air behind him; she stumbles, and he catches her by the arm, then immediately lets go. They are not lovers, it seems, but might soon be. The woman is looking into his face as he talks; she laughs. This might be an episode, it occurs to Kate. From a distance, Jakub is observed by Dorota; he is walking with a young woman; there must be some indication of the closeness of their relationship – a hand that touches her back as they cross the road, perhaps. Kate makes a note to this effect. And there would be some doubt, of course, as to whether or not this is in fact Jakub; and some sort of obstacle is necessary, to prevent Dorota from pursuing them. They could be on the opposite bank of the river; or perhaps the river is too wide. The carriage might be better employed here, she thinks. The carriage in itself would be a sufficient sign of intimacy. A boat would be another possibility. *Pleasure boats on Vltava, c. 1920???* she writes. *A boating lake in Prague?* Immediately the boating lake seems to have the fullest potential. She pictures it: Jakub rowing, the woman holding a parasol; the water sparkles in the sunlight, making it difficult for Dorota to make out what is happening. Details offer themselves: on the path, governesses with over-dressed children; a young boy in a sailor suit; a bandstand; the gleam of brass instruments; straw hats, canes, moustaches; perfumes of pipe smoke and eau de cologne and mown grass. There is research to be done here. What style of dress would a governess be wearing? How would a smart young man of that time be attired? Would couples have held hands as they walked in the park? Does such a park exist?

The work of research is something that she has always enjoyed. At times, she has wondered if it might be the part of the process that gives her the greatest pleasure. The satisfaction of completion is immense, but the conclusion of a book never has the excitement of the beginning, when the material proliferates week by week, taking form in different ways from day to day, from hour to hour, like the changing shapes of clouds. On the shelves of her room are ranged the books from which her own books grew. The notebooks have a case of their own, beside the desk; within each one are the seedlings of a dozen novels. Without looking, she reaches down and takes one out: it's the maroon notebook, bought in Paris, for the project that became *The Women's Palace.* It comes open at a page of names: John Sedgwick; Caroline McGhee; William Arbuthnot and others, each annotated with a description and salient points of biography. These were to be the members of a company of actors, performing in London in the early days of gas light. There were to be intrigues and betrayals of various kinds, and a fatal accident, possibly not an accident. But what emerged instead was a book set in Chenonceau, the chateau that spans the River Cher, which for several years was the home of the irresistible Marguerite Wilson-Pelouze, the daughter of the Scottish engineer who put gas lights on the streets of Paris and made so much money from the enterprise that he could give the chateau of Chenonceau to Marguerite as a wedding present.

She takes down a copy of *The Women's Palace* and skim-reads the scene that one reviewer selected as a highlight, the scene that she too regards as the most successful: Madame Wilson-Pelouze daydreaming as she listens to the playing of the pianist she has employed for the summer of 1879. The pianist is a teenager; he is Achille-Claude Debussy.

The real Marguerite was 'as sensuous and intoxicating as a magnolia', wrote Robert de Bonnières, and Kate is still pleased, quite, with the character that she made of her; her Marguerite might not intoxicate, but she is forceful and intelligent, and a young man might readily have fallen under her influence. The scene has an air of veracity; the period details are not overdone. Kate glances at other pages. The book has a tone that is hers; in the back-cover quotes, the adjective 'atmospheric' appears. On the cover of *The Whore of Augsburg* the author is praised as the creator of 'remarkably atmospheric' prose. She turns to the chapter in which Gregor completes his limewood image of Mary Magdalene; she reads it as if the writer had been someone other than herself; these pages, she finds, do succeed in creating an atmosphere; this is how things might have been in Augsburg in the sixteenth century, when Gregor Erhart, the master sculptor, was at work. And *Giulia the Beautiful*, opened next, does not disappoint. In a bedroom of the castle of Carbognano, a conversation is taking place between Giulia Farnese, the governor of the *comune*, and a man called Paolo Bortolo. He is an invention of the author's, but an invention with some historical warrant: *Giulia la bella* is known to have had lovers between the death of her first husband and her marriage to her second. The conversation concerns – among other things – the Borgia pope, Alexander, formerly Giulia's lover; Paolo and Giulia talk about Cesare, recently killed at Viana, and about the circumstances of the pontiff's death, and the scandalously horrible state of the papal corpse. In places the dialogue is perhaps a little stilted, but for the most part the conversation is the conversation of real people; the research is evident, but not ostentatiously so; Paolo and Giulia don't tell each other things that they would already have known. This is something more than costume drama;

it is more than escapism, Kate tells herself. She can permit herself some satisfaction.

Her readers now have certain expectations of her, as do her publishers. The word 'brand' has been used. Every two years she has delivered a new book, and this cycle has become established, as if her productivity were merely a matter of biological gestation. A book bearing her name will have a strong story, an emotionally engaging story, with a woman at its centre, more or less in command; the location will be foreign, both geographically and temporally; a rich social milieu will be evoked, replete with fixtures and fittings; it will be atmospheric. So far, there have been seven; Kate ticks them off, reading the spines, as if it might be possible that she has misremembered the number. A great deal of work has gone into them and the work has been rewarding, in every sense, so it perplexes her a little that she should now seem to be hesitant. If there is a problem, it is not, she thinks, that the subject is weak. The idea of the revenant husband, seen in broad daylight, in that year, in central Europe, has had a feeling of rightness since the moment it occurred to her, with all those elements in place. It is possible, of course, that this rightness will prove to be illusory; this is what has happened before – ideas that seemed perfect at the outset began to fail as the work proceeded. At the moment, however, the dead/living husband, in Prague, around 1920, seems a strong foundation for a book – stronger, much stronger, than all the other possibilities that passed through her mind before this one arrived. And yet she has not begun to work properly on it; she is idling. At this stage she should be reading, planning, taking notes; there should be some exhilaration at the prospect of what lies ahead. Before, it has felt like arriving in a city for the first time.

Instead, it is as if she were sitting on a train that has just come to a halt; she can see towers and domes in the mid-distance; the city of the book awaits her; its streets begin on the other side of the station – from her seat she can see, through the windows of the ticket hall, the trees of a wide avenue and a slow flow of traffic. She does not move. Time could be spent profitably in this place, she knows; it would give her pleasure to explore the streets, however busy they may be; but she would rather be where she is, in this carriage, on her own.

This image appeals to Kate, and she makes a note of it. *People are waiting for her in the city*, she writes, *but perhaps, instead of going to meet them, instead of spending time here, she will stay on the train until the next stop. And what is the next stop? She doesn't know. Maybe it's only a little village, where there's nothing to see except the hills around it.* This might be something that Dorota might think, or it might be a notion conceived by some other character who has not yet appeared. *But*, she adds, *someone is speaking to her. At first, in her reverie, she had not heard him. She is being told to disembark. This is the end of the line.* She reads what she has written, and takes a pencil to score it out; she puts the pencil down without using it.

On her computer she has thousands of family photos. Here are the pictures from Prague: Lulu and Martin, with the Powder Tower behind them; herself and Martin, out of focus, at the Josefov cemetery; little Lulu in her powder-blue raincoat, wading in blossom by the castle; Lulu with an enormous ice cream. It was a wonderful holiday. One day a book would come of it, she had thought while they were there. She would use the station as a setting, somehow, and she would try to make use of a strange scene that they had witnessed.

A smartly dressed man, fiftyish, had stood as still as a statue while a very pretty woman, about twenty years younger, standing less than arm's length from him, spoke fiercely but quietly into his impassive face, until the man turned and walked away; whereupon she followed him, one step behind, neither of them hurrying, as the young woman continued to talk at the man's back with barely a pause, as if reciting the catalogue of his offences against her.

Kate closes her eyes again, to return to the lake in Prague. What music would the band be playing? There must be flowerbeds, but what flowers would be growing there? She sees Jakub in the boat: he takes a cigarette case from the inside pocket of his jacket; the sunlight flashes off the silver. With a seducer's smirk – an expression that looks completely wrong on Jakub's face, thinks Dorota – he touches the wrist of his lady friend, and as he does this he glances in Dorota's direction, as if he knows that she is observing them. He says something, and the young woman lowers the parasol to look at what Jakub has seen; she laughs, too extravagantly, like a bad actress; she is wearing a great deal of make-up; her lips look almost black.

But here the action is halted. Kate can see it all so clearly – the parasol; the actressy young woman; the young man, smoking, now wearing a boater hat – that suddenly she is seized by the suspicion that she is recalling the scene at the lake, not creating it. The suspicion quickly gathers force. Has she seen this couple, on the boating lake, in a film or on TV? She replays the sequence in her mind. The sense of its familiarity becomes stronger, but without bringing any information from which she might identify what it is that is being remembered. One moment it seems likely that she's seeing characters from a film set in Paris, a film from the 1940s or 1950s, monochrome; the next moment she suspects that she is making this assumption on the basis of nothing more than the scene's ambience of old-world elegance and illicit romance. Could it even be, she wonders, that the essence of the story – the mystery of the husband who may or may not have been killed in the war – is not in fact hers? Within a minute she is almost persuaded that she has read such a story somewhere, and is merely filling it in with borrowed costumes and backdrops.

30.

A fortnight after the delivery of the photograph, a postcard arrives, in an envelope that has been franked in Fort William. On one side is a picture of a golden eagle. On the reverse, Naomi has offered a report, of sorts: *Life could not be better – no need to worry – whole days of saturated silence – Larder well stocked, so no imminent risk of death. Am at work, as I trust are you. Once in a while I will go into town – can get a signal there, so will text.* No address is given; by 'town' she must mean Fort William, Kate assumes.

31.

At irregular intervals, text messages arrive. In November: *Thrashingly windy days – ash trees sounding like surf with every gust – we have owls at night and buzzards during the day, and a fearless fox – a kiss for you & a kiss for Lulu & one for Martin too.* Ten days later: *Rain rain rain rain rain, a glorious noise, the infinite symphony of the sky – am in good shape – have muscles now, thanks to the axe work – enough wood to burn till Easter. Mum OK? You?* And Kate replies, immediately: *Mum much the same. I'd like to talk to you.* There is no response; she tries calling, and of course is diverted to voicemail. At Christmas, Naomi sends a card with a clumsy drawing of two huts amid hills on one side, and on the other a message: *Season's Greetings from the charterhouse – all is exceedingly well – we now have a sauna, and some snow in which to roll – reading bee-books in preparation for spring & the arrival of the hive – picked up the flute yesterday & had some pleasure playing again – working on the translation & should have something for you soon – a Happy New Year to you all.* In the New Year, two texts are received within a week. There is no mention of Bernát, nor of any intention to come south.

32.

Scanning the TV pages in the Sunday paper, Kate sees a familiar name: Daffyd Paskin. Part one of *The Never-Ending Conquest*, his new documentary, is being broadcast the following Wednesday. It will 'reveal the appalling human cost of our exploitation of the Amazon wilderness', the previewer writes.

On dark and glassy water, a narrow boat slides between high trees; sitting in the stern, Daffyd Paskin surveys the welter of vegetation that obscures the banks of the river; he is humbled by the magnitude and fecundity of it, we can see. Addressing the camera face-on, he tells us that we think of the Amazon as the 'ultimate jungle'. A bird of ultrabright plumage is spotted; an unseen creature disturbs the water underneath an impenetrable canopy of leaves. 'This is one of the richest ecosystems on the planet, and people have been part of this ecosystem for many many centuries,' he states. 'The Amazon is not just about natural history. It has a human history – a terrible history,' he tells us, as if bringing news. His face is slightly fuller than in his gypsy days, and the stubble is a little more lush; a blazingly white shirt offsets the bristles nicely. The vocal style is more portentous too.

We have come to a bend in the river; looking ahead, into the gloom of the undergrowth, we distinguish a group of grass-roofed dwellings. The jungle village is located somewhere on a tributary of the Rio Negro, Daffyd tells us. In the sixteenth century the Europeans arrived here, he goes on; this was the start of a 'perpetual disaster' for the peoples of the Amazon. At the time of the invasion, the rainforest supported a great number of settled societies of great complexity; within a hundred years, these societies had lost ninety per cent of their people. When the Spanish first ventured into the forest, more than one thousand languages were spoken in the area that is now Brazil; today the number is lower than two hundred, Daffyd informs us, as sombre as a doctor bringing a gloomy bulletin from intensive care.

The entire population of the village is gathered into the frame of the lens. 'You are looking at half of all the people in the world who speak this language,' says Daffyd. An elder of the village has placed three stones on a log; the stones vary in size, but all can be held easily in the hand; to us, says Daffyd, the three stones are all just 'stones', or 'pebbles', but these people have a different word for each. Since coming into contact with the modern world, the villagers have become prone to illnesses to which they had previously never been exposed. The population is in steep decline; it seems inevitable that their language will expire sooner rather than later, and it will have left no traces, other than in the notebooks of a few ethnologists. Daffyd has such an ethnologist to hand, a man called Walter Doniphan. Why should it matter, Daffyd wonders, if this fragile and small language becomes extinct? Change, after all, is the essence of life; extinction is inseparable from survival. It matters, Walter Doniphan believes, because language is the greatest natural resource of the human ecosystem, and the human ecosystem, like any ecosystem, thrives on diversity. The loss of any language is a loss of information, of vision. Every language is charged with knowledge: the language spoken in this village is the embodiment of a unique way of seeing the world. These people, says Walter, have more words for cloud types than any Western meteorologist. We return to the image of the three stones on the log, before being shown some women talking energetically; from the rhythm of their exchanges, it appears that they are taking turns to add details to a lengthy reminiscence; they laugh loudly. Walter explains that they are talking about their mother. We observe the incomprehensible sisters; one of them is dabbing her eyes as she laughs. Another thought from Daffyd Paskin: Homo sapiens is the only species that can recover its past, and language, more than images, is what makes this recovery possible. He asks us to imagine a world in which everyone speaks the same language – a linguistic prairie, a world in which billions have been exiled forever from the culture of their forebears.

Suddenly, Daffyd Paskin has been transplanted to a traffic intersection, before a backdrop of office towers. He might be somewhere in the USA, but in fact we have moved some unspecified distance downstream from the endangered village. We are in Manaus, the city that grew twentyfold in the space of just three decades, in the latter part of the nineteenth century, when Brazil monopolised the world's production of rubber, and Manaus grew rich on the proceeds. So wealthy did the elite of Manaus become, Daffyd Paskin tells us, that more diamonds were bought here, per capita, than in any European city. Clothes were sent all the way back to Europe to be laundered; an opera house was built here, almost a thousand miles from the ocean; thousands of prostitutes were brought to the jungle city from Paris, Budapest, Moscow and Tangiers; 'they bathed in champagne, literally', Daffyd Paskin marvels, half-appalled. 'And this is what paid for the decadence,' he pronounces, and the screen is filled with a picture of dark-skinned men in chains. 'This is what paid for the diamonds,' he says, before reading an eye-witness account of the rape and mutilation of slaves on the rubber planta-tions, of workers being thrown onto fires alive, of slaves being used for target practice. He quotes the words of a plantation supervisor: 'Kill the fathers first, then enjoy the virgins.'

The horrors continue: Daffyd Paskin peers into the pit of an illicit gold mine, where scores of desperate men, slathered in mud, are panning for gold in slurry that has already been panned; he wades through slicks of oil in ruined waterways; he encounters the displaced, the crippled, the ailing, the destitute. In case we do not understand how calamitous this all is, Daffyd Paskin's sorrowing face is repeatedly displayed. In a preview of next week's programme, a small plane bears the presenter over a soybean plantation that extends almost to the horizon, to the shore of the disappearing jungle. Only then does Kate remember why there is something familiar about Walter Doniphan's name.

33.

Though concern for her sister and for their mother – and, sometimes, some resentment of Naomi's refusal of communication – combine to make concentration difficult, Kate carries on with the story of Dorota.

After again sighting Jakub with his former workmate, Dorota sees a man she knows to be dead rather than missing – he was killed in Galicia and buried there. He is definitely dead; he has a tombstone. Yet he is seen near the station, like Jakub, and like Jakub he eludes her in the crowd. Perhaps she then sees another man, also certainly dead, also in the vicinity of the station, walking away from her quickly. At home, she suffers headaches and nightmares; she walks in her sleep. One morning Julius wakes up to find that every drawer in their flat is open; for a moment he thinks they have been burgled while they slept. Three or four times Dorota is not at home when she should have been. Julius's suspicions are becoming intolerable. *Sunday afternoon*, writes Kate, *D tells J she has to visit her sister/cousin/parents – J follows – walk along the river – weather & architecture – D's point of view: she sees the ex-workmate (another J? or is this too much?) & catches up with him – introduces herself – he claims not to remember Jakub – seems v ill at ease in her presence – some talk about the war & then D mentions his wife – man says that he has never been married – D's consternation – man leaves her, hurriedly – & switch to J's POV – his wife accosting a man in the street & the man's wariness & D's bewildered reaction to something he says.* This scene might be powerful, she thinks, but the thought lacks strength. *Man that Julius sees does not resemble in any way the former workmate, as described from D's POV earlier*, she writes. Her novel proceeds no further.

34.

She contemplates a new story, set in Germany, in the 1830s, amid lakes, mountains and forests; the central character would be some sort of false messiah, and there would be a schism among his disciples, leading to a murder perhaps. This idea soon expires. A portion of a chapter of Afonso's life in London is written; he works in a hospital laundry, with people who have no idea how remarkable he is; something horrible happens – *foetus in a drying machine?* – *hand reaches in & touches something like warm vinyl* – and Afonso is dismissed, though blameless. Nothing comes of the story of Afonso. Kate reads several books for a novel set in the rubber plantations of Brazil; she fills pages with notes about Walter Hardenburg, Roger Casement and the unspeakable Rafael Calderón. She writes a ten-page sketch of a big set-piece: a party at the home of Waldemar Ernst Scholtz, Austria's honorary consul in Manaus, at which guests drink champagne from a bath occupied by a beautiful naked woman – Scholtz's mistress, Sarah Lubousk. Nothing comes of it; nothing comes of any of these ideas.

35.

At the end of April, the postman brings a package, franked in Fort William. It contains two batches of text. The first consists of twenty photocopied pages, in Bernát's extravagant hand, in Hungarian; a cover sheet bears a single word: *Gyermekjelenetek.* The second batch is another photocopied manuscript, in English, written by Naomi with evident care; there are no revisions, no smudges. A card is attached: *The translation, at last – apologies for the delay – to repeat: Bernát is happy for you to do what*

you want with this material – he asserts no claim to it,
and neither do I – use it as a quarry, or whatever – treat
the words as if they are anonymous – bees installed &
thriving – I thrive too – 'Therefore, happiness does not
consist in the activity of prudence.' N xx.

Into the 'Enter text' box of an online translator, Kate
types the title: *Gyermekjelenetek.* The result: *children*
scenes. She types the first four sentences, and they are
converted into this:

Waking up, I remember waking up in my room at
home, in the bedroom of a half-century ago, in the
winter, and I see the curtains in the room: the colour
of the white light glowed so weak blackcurrant cordial.
Feathers was ice on the inside of the window, and the
wide range of satin duvet was cold to the face. It was
the satin scarlet border. The bedspread, candlewick-
patterned, was burgundy. I see the headboard of
the bed, painted to resemble mahogany, three deep
scratches, close to each other, as the traces of a claw.

Kate sends a message – *I would like to talk about what*
you sent me. Intrigued. Please call. I really need to talk to
you. Eight days later, she gets this: *Nothing to say about*
G'tek – it is what it is. But glad you got something out of
it. All is well. Nxx. And so it goes on, week after week:
All is well; Am very well; Everything is wonderful. The
condition of their mother deteriorates as autumn arrives,
and Kate informs her sister; the bulletin is acknowledged,
without comment. Two weeks later, at The Willowes, Kate
learns that her sister has been there. 'How did she look?'
she enquires. A bit thinner, Kornelia tells her. Naomi had
been wearing a kind of smock, grey, ankle-length, shapeless; and a headscarf, which stayed in place throughout

the visit. She was with a man, the same man as before. He sat in the car for the entire hour, looking at the scenery, it seems. Kate talks to her mother. Her mother has no memory of a visit from Naomi, but she might remember being visited by a nurse who wore a headscarf. 'Last week, I think,' she says, then she returns to silence, then to sleep.

36.

Katie, Naomi writes, on a postcard showing a view of Loch Linnhe:

I have decided to stay here for the foreseeable future. I mean that I shall not be leaving the retreat and its immediate environs. The town is now Bernát's domain. So the phone is henceforth of no use. Our plot is productive and the bees are earning their keep. I am healthy, I promise you. Should anything untoward happen, Bernát will let you know. And vice versa. But nothing is going to happen. This is where I have to be. Sorry I am not equipped for family life. Please try to accept this. Be happy that I am happy, and be happy with Martin & Lulu & your work. And I won't be here for ever.

More than a year has passed since Naomi left.

VII

Gyermekjelenetek
[Scenes from Childhood]

Bernát Kalmár / Naomi Staunton

Awaking, I remember waking up in my bedroom at home, the bedroom of half a century ago, in winter, and I see the curtains of that room: in the pallid light they glowed with the colour of weak blackcurrant cordial. Feathers of ice were on the inside of the window, and the wide border of satin on the eiderdown was cold to the face. The satin border was scarlet; the bedspread, candlewick-patterned, was burgundy. I see the headboard of the bed, stained to resemble mahogany, with three deep scratches, close together, like the marks of a small claw. On the chest of drawers stood the old radio; it was as wide as the kitchen sink and could not be lifted easily. On the black and gold glass pane of the radio were marked, in echelon formations, the names of many mysterious stations; when the cursor was moved across the names, incomprehensible voices would rise and fall against a wail of interference, like messages in wartime; in the top right-hand corner of the radio, a tiny deep-set window, like a miniature radar screen, had a fan of green light in it, which would become narrower and brighter when a station came into focus. And I can see the wallpaper, on which was depicted, on a white background, children at play under trees, with hoops and balls, on rope swings, in a tree house. There were half a dozen scenes, repeated over and over again, but the repetitions were imperfect: here was a tree with leaves that were smudged in one place; here a child's hair was like a cap made of brass; this yellow ball, misshapen, resembled a lemon; here, above the dog's muzzle, were two tiny dots that might have been flies; in half a dozen places the girls' skipping rope was a string of dots and dashes, like Morse code, and no two pieces of code were the same.

From the windows of this room, at the front of the building's top storey, the entirety of the market place was visible: four rows of stalls, arranged as two lines, back to back, with a cobbled avenue separating the two inward-facing rows. Striped tarpaulins, red and white, covered the stalls, and at one end stood the fountain, from which two stone horses arose, high above the pavement: the sentinels of the street. If you awoke late, you would hear the murmur of the shoppers below, a sound as easeful as a breeze through leaves. A storm one night made the tarpaulins snap and crack; they flailed in the wind, and at last flew away. The bedroom door trembled against its frame with the thunderclaps. Rainwater falling from a broken gutter struck the pavement with a noise like turnstiles. A fire engine rushed through the rain, towards Top Church, raising huge wings of water from the road. The sound of the siren was always thrilling; it was the moment of passing that you so enjoyed, the voluptuous instant of mournful decline. In the morning, after the storm, the weathervane of Top Church dangled from the spire, like an almost severed head.

The bedroom had two doors, one of which opened onto a windowless storage space. Boxes and suitcases were stacked in here, on three sides. A navy blue trunk with wooden corners formed the base of one stack. You would close the door of the little room, then prise open the trunk and climb in. It was difficult to raise the lid, with the boxes piled on top, but the effort was rewarded. Inside, it was as dark as the deepest corner of a mine, and nothing but your breathing could be heard.

A window at the top of the uppermost flight of stairs opened onto a light well, which was traversed by a washing line. In the coldest days of winter, shirts taken off this line were as stiff as balsa, and furred with frost: I see them lined up along the corridor, at an angle to the wall – a cloche of rigid clothes.

The frozen shirts were like the torsos of mummified corpses, raised from frozen earth; you would crack the arms one by one.

At the bottom of the main staircase, opposite the triangular space below the stairs, a wide window gave a view of a complicated landscape of flat roofs, chimneys, vents and low walls. After rain, large shallow puddles remained on the roofs for days – cloud shapes, with real clouds mirrored in them. A pale russet stain spread out from a spool of wire that lay beside a rotting ladder. Three or four doors, in cabin-like structures, opened onto the roofs, but nobody was ever seen to emerge from them. There were no gaps between the buildings, so it would have been possible to walk for a long way across this zinc-coloured plain. The window, however, could not be opened.

A thin carpet covered the floor of the hallway, and the boards underneath were loose in places, and uneven, so a ball or marble would not run straight along it. There was one spot, an inch from the wall, midway along, where a board was loose, so the floor would make a tiny scream, like a mouse in a trap, when lightly trodden. Near this spot, above the skirting board, a box of thick black plastic was attached. It was the size of a large book, and the plastic had the sheen of ebony. By pressing an ear against it, you could hear, faintly, the sound – but rarely the words – of conversations on the telephone line of the shop below.

Daylight came into the dining room through a single window, which opened onto the light well, which was deep and narrow, so nothing of the sky could be seen from the dining table. Even in the middle of the year it was sometimes necessary to use the electric light that hung from the centre of the ceiling; the lampshade was a shallow bowl of opaque white glass, with a large pale yellow stain in it, like the body of a jellyfish. The only old piece of furniture was in this room: a sideboard of dark wood, surmounted by a clouded oval mirror and a cornice that was supported by four columns carved into barley-stick spirals. Below the drawers, two doors closed a compartment in which were stacked copies of the Reader's Digest, some science fiction novels, an atlas, and a medical book in which there were pictures of a pregnant woman, naked but for her knickers, with nipples as big as biscuits and dark as liquorice.

In the centre of the living room stood a grass-green settee. The fabric was nylon, and the pattern of the fabric was formed by narrow cables laid closely together in diagonal lines. On the day you came back from the opticians with your first pair of glasses you came into the room and saw the settee in bright sunlight. From the distance of the doorway you could discern the strands of which each cable was composed; coming closer, you saw the dust that lay in the twists of the material, like grains of sand amid ribbons of seaweed. You cried at this astonishing sight.

The fireplace was clad with thick ceramic tiles, the colour of caramel and plain chocolate, in a chequerboard array. Over the mouth of the fireplace was placed a metal mesh fireguard. Now, as I write these words, the sensation of touching my tongue to the metal is renewed, and saliva springs in my mouth. It is akin to the sensation created by putting one's tongue across the terminals of a nine-volt battery. Later, an electric heater was installed in the fireplace. Above the twin elements, a pile of fake coals – a single piece of fibreglass – lay in front of an undulating backboard of polished metal. Two light bulbs burned beneath the coals. Perforated parasols of thin metal were pivoted on pins above the bulbs and turned in the heat that they generated, creating on the backboard an approximately flame-like effect, which invited contemplation, despite the clumsiness of the artifice.

The television – an object as bulky as a jukebox – had a screen that was convex and grey-green, and little larger than a closed magazine. A thick casing of something like cardboard covered the back of it, pierced with many slits. Peering through these slits, you could see valves glowing faintly above the plateaus and canyons of circuitry, like a city of the future at night.

A small platform, perhaps three feet high, was enclosed by the bay window of the living room. On days of warm sunlight, you would sit on this platform to read, on a seat of cushions. Net curtains covered the windows, and in hot weather these curtains held a perfume that was sweet and musky. For the summer carnival the windows were opened so that you could dangle your legs above the parade of pirates, Aztecs, cowboys and Indians, as they followed the brass band along the high street. One year, an Aztec girl stopped below the window and smiled up at you; she was as lovely as an actress. For weeks afterwards you looked at every girl you passed in the street, hoping that she would be the Aztec girl. You never saw her, except by thinking of her, which you did every day, for a long time, until she began to blur, as if her features were being worn away by your thinking, like the face on an old coin.

In the bathroom there was a small wall-mounted heater, which warmed only the air directly below it. The flooring, of synthetic linoleum, was cold for most of the year, but beside the bath a rectangular rug was placed, on which was shown a lion, standing in a jungle clearing, below a sky that was as red as tomato ketchup. The rug had been bought from a man who came to the shop one day, a man from India. It had an underlay of thick orange foam, which disintegrated over the years, releasing granular pieces of rubber, like cod's roe. A cabinet stood behind the door, and in the lowest compartment of this cabinet was kept a milk bottle into which every powder in your chemistry set had been poured, with water, in the hope of creating a spectacular effusion, like one of Dr Frankenstein's concoctions. The brew had proved to be inert. The bottle remained in the cabinet for months, with an inch-thick stratum of sludge, catfish-brown, at the base.

A curtain of red and white chequered cloth, hung from a wire, covered the space below the kitchen sink, and in this space, in a plastic bucket, could be found a stiff yellow stick of leather which, when dropped into water, performed a transformation that always fascinated. You would fill the bucket with warm water and let the stick slide into it, as though releasing a creature that rightfully belonged there. You scooped it out on the back of a hand, for the feeling of the delectably repulsive adhesion, like the belly of a huge warm slug.

Opposite the door that connected the kitchen to the hallway another door opened onto a staircase, which turned sharply to the right, at the top. At this turn, a narrow ledge was occupied, for many years, by two objects of unknown origin: a Toby jug, with a face expressive of gleeful malice; and an elephant of hard black wood, four or five inches tall, which had a single tusk of fake ivory and a circular cavity where the missing tusk would have gone. At the foot of the staircase, three steps turned to the left, to the door that opened into the back yard, and three turned to the right, to the door that opened into the stock room of the shop. The last three steps on each side were steep and narrow. One night you were carried down the stairs and manoeuvred with care around the angle, into the arms of a man who came forward from the bright open door of an ambulance. I remember the oxygen mask: gelid, cold, the colour of dishwater.

The front office of the shop was furnished with a table and four chairs. On the table was an ashtray, in which cigarettes were left burning when a customer came into the shop. Sometimes you would lift the cigarette to sample it, putting it to your mouth very lightly, so as not to smudge the fine imprint of the woman's lips. The ashtray was made of glass, and within its base was encased a passenger plane, with a bulbous fuselage and two propellers. The wings were as slim as razor blades, and you would angle the ashtray close to your eyes, to marvel at how the plane came to be there, like a bizarre insect inside a colourless amber.

A second office, at the opposite end of the stock room, was where the wallpaper was trimmed. The trimming machine had a treadle to control its speed, and two circular blades that could remove a finger in an instant, you were told. The room was unheated and had a single small window, which had bars like a prison cell's. In the days preceding November 5, the guy for the bonfire was kept here. Once, at night, you visited him, in his moonlit dungeon. His limbs and torso were stuffed with offcuts of wallpaper, so he crackled when embraced, and his face was a mask made of card that had the texture and smell of an egg carton. The walls of this office were whitewashed and the plaster had blistered in many places; the lightest tap would shatter it, exposing liver-coloured brick.

The outside toilet was used for storing the waste cardboard from all the shops that backed into the yard. The boxes were broken down and piled horizontally. The stack resembled a segment of rock, with dozens of thin strata. A smell of dampness and rot came out of it when the door was opened. A latch with a spoon-shaped and rusty thumb-pad kept the door closed. When you released it, sometimes, a scurrying would start. Once, after the cardboard had been pulled out for burning, two dead mice, pink and hairless, were found on the concrete floor; they looked like boiled sweets, gone soft with age.

For November 5, the bonfire was built in a corner of the yard that had high walls on three sides. When the fire was in full spate, giant shadows moved across the bricks, and the walls glowed from top to bottom. The shadows made you think of Shadrach, Meschach and Abednego in the fiery furnace. In the morning, tiny wisps of smoke still seeped from the crevices in the silken charcoal that covered the remnants of timber.

One Sunday, after a night of snowfall, the door to the yard could not be opened: the wind had created a drift that came to the height of your shoulders.

On one side of the yard, against the wall, the snow was so deep that a burrow could be dug in it. You excavated a chamber inside the snow and sat there for a long time, under a glowing white roof, telling yourself that you must be careful not to fall asleep, because if you fell asleep in the snow you would die. But dying in the snow, you also knew, was the most peaceful of deaths.

One of the walls of the yard had been blackened by the smoke of bonfires and some of its bricks had crumbled, creating holds for hands and feet. The top of the wall turned out to be the parapet of a wide flat roof; from here, unobserved, you could observe the comings and goings in the yard. In the middle of the roof rose a construction like a small tent of rusted metal, but in fact it was glass, coated with oily soot. With a finger you scoured a hole in the soot, and what you saw through this hole was a workshop, in which a man wearing a helmet as heavy as a medieval knight's, and gloves that could have been used in battle, was holding a long thin rod that ended in a point of white flame. The man moved the flame slowly over a large plate of steel, which burned and reddened where the flame touched it. It was like an old story, in which a boy discovers a crack in the earth, and a forge hidden deep within it.

A short tunnel, square in cross-section, connected the yard to the street, and above this tunnel ran two storeys of flats, reached by iron stairs. The huge vats of a Chinese restaurant stood below one flight of steps, and sometimes the lid was removed from them, and you could look down into the yellow water that was seething inside. Underneath these steps hung buds of dusty grease, all of the same size and shape – a hemisphere, extended slightly at its lowest point by gravity.

Emerging from the tunnel on a Sunday morning, you looked to your right, where the road rose slightly towards the high street, then to the left, where it descended at the same small gradient, past the police station and on to the public gardens. A cat strutted across the road, and paused for a few seconds in the middle, to stare at you. In the sunlight, the tarmac was as pale as sand. You stood and gazed down the road. The day was warm and clear. When the cat was gone, there was not another living thing to be seen on the heavenly street, for a full minute or more.

The tall folding doors of the fire station were blood-coloured, and looked perpetually wet. A square window of four small square panes was set into each door, and the glass in every door was as clean as tap water. Inside stood the mighty vehicles, parked always in the same positions, to the inch. The bodywork was as slick as nail polish, without blemish. Every door of the fire engines was open, all of them at an angle of forty-five degrees. The tyres, deeply incised, gleamed like fresh tar, and every tyre had a small bulge in its inside and outside wall, of identical size and curvature. Underneath each engine, placed midway between the front wheels, lay a shallow steel tray, in which might be seen a tiny pool of oil, the black blood of the machine. Everything was readied: the tightly wound hoses, with nozzles that shone like trophies; the silver-bladed axes; the helmets, arrayed in perfect and unchanging order. The aura of the fire station was like the aura of an empty church.

Opposite the fire station was the barber's shop. There, waiting, you watched the operation of shaving: the swaddling of towels, which were wound around the neck and jaw as thickly as a winter scarf, emitting a thin steam; then the quick unwinding of the towels and the painting of the skin with lathered soap. Sometimes, where the blade had wiped a track through the lather, a bud of blood would appear and a small white stick, of a radiant and crystalline whiteness, like the marble of a gravestone in rain, would be touched to the wound. The stick caused a sting, you could see, but the sting seemed to be refreshing, as the tartness of lemon juice is refreshing, and immediately the skin was healed.

The fountain in the high street had two large granite bowls at ground level, at the side, from which horses and cattle would once have drunk, and two smaller bowls, on pedestals, at the front and back, which would have held water for the market traders. There was no longer any water. Above each of the smaller bowls there was a lion's head, with a dry spout inside its mouth. Water for the animals would have come from the mouths of two large white stone dolphins, which were stuck on the sides of the fountain's main arch, head down, like squirrels descending a tree trunk. The arch was made of the same white stone, and was covered with carvings – of angels, sea shells and swags of fruit. Above each dolphin, a half-horse pressed its front hooves to the parapet, as if clambering out of the monument. Inside the arch, in niches, stood statues that could not be properly seen from the street, and for that reason had an air of secret meaning. And what was the significance of the two figures that stood at the summit? Who were they? You imagined the fountain to be ancient. It was in the nature of ancient monuments to be massive and incomprehensible and no longer useful.

In the centre of the high street, two department stores stood side by side. In one the floor was shiny, like the floor of a hospital, and a smell of cold meat was everywhere. In the other, the floor was made of dark wooden tiles that clacked when you stepped on them; at the back, the town's first escalator took you down to where the toys were. It was here that you bought a racing car of so gorgeous a blue that you never played with it, for fear of damage. Many years later, in a museum, you at last saw an object of the same hue and lustre: a Byzantine angel, of vitreous enamel.

At the rear of the department stores, a factory was being demolished. A bulldozer was parked on a mound of bricks, its blade raised to the sky in a gesture of threat. Swung from the gantry of a crane, a gigantic ball went into the one high wall that remained upright. When the ball struck, the bricks curved inward to take it, as if making a catch, then everything came down with the noise of a breaking wave. Dust smoke flew up from the rubble and when the smoke had fallen back it was surprising that so small a pile of rubble should have been created. Behind the pile a door was still standing; a grey overall hung from a peg. It was unsettling, the sight of this overall; it suggested to you that the factory had been demolished before it was ready.

When the factory had been removed a new car park was laid out. It was a small shallow valley of tarmac, and at the top of the far bank, for many weeks, there was the wreck of a car that had been set on fire. Its bodywork was scorched all over, and only in three or four places could it be seen that it had once been green. The bonnet was ajar and could not be closed. The engine had gone, as had the wheels. Inside, the seats were naked wire and the steering wheel was a hoop of bare metal. Something plastic, in the glove compartment, had melted and was stuck in the cavity, like a large black barnacle. On the floor lay hundreds of little cubes of glass, which you would grind with your feet as you drove. When the car was taken away, it left a print of its chassis on the tarmac, which never disappeared completely.

Water gathered between the cobblestones where the buses pulled in, and there was often a skin of oil or diesel on these narrow little pools. Waiting for a bus, you would watch the colours swirling in the water. The colours would always be in motion, no matter how still the air. Where the buses turned onto the road, a short length of tram line had been exposed. Their tyres had worn away the tarmac, and had polished the steel so that it gleamed like the leg bone of a prehistoric animal, exposed in a bed of peat.

In a clothes shop in the vicinity of Top Church stood three female mannequins. Their faces did not smile, unlike the mannequins in other windows, and their hands were more elegant. The fingers pointed downwards, as if the women were ordering someone to pick something off the floor. You thought of them as three sisters. The mouth of one had an expression of disdain, and her eyes were different from the eyes of the other two. The difference was slight, but enough to give her a furtiveness that was exciting. You would exchange a glance with her whenever you passed.

In the graveyard of the church you uncovered, under vines and bindweed, a headstone that was blotched with thick pads of moss. At first, all that could be read was a portion of the date and a name: Jean. With a penknife you cut the moss away. Here lay the body of Jean-Paul Deverell and his wife, whose name, in smaller letters, was Katharine. He had died in 1771; the year of Katharine's death was illegible, as were the words beneath the dates. You would murmur his melodious name, to which the hyphen gave such glamour. You would trace the lettering with a finger. The letters were not chiselled squarely, but were irregular and fluid, as if someone had written freely into the stone with a magical pen.

The name of Marsh & Taylor, the ironmonger, was spelt above the windows in thick letters of gold-painted wood. The richness and solidity of the letters guaranteed the quality of the things that were sold there. The shop was an armoury. Heavy tools, with blades and prongs, hung from chains that crossed the ceiling; it was dark, and the smell was of oil and metal. Huge bolts and screws and nails, such as might be fired from crossbows, were heaped in cartons behind the counter. But the bell that hung from a coiled spring above the door made a small and dainty sound when someone came in, and it danced on its spring like a jubilant little puppet. At the sound of the shop's peculiar name, you would imagine an outfitter on a space station: Martian Tailor.

A pounding noise came out of the newspaper office throughout the day. Frosted panes filled the windows, but sometimes the door would be left ajar, and then a huge contraption was visible, a kind of loom with many levers and chains and wires. It was larger than a car, and almost filled the room. How had it been put there? Parts of the machine leapt up and down in a frenzy, as if to pulverize what was inside it. A man would always be standing in front of it, with plugs in his ears, like a hero of some myth, whose survival depended on his not being able to hear.

It was a test of resolve to breathe the air of the butcher's shop. A nausea arose when you inhaled the smell of the meat and the blood, and of the sawdust that covered the floor like filthy snow. Flesh was always being hacked on the chopping board, and you would force yourself to watch, as if this were some form of instruction. With a single stroke, the blade of the cleaver passed right through the bone, to embed itself in the pink-tinted wood. At one end of the shop there was a cold room, like a dungeon, with huge steel levers and chains on its door. Hearing the clank of the levers you would turn for a glimpse of the interior, where huge pale corpses hung from rails, their ribs gaping.

On the upper floor of the toy shop, behind the counter, there was a door that was set flush with the wall. One day the door was unlocked for you. A large room was behind it, with a high ceiling supported by triangles of black wooden beams. Cobwebs as thick as tea towels hung in the angles of the beams, and the glass of the windows was grey. A café had once been here. A poster, held onto the wall by a single rusted pin, had curled up into a cylinder. On the outside the paper was brown, but when you flattened the poster with your hand you found that the colours inside were fresh; it was an advertisement for holidays in Cornwall, depicting white-walled chalets above a buttery beach and royal-blue sea, with white waves rolling towards the sand in well-ordered ranks.

The pubs in the high street had windows of mottled and coloured glass that was thicker than the glass in any other windows, so that all that could be seen through them was the movement of dark shapes. It was like peering into a fish tank that had never been cleaned. Sometimes a door would open as you passed, and you caught sight of men peering into glasses of beer, or the brilliant baize of a snooker table under a block of grey-veined light. The noise that came out was the sound of many voices complaining; an air of adulthood flowed out. It was a mystery, what went on in these places, and that the pubs should have names that belonged to legends and adventures: The Green Man, The Red Lion, The Golden Fleece, The Saracen's Head.

In the shop that sold record players and radios and music there was a shelf on which were ranged a dozen valves, like a display of closely related species in a museum of natural history. The valves were of similar size but none was identical to any of the rest: some had a tiny tip, like a thorn; some were domed, some flat on top; some had a silver cap, others were entirely clear; most were cylindrical, but some were swollen in the middle, like skittles. You could not conceive of any function for the valve that stood apart from this row of specimens, on a plinth of its own. This singular item was the size of a vase, and inside it was a plate of metal that was as big as a playing card. Perhaps it had no purpose? This seemed possible, because nobody bought it. Until the day the shop closed down the colossal valve was always on show. In the back of the shop, above a low flight of steps, customers stood in two transparent booths, nodding their heads and tapping their feet to music that no one else could hear. They could be mistaken for mad people, or the subjects of some experiment.

The name of the Hippodrome, you learned, had something to do with horses, and so, for a time, you imagined that horses had once galloped around inside it. The building was big enough: it was larger than the town hall, and the wall at the side was as high as a cliff. Wrestling happened there, and sometimes people from television appeared there too. You could tell how famous they were by the style of the posters that were put up in the glass cabinets at the entrance: the most famous had photographs underneath their names, whereas the names of the others were painted in red on lime-green card, surrounded by painted stars.

Once a year the circus would occupy the car park behind the Hippodrome. On the morning before the first show you would go down to the car park to see the encampment: the red lorries, with the name of the circus in big sky-blue letters; the wagons, like train wagons, on which were written, in the same style, *Lions*, *Tigers*, *Horses*; and the crane with the high curved sides, which would hoist the Big Top. The vehicles were parked in a ring, like the camp in a cowboy film, and the guy ropes and the pylons were heaped in the middle. It was astounding that in the space of a day the huge tent could be raised, and seats for hundreds of people put in place, and the ring and cages constructed. On taking your seat you would look up into the darkness of the roof, to study the trapezes and the high wire. Up there was where the best part of the show would happen. The clowns were cruel and stupid; the big cats, cringing and snarling at the whip, were pitiful and terrifying; only by the acrobats were you roused to rapture. The woman on the trapeze was an object of adoration: the lights flashed on the sequins that covered her body; her legs were ink-coloured and as muscular as a man's. You watched her as if her survival were dependent on your attention. It made you shiver with pleasure, the moment when she let go of the trapeze and fell. You would glimpse the elation in her face as she came down into the net. She was so fearless, so graceful, so powerful. Dark feather-shapes were painted on the outside of her eyes.

It was said that the hotel at the bottom of the hill was haunted by a woman who had been murdered there, and then buried in a barrel, by a man who had been the manager. You never knew anyone who had been inside the building. A long time ago, when the town's theatre had been famous, film stars had stayed in the hotel. Laurel and Hardy had once visited. Bob Hope and Bing Crosby had been guests. When George Formby was here, a crowd gathered outside and he performed a song for them, from a balcony that no longer existed. Wrestlers who fought in the Hippodrome now stayed in the hotel, but none of the men you saw coming out of the building ever looked like a fighter.

In one part of the rose garden the bushes were very deep. A high wall stood behind them, and at the foot of the wall was an area of bald earth, a cockpit among the vegetation. The shortest route from the path to this patch of bare ground was impassable, but you could reach it obliquely, sidling through the loops of thorns in a sequence of turns and twists which you memorised, like the combination of a safe. One day, under a bush that was passed by this approach, something stank: a rat, with globules of white fatty stuff where its eyes should have been, and ants running out of its mouth. Many times you returned to observe the progress of its change, as the body shrank and the bones emerged through the fur. The angle of a paw changed day by day: it rose, then subsided. The skull began to show at the tip of the nose. Soon after, the carcass disappeared, leaving only an oval of darkened earth and a sour fume that soon vanished too.

The paths in the public gardens converged at the fountain, which stood on a platform above the lawns and flower gardens. On the top of the fountain a muscular metal man, completely naked and entirely green, held a stringless green bow in one hand; the other arm was drawn back, and two fingers of that hand were straight, because he had just released the invisible string, aiming at the ruins of the priory. The wide basin at the base of the fountain was made of a pale smooth stone, and the shallow water, in sunlight, created a net of shadows that was full of sparkling lights. But a chemical had been put in the water, you were told, which would blister the skin of anyone who paddled in it. The water could only be looked at.

In the absence of the park keeper, the bowling green was used for football, in plimsolls rather than boots, out of respect for the perfect surface. Nowhere else was there grass so smooth, so tight, so flat, so intensely green. A game of football was played there on a day in August, a cloudless day, and very hot. At the end of the game, exhausted, you lay with your cheek on the warm grass as the ball rolled towards the gutter. Watching the milk-white ball as it rolled away, perhaps you thought, as now it seems you did: *This is beautiful; this is becoming a memory.*

In summer, towards the end of the day, the chestnut trees in front of the priory caught the sun in such a way that the leaves were turned to tangerine; the grass beneath them was covered in shadows of multiple blues and greys, like the plumage of a pigeon. It had the allure of an imaginary land, a paradise, a place of absolute tranquillity. But when you arrived there, and stood upon the shadows, the atmosphere of the place was no longer the one that the sight of the sun-struck leaves and the darkened grass had created. The paradise had disappeared as you entered it.

The approach to the ruins took you past a row of crab-apple trees. You would linger there, beneath the dark pink blossom, and in spring there was something horrible to see: newly hatched birds would fall from their nests onto the paving stones. You compelled yourself to inspect these monsters. The naked yellow bodies looked like scraps from the butcher's bin, and the blue-lidded eyes were the growths of a terrible disease. Once you were looking at one when its hideously wide beak made a movement. For weeks afterwards you walked on the other side of the road.

At the edge of the ruined priory rose the stump of a spiral staircase, encased in rough masonry – only six or seven steps, but enough to make a tower. To climb the steps you sometimes had to step over a patch of gritty black mud, which gave off a tang of urine. The steps smelled of urine too. You breathed the bad air, knowing that this was how the air would have smelt in the days when the priory was not a ruin.

A rectangular pond of unknown depth, surrounded by a wall of large stones, lay at the bottom of the slope on top of which the priory stood. The surface of the water was covered by lily pads and weeds; occasionally a ripple would appear between the leaves, and you might glimpse a huge goldfish. At an angle of the wall, rainwater drained through a small iron grille; often, when you lifted this grille, you would find a frog in the hole. The frog would never jump out. It squatted in the shallow water, quivering in terror.

Plevna Road was a street of identical houses, indistinguishable from the houses of the neighbouring streets, but the name gave Plevna Road a character that no other street possessed. You thought of Plevna as a girl of exotic beauty, black-haired, black-eyed; she came from some island in the tropics; she might have been an orphan; piracy was sometimes involved. The first house on the left, as you came to Plevna Road, had a cherry tree that produced immense quantities of delicate white blossom, befitting the romance of the beautiful girl.

You would often dream of a road called Firs Street. In this dream you would look to left and right, and then, seeing no traffic, you would begin to cross. When you reached the middle of the road your legs would no longer work; your feet seemed to be glued to the ground. Under the strain of trying to move, you collapsed; now a car was speeding towards you; kneeling on the road, you scraped at the tarmac, frantic with fear; in seconds, you would be struck. Here, always, you woke up. Why this road? Nothing had ever happened to you there, and there was nothing remarkable about it, other than the fact that you dreamed about it again and again, and that it was called Firs Street, though there were no firs.

Alongside your school, separated by a wall that was topped with broken glass, was the Catholic school. You knew nothing of what went on there, other than that the children had nuns instead of teachers, and that they worshipped statues. At lunchtime the Catholic children could be heard at play. Their games seemed quieter than yours; the bell that summoned them back to the classroom seemed to be rung more fiercely.

To enter the zoo you passed under a canopy that was formed of five overlapping concrete waves. The five curves of concrete looked like nothing else in the town, but within the zoo there were similar things. The polar bears dived from a swooping ramp of concrete; the lions and tigers basked on curving concrete shelves; the tropical birds lived in a house of white concrete that looked like a flying saucer; at the brown bears' ravine a concrete platform jutted out like the prow of a ship. There was a concrete kiosk, circular, with a concrete counter and a roof supported by thin pillars, and a café with a wall of windows that had as many curves as a snake. At night, in bed, you would close your eyes and walk around the zoo, passing every building, taking every staircase and every path. You could hear, in the darkness, the ripping of the grass as the bison grazed; you could hear the screaming that came from the aviary, and the sighing of the elephants; you heard the leopard, pacing its cage, making a noise in its throat that was like a machine in which parts had become loose.

The aquarium had an outer and an inner room. No sunlight came into the inner room – light came only from the boxes of illuminated water. It was always warm in there, and everyone spoke in whispers, so you could hear the burbling of the bubbles in the tanks. Freaks were to be seen here: eels as big as a man's leg, with teeth like pieces of crystal; fish that were rocks with tiny eyes; fish with mouths that never closed, rimmed with needles. There were delightful creatures too: tiny fish emblazoned with dashes of luminous red and blue; and others with long transparent skirts for fins, which moved without effort, like coloured tissues in a current. But the creature that always held you for the longest time was the axolotl, the smooth pink lizard-fish that had gills like frills of seaweed. The axolotl was blind, and you would watch it for minutes on end as it groped over the stones that were piled in its tank; its mouth was fixed in a smile that meant nothing.

The gorillas had a den in which to sleep, one wall of which was made of glass. It was a special kind of reinforced glass, you were assured. The gorillas could not break it and they could not see you through it, though you could see them. But one day the male, resting his cheek on the glass, slowly turned its head to look straight at you, intent on revenge.

In the reptile house the crocodiles lay on a bed of gravel, behind thick glass, at a height that was level with your head if you knelt on the floor. You would kneel to gaze into their dinosaur eyes. The eyeballs were like balls of onyx, and the lids that wiped them clean were like sausage skin. They never seemed to see you, or anything.

The brown bears occupied a ravine in the flank of the limestone outcrop on which the castle stood. Caves and mine shafts and a canal tunnel riddled the hill overlooking the ravine. Many years ago, it was said, a landslip had opened a hole in the side of the ravine, and the bears had escaped. Not all of them had been recaptured.

The hill above the canal was where the countryside began, but the water of the canal was unnatural: it was the colour of jade and there was no movement in it. If you fell in, and some of the water went into your mouth, you would be poisoned. If you sank, the water would close over you like oil. There was a tunnel that had a path running through it. One day you walked into the tunnel until you could see nothing but a small half-moon of light in front of you and another small half-moon behind. The water was invisible there. You turned back, and never had any idea what was at the end of the tunnel.

On Sunday you might be taken to the hills where people had lived in caves until recently. Around the caves the woods were filled with bracken, and you might be left to lie in the midst of it, engrossed in the intricate vegetable mechanism of the unfurling leaves. Up top, the turf had been shaped into tuffets, where the soil had slipped and been washed away. Sitting on one of these, you looked towards the horizon, where there was a town, the one you lived in. The tip of an outstretched finger could blot it out. Horses were ridden on the hills. Their manure lay on the close-cropped grass: fibrous loaves, as big as your head, stinking sweetly. Whenever the horses approached at a gallop, the thunderous crescendo of their hooves gave you a fear that was delicious. Sometimes the horses would be halted near where you sat; the animals stood still, under the control of their riders, but their breathing was a wild sound and their staring was furious. The horses were what you hoped to see, every time you were taken to the hills.

A vision of a river: on the opposite bank, weeping willows; motionless water and motionless air; a long oval of sunlight on the surface of the river; a bright haze of midges in midstream; you lie among rushes and long grass; mayflies; an afternoon of silence; warmth. What is being remembered? When was it seen? Where is this place? It is here; it is only here.